The Summer of Chasing Dreams

A gorgeously uplifting and heartwarming
romantic comedy to escape with

Holly Martin

Published by Holly Martin in 2019
Copyright © Holly Martin, 2019

Holly Martin has asserted her right to be identified
as the author of this work.

eBook ISBN 978-1-9160111-0-6
Paperback ISBN 978-1-9160111-1-3
Large Print paperback ISBN 978-1-9160111-2-0

This book is a work of fiction. Names, characters, businesses,
organisations, places and events other than those clearly in the
public domain, are either the product of the author's imagination
or are used fictitiously. Any resemblance to actual persons, living
or dead, events all locales is entirely coincidental.

Cover design by Emma Rogers
Formatted by Polgarus Studio

Chapter 1

Eva Blue walked down Clementine Avenue with the late afternoon spring sunshine on her back. New flowers were dancing on the plants that tumbled over the walls from hanging baskets or flower pots attached to the wrought-iron fences. The blossom trees were just beginning to bud, but it would be a few weeks before their beautiful pink flowers started to bloom. The branches were leaning over the fence from the private communal garden in the centre of the street, giving a tantalising glimpse of the secrets that lay beyond the locked gates.

When Eva was a child, she and her mum used to lie on the grass in there as the blossom petals gently fell on them like confetti. Her mum loved the blossom trees and was always sad when the flowers wilted and died shortly after they appeared.

It had been a long time since Eva had been inside the private communal garden. Her mum had put the key somewhere safe many years before and it had never been seen again – like many of her mum's belongings, which all seemed to go missing and then end up in unusual places. Eva smiled fondly as she remembered the many times she would pop by for a visit to find her mum had misplaced her phone, her keys, her purse or her shopping list.

Juliette always seemed to have her mind on a hundred other things she needed to do. She was busy with yoga, Zumba, salsa lessons, pole dancing lessons, painting, pottery, mosaic making or jewellery making. There were always crafty bits everywhere, unfinished paintings, half completed pots. She was scatty and flighty, her head permanently in the clouds.

Her mum always blamed Gladys, the ghost that she said lived in the house, for the things that got lost. Although, apart from the missing items, Eva had never seen any evidence of spectral beings. Juliette had never seen her either but it didn't stop poor Gladys getting the blame. Juliette used to talk to Gladys, ask her for advice, and though Juliette never heard any answers, she said that after talking things through with Gladys she always knew what the answer was to any problem. Eva wondered idly whether Juliette and Gladys were off somewhere else together now, causing mischief.

Eva walked up the stone steps of her mum's four-storey Victorian townhouse and let herself in through the blue front door. She closed it softly behind her and listened to the complete and utter silence of the house for a few moments. If her mum was now a ghost, rattling her chains somewhere, it most certainly wasn't here. There was no life here, nothing to remind Eva of the colourful exuberant woman that Juliette had been. Music was always playing in this house, something classical like Beethoven, something contemporary like Ed

Sheeran, or Calvin Harris, some belting seventies track from Abba or some musical soundtrack from *The Lion King*, *Wicked* or *Les Mis*. Quite often one song would be playing in the lounge while something else entirely played in the kitchen. At the same time her mum would sing along to some other soundtrack that was only in her head as she danced from room to room. She was always dancing.

The bright colours that adorned the walls of each room were still there, shades of red, purple, gold, and turquoise, though they seemed duller somehow without the person who had lovingly painted them. While Eva liked to add colour to her home with the odd scatter cushion or a colourful painting on the walls, there was colour everywhere in her mum's house; all the doors were in different shades of gloss, the carpets and furnishings were colours that Eva would never have chosen to display side by side, but somehow, together, it all seemed to work.

Eva hadn't the heart to paint over them yet, even though she knew she needed to if she was going to sell the house. She'd choose something practical, maybe a nice cream or magnolia like she had in her flat. But eradicating this kaleidoscopic theme would be removing the last influences of her mum from her childhood home. She couldn't bear the thought of it.

Over the last few months, Eva had slowly packed away her mum's life, taking clothes to charity shops, boxing up Juliette's beloved knick-knacks and moving some of them to her own flat, selling furniture and paintings. This was the sensible thing to do. It had occurred to her that she could move back into her childhood home, but that wasn't practical

– what would she do with such a big house all by herself?

She cringed. She was getting a little bit annoyed with her sensible, practical side lately.

But what would be the point in moving in here, living her life with all these memories – making cakes in the kitchen, helping her mum paint her childhood bedroom with giraffes, elephants, lions and tigers, having a water fight in the garden, snuggling on the sofa together and watching movies. The life she and her mum had here was seared into every corner of every room. She had even been born here, in her mum's bedroom, twenty-seven years before when she had been so eager to enter the world she couldn't wait for the paramedics to arrive. Did she really want to live here again? Wouldn't it hurt too much? Or would it be a way to stay connected to her mum now those memories were starting to fade? She'd spoken about it with her beloved Aunt Laurel at the solicitors that morning. Laurel thought Eva should keep the house but that ultimately it was up to her.

She didn't want to make that decision but probate had finally been agreed, the will had been settled and, as of that morning, the house was officially hers to do with what she wanted, as was the huge sum of twenty-six thousand pounds which was half of her mum's estate, the other half going to Juliette's sister, Laurel.

Eva had no idea what to do with the money. Four or five years ago, the money would have been very handy. She had been an artist, doing a bit of cover designing on the side, mainly to help with the costs of her paints and canvases, and living in a tiny rented flat, trying to scrape together enough to pay for a deposit on the house. But then her job as a cover designer started to take off in ways she had never imagined and she was able to buy a small two-bedroom flat. She'd quickly become one of the top cover designers in the publishing industry and it paid her a really nice wage. Just a few months ago, after years of saving, she had even been able to pay off her mortgage. She was by no means rich but she didn't have any debts – no credit cards or loans to pay off – so she didn't *need* the money.

It seemed wrong that she should benefit from her mum's death when she would have paid a hundred times that amount to have her back. It had been eighteen months since Juliette had died and, though Eva didn't think she would ever reach the day where she was over her death, it was slowly becoming slightly easier to deal with.

She supposed she would put the money in a savings account for that proverbial rainy day.

She glanced at a framed photo of New York at the bottom of the stairs. It was somewhere neither her mum nor she had ever been to. It was hung there as a reminder of dreams that might one day come true, or so her mum had said. Looking at that photo every day when she was growing up made Eva yearn to experience the bright lights of this distant city too. Juliette had talked to her about the restaurants and shops that were open twenty-four hours a day, being able to buy a pair of trainers at three o'clock in the morning if you so wished. Juliette had spoken about the different food you could eat, the sights and smells of the city. She'd talked to Eva about how one day they would go together but that had never happened and now it was too late. Maybe she would use some of the money and go there for a weekend. God, the thought thrilled her and scared her in equal measure.

Eva was different from her mum in so many ways. Her mum had the most beautiful singing voice and could dance gracefully, while Eva sounded like a strangled cat when she tried to sing and was clumsy and ungainly with no sense of rhythm. Juliette had been tall, blonde and willowy, while Eva was short with dark hair and at best could be described as curvy, though many people might have said pear-shaped.

But the biggest difference was their attitudes to life. Juliette would grab life by the horns, jump up into the saddle with a cowboy hat in one hand and a glass of wine in the other and ride that bucking bronco with a huge smile on her face. She grabbed every opportunity, never said no to anything and wanted to see every corner of the world. She'd make friends so easily, chatting happily to perfect strangers. Eva preferred her own company, was more than happy spending the night in her own flat and was, quite honestly, a little bit scared of the world outside her little bubble. She'd seen the news; the world was a cruel and scary place. And though there were places, like New York, she'd always wanted to visit, she always thought she'd go with someone. Being an introvert she didn't have a lot of friends and those she did have were all married with children. Travelling companions were a bit thin on the ground.

Holidays with her mum had always been a bit of a disaster when Eva had been growing up. They wanted very different things from their trips away. There was no lying on a sunlounger and reading a book for Juliette.

Her mum would hire a dirty old jeep and bundle Eva into the back and drive along precarious mountain roads to visit some monastery tucked away in some vertigo-inducing village. They'd go jet skiing, surfing, bare back horse-riding, zip wiring, quad bike riding, none of which appealed to Eva. She'd ended up with more broken bones than she could count over the years due to one of her mum's madcap schemes. Eva's trust in her mum to keep her safe had been slowly eroded away until it had vanished completely.

When Eva was older, she never felt inclined to join her mum on her travels. Her mum had sent her postcards from each location she'd visited: sometimes a few scrawled hasty lines before her mum went off on her next adventure, sometimes there was so much writing as her mum tried to cram in everything she had done that the words were almost too small to read. Every one ended with the clichéd line *Wish you were here*. And she knew her mum really did wish for that.

At the time she had turned down her mum's offers to accompany her and blamed work commitments. How she regretted that now. She'd ride on the back of a motorbike, wrestle a crocodile, bungee jump from the world's tallest bridge if it meant she could have one more hug from her mum, one more late-night chat over a bowl of bananas and custard.

She looked at the twinkling lights of the New York skyline and shook her head. No, she couldn't go there on her own. Maybe she would use the money and invest in some stocks and shares. She would do something sensible with it, she had no doubt of that, not something silly and fanciful.

She moved up the stairs, past the photos that hung from the walls, not one of them hanging straight. There were many pictures of sunsets and sunrises. Juliette loved a great sunrise or sunset. She said sunrises were a new beginning and the possibilities for the day ahead was always endless. And she said a beautiful sunset was the perfect end to a brilliant day.

She knew she needed to pack these photos away, the last evidence her mum had lived here, but that was a job for another day.

Eva stopped and smiled as she looked at one photo of her mum sitting astride a large Harley-Davidson.

When Eva had received the call that her mum was dead, it hadn't been the greatest surprise. Heartbreaking, of course, but not a surprise considering how Juliette lived the last few years of her life. Bungee jumps, riding elephants, hugging a lion, hang gliding, Eva had almost been waiting for the call to say that her mum was never coming home. In the end she had been knocked over by a car, which seemed far too dull an ending for someone as glorious and colourful as Juliette. She always said when she died, she'd go out in style and that her death would be so spectacular it would make the papers. She hadn't even achieved that.

Eva made her way to the top of the house, looking through the rooms that were devoid of anything that made this house a home. The only room left to tackle was the loft, and Eva had no idea what to expect.

When Eva had lived here as a child, the loft had been a place to keep the Christmas decorations and that had been it. She'd never been up there and, as far as she was aware, her mum hadn't been up there since the ladder broke when Eva was a kid. Juliette had never got round to having it fixed, so hopefully there would only be a few boxes of tinsel and baubles to sort through.

Eva had had the foresight to borrow a ladder from Laurel a few days before and that was waiting for her underneath the hatch. She unfolded it and carefully climbed up, releasing the bolt on the door and letting it fall open to one side.

Little motes of dust sparkled in the air as if released from a place that had been long forgotten. If this had been one of the fantasy children's books she was designing the cover for, there would be a mystery book up there that took the reader to a distant land, a forgotten relic that held mysterious powers or maybe even a fallen angel, hidden amongst the cobwebs. Eva's practical mind knew there would be no such treasures.

She stepped up onto the loft floor and looked around. There was a small air vent that let tiny ribbons of gold play across the dusty wooden boards, but the rest of the loft lay in darkness. She fumbled around and found the light switch. A lone bulb sprang to life in the middle of the roof but surprisingly the light filled all the nooks and crannies.

There were three neatly stacked clear plastic boxes that quite visibly held baubles and tree decorations. There was even an old artificial Christmas tree propped up against one of the beams. There were a few other boxes near the loft door. One looked like it might be filled with baby clothes in various shades of pink. Another looked like it held all Eva's old baby toys, even the broken ones. Beyond that there didn't seem to be a lot up there.

She cast her eyes around; there was definitely no mysterious object that contained super powers. This would take her a lot less time than she'd thought.

She moved over to the box of children's toys and picked a few off the top. There were two dolls, their hair tinted green and blue courtesy of Eva's felt-tip-pen dye job. She smiled as she remembered her mum's reaction to the new hair style, Juliette declaring the two dolls to be mermaids, and they'd spent the rest of the afternoon making mermaid clothes for them.

She shifted a few other toys around and found a dirty yellow, crochet donkey which Eva distinctly remembered was called Joshua. She had carried him around everywhere when she was growing up.

She moved a few other toys off the top, some of these quite clearly baby toys, and found an envelope. She picked it up; it felt heavy. She slid it open and realised it was her first birthday card from Juliette. She ran her fingers over the shiny pink writing that said, 'To my beautiful daughter.' She smiled at the mummy and baby bear hugging on the front, the baby bear clutching a number one.

She opened the card and saw a long letter scrawled across the inside of the pages.

Eva took in a sharp breath.

A letter from her mum to her. Even though it had been written over twenty-six years before, that bond between them that Eva feared was fading away was now as sharp and as clear as it had always been.

Eva sat down on a nearby box to read it, clutching Joshua to her chest.

My darling Eva. Today is your first birthday and I have so many hopes and dreams for you. I wish for you the biggest adventures, the ones that will make your heart beat faster and take you to distant shores and exotic lands. I wish for you complete and utter happiness that fills your entire being and soul. I wish for you the greatest love, I want someone for you who will make you laugh, will treat you like a queen and will hold your hand on this wonderful journey through life. Find something you love, something you're passionate about and do it. Life is too short and we never know what is around the next corner so be silly and wild and wacky and never fear what people will think of you. Those that judge you will not be important to you and those that are important to you will be silly right along with you. Be kind, be hopeful, never stop learning, read everything. Be brave and chase those dreams. I love you, my beautiful girl. Mum xx

Tears filled her eyes as she traced her finger over the words, reading them again. She wondered if her mum would be disappointed with the life Eva led, tucked up in her own bed by ten o'clock most nights with a cup of hot chocolate and a good book. There were no big adventures, no chasing dreams, there was no great love and there was no silliness. She did have a job she loved so that was something, she supposed.

When had her life become so... mundane? Where was the excitement that her mum used to chase, filling her life with risks and thrills and laughter? She looked around the dusty loft and down at Joshua. This was not the life her mum had wished for her, not even close.

She pushed the card into her jeans pocket, not sure what she was going to do with those words, those hopes for a future that Eva had never claimed.

She stood up and wiped her eyes and then carried the toys and baby clothes down the ladder. She would take them all to a charity shop.

She went back up into the loft and moved the three boxes of Christmas decorations carefully down the ladder. She would go through them later and pick out any decorations that held any sentimental attachment. She went back up to collect the tree and that's when she spotted it. Her heart leapt because, tucked against one of the supporting beams, was literally a small treasure chest. It was made with dark wood, had a curved lid and gold leaves carved into the sides. And although it was very unlikely that the lost treasure of Long John Silver was in the loft of her mum's West London house, Eva couldn't help moving towards it, running her hands over the smoothness of the wood before flipping the catch and opening the lid with a tiny creak.

Inside were tiny strips of faded pink paper. She rooted around inside the paper, looking for any doubloons or rubies the size of her hand. But there was nothing in the box at all.

Eva sighed and sat back on her heels. Then she noticed a lined piece of paper tucked into the lid.

In felt-tip pen, in her mum's distinctive curly handwriting, were the words, 'My box of dreams'. At the bottom of the paper was the date. A quick calculation in Eva's head made her realise the note had been written by Juliette, the night before her eighteenth birthday, when she'd had her whole life ahead of her.

What had the box of dreams once held amongst the pink confetti?

She stared at the strips of paper and noticed that one of

them had faint curly writing on. She quickly snatched it up and held the paper up to the light.

Swim with dolphins.

She looked at the other bits of paper and realised they all had writing on too. She grabbed another.

Visit the Grand Canyon.

She picked up another.

See the midnight sun.

These were her mum's dreams. Each dream written on a separate piece of paper. There must have been forty or fifty pieces in there.

She started picking them all out, reading each one.

Sing on top of the Eiffel Tower.

Find lost gold in Egypt.

Swim in Lake Superior.

Sing in front of the Queen.

She read every one and she couldn't help smiling at them. She knew Juliette had done a few of these things but most of them had never been achieved.

A year after she had written these hopes for her future, Juliette had fallen pregnant with Eva and that had clearly put an end to all of these things. Juliette had planned to travel the world and lead an adventurous life and, though in more recent years, her mum had started doing just that, she had never done most of the things in this chest. Eva had stopped all of that.

Eva had known she had not been a planned pregnancy. One night with a man who Juliette had completely fallen in love with and never seen again. Juliette always said Eva had been this unexpected but wonderful gift but had she actually ruined her mum's life?

She closed the lid and rested a hand on top of the box.

What could she do with these forgotten dreams? She couldn't throw them out, but now that she had seen them, she couldn't lock them away in the chest for these dreams to never see the light of day again.

A glimmer of an idea started to bubble in her mind but she pushed it away. She couldn't do that. It was ridiculous.

A board creaked in the furthest corner of the loft and she looked over in that direction. There was nothing there.

'Gladys?' Eva said, feeling beyond stupid. She swallowed. 'Mum?'

Silence.

'What should I do with these dreams?'

Silence.

Eva fished the cheque the solicitor had given her earlier from her pocket. Twenty-six thousand pounds. She looked back at the chest and, whether it was Gladys, her mum or just her own clarity of thought, suddenly she knew exactly what she was going to do.

Chapter 2

Laurel placed a mug of tea and a slice of pineapple cake in front of Eva and then sat down opposite her niece at her kitchen table.

'So tell me again what you plan to do with your half of the money?' Laurel said.

'I'm going to travel the world,' Eva said, the wobble in her voice betraying that she was losing the confidence in her decision as every minute ticked by.

Laurel stared at her and then made a show of feeling Eva's forehead. 'OK, where's my Eva and what have you done with her?'

'Very funny.'

Laurel laughed. 'It's just not something I ever thought you would do. I thought you would invest in some nice safe shares or stick it in an ISA or something sensible like that, or even just give it all away to charity.'

'I need to do this,' Eva said, touching the small treasure chest she had brought with her.

'Is this to do with the Lost Ark here?' Laurel gestured to

the chest. 'Are you going to go all Indiana Jones on me and start searching out the world's missing treasures?'

'Did you know Mum wrote a list of dreams, the things she wanted to do with her life?'

Laurel frowned. 'When?'

'The night before her eighteenth birthday.'

Her aunt shook her head, all humour now gone. 'I didn't know.'

Eva flicked open the chest and gestured for Laurel to look through the pink leaves of paper. Laurel picked up one and read it, then she picked up another and another and read those too, spreading them all out on the table between them.

'This is the life she should have had… if she hadn't had me.'

Laurel's eyes snapped up to hers. 'Your mum adored you. She never regretted having you, not for one second.'

'I need to fulfil these dreams for her. She gave up her entire life for me, all those plans, her hopes and dreams. I need to do these things for her that she never got round to doing. There are five things in here that she did before she died. That's what she was doing with all her crazy travels. She was trying to do all these things on her list that she never had the chance to do. She died before she'd even done a quarter of the things she wanted to do. I need to finish this list for her. That's what Mum would want me to do with the money and that's what I'm going to do.'

Laurel hesitated for the longest time before she spoke. 'Your mum would want you to spend the money on what you wanted, not what she wanted. But… as I can see you've made up your mind, I do love the idea of you travelling the world.

You've sounded so excited over the last few days and I love hearing that in your voice again.'

Eva looked at the dreams on the table. 'Some of these, I have no idea where to start.' She picked up one. '"Go back to Skagen." Where is that?'

'Denmark and it's pronounced *Skayne*.'

'I didn't even know Mum had visited Denmark. Why did she want to go back there?'

'Remember her telling you about her doing a tour of Europe with a theatre company and she was Dorothy from *The Wizard of Oz*?'

Eva nodded. 'She went to Denmark on that trip?'

Laurel nodded. 'She was seventeen and I think that tour gave her a taste for travelling and seeing different countries.'

'And what did your dad think of her travelling around Europe?'

'Of course he disapproved. He never approved of anything your mum wanted to do, which just made her want to do those things even more.'

Eva smiled at that rebellious streak. Her nan had died before Eva was born so she'd never known her or how she would have reacted to Juliette's more crazy plans. Her grandad had pretty much kicked Juliette out of the house once she fell pregnant with Eva. Juliette had even changed her surname so she was no longer associated with him, taking her stage name of Juliette Blue. When Eva had come along, she had inherited that name too. Eva had only met him a few times growing up and she remembered only an angry and bitter old man. Disapproving was his middle name. He'd died many years before and Juliette hadn't shed a single tear.

17

'Juliette loved Skagen, but from what I can gather there was a man there who she completely fell in love with. She was only there a week, but from what she told me, it was quite clear she was head over heels for him. I think he was the first person she made love to.'

Eva leaned in, keen to get the lowdown on this relationship she had never known about.

'What was his name?'

'I don't know, Juliette didn't tell me a lot. Dad overheard us speaking about it once, not long after she came home, and he went ballistic. He said no daughter of his was going to be sleeping around and getting pregnant. She didn't really speak much about him after that.'

'What happened, why didn't they get together?'

Laurel shrugged. 'I suppose long-distance relationships are hard. This was nearly thirty years ago, so we didn't have social media or Skype or the other forms of contact that we do now. She wrote to him a few times but he never replied. They never saw each other again. Maybe he just didn't love her as much as she loved him.'

Eva sighed. 'Urgh, why are men so rubbish!'

'That's a huge generalisation,' Laurel frowned. 'Not all men are rubbish. I know you feel let down by your dad but I think a lot of those circumstances were out of his control. And it doesn't mean every man is like that.'

Eva thought about her dad. She'd inadvertently seen an article about him and his new autobiography in the paper the other day, where he'd shown off his LA home, complete with swimming pool and a mini golf course in the back garden. There were pictures of his doting wife as they celebrated twenty-seven years of a loving marriage. The world didn't know about Eva, his dirty little secret. She'd never even met Thomas Connor, despite asking her mum to invite him to her birthday party when she was seven. Apparently he'd been too busy. That had probably shaped her view of men from an early age. Though she supposed she should be somewhat grateful to him. He'd given Juliette enough hush money, after Eva had been born, to buy the house in Clementine Avenue outright.

'No, I know you're right. I'm sure there are some lovely ones out there, I guess Mum was just bad at picking them,' Eva said. Although she hadn't exactly had a great track record with men either. Her relationships never lasted long. She glanced over at a photo of Laurel's husband, Michael. He had died many years before and he had been a wonderful man. Laurel hadn't been with anyone since until very recently, when she'd started dating a very nice man called James; it seemed to be going well. Maybe not all men were rubbish.

'So, apart from Skagen, where else are you going? Tell me, what are your plans?' Laurel said, breaking into her thoughts.

'Well, New York definitely. It's on Mum's list but it's also been one of the places I've always wanted to visit. I want to see the cherry blossoms in Japan. I've been looking at photos of it pretty much non-stop over the last few days and it just looks magnificent. Some of the places in Japan have thousands of cherry blossom trees all in one place. It's a complete phenomenon over there, they paint it, write poems about it, they even have it in their food and drink. I really want to go there and experience all of that. But beyond that, I'm not sure.' Eva pulled her tablet out of her bag. 'As you know, the furthest I've ever been is France, Spain and Germany. I've never been further afield, never really wanted to. I'm not sure where the best places would be to do some of these experiences, I'm not even sure where some of these locations are. So I decided I'm going to go through a tour company, get them to organise some of these excursions for me. And I found one that does escorted holidays, so I'll have someone to go with, someone who will know the lie of the land, the various cultures and can guide me around the different countries with an expert eye.'

Eva eagerly flicked through her screen to find the right website. Although the thought of travelling the world scared her half to death, it excited her too. Despite what Laurel said, she wanted this.

'That's a good idea,' Laurel said. 'Do you get to choose who you can travel with?'

'Yes, that's the best bit.' Eva found the website for The World Is Your Oyster. 'They have six members of staff to choose from.'

Eva turned the tablet round to show Laurel the different guides she could choose.

'Wow! He's hot,' Laurel said, pointing at the tablet.

Eva didn't need to look to know who Laurel was pointing at. Thor Anderson. The man looked like a god. And not in a 'oh he's really nice-looking' kind of way. He looked like he had been carved from the finest marble by an expert sculptor and then brought to life. He was ridiculously huge, filling the tiny frame of the photo. His eyes were the deepest blue, as if the artist who had made him had picked the colour from the seas of Bali or the Maldives. He actually had chiselled cheekbones and just enough stubble to be sexy without looking untidy. His longish blond hair was perfectly styled as if it had been painted on. He was flawless. And from the smug smile on his face, he totally knew how he looked as well. This was a man who knew he was god's gift to women. Definitely not her type. At all.

'His name is Thor, Laurel. The god of thunder. What kind of idiot is actually called Thor? I bet it's a fake name just to make him sound more impressive.' Eva clicked on his profile just to prove her point. There were several more photos in here. Thor standing on an expensive-looking yacht, relaxing in a huge Jacuzzi, his strong arms stretched out over the sides, that cocky smile on his face. There was another of him dressed in a tux, as he stood in some skyscraper bar that overlooked the twinkling city below, a glass of champagne in his hand. There was another of him in the driving seat of a silver-grey Aston Martin. 'He looks like an arrogant, stuck-up knob.'

Laurel nodded. 'He does look a bit haughty and superior, I'll give you that. But maybe he has a soft side that doesn't involve fast cars and a glamorous lifestyle.'

'Can you imagine spending a month or more with him. Did you read his bio? "I love showing people the finer experiences in life. From gambling in Monaco, to an exclusive resort in the Seychelles, I'm the one who has the magic key to secret clubs and can get tables at the most exclusive restaurants in the world",' Eva quoted. 'Posh restaurants, casinos, secret clubs. That is absolutely not me. I get hives thinking about which fork to use. I don't have any formal clothes, most of my working life is spent sitting in my bed, in my pyjamas.'

'You're probably right. You need to find someone more on your wavelength and I hate to say it but sexy Thor is definitely not, even if he does look like he knows how to wield his hammer,' Laurel said.

Eva laughed.

Her aunt clicked out of Thor's profile and back to the main screen. 'How about Simon?'

Eva grinned. 'I know what you're doing. I don't need a man to escort me around the world. I've chosen Rebecca.' She clicked into Rebecca's profile. '"I love exploring the world and finding all those nooks and crannies off the beaten track. That tiny little Italian restaurant in the back streets of Rome that serves the most amazing pizza, the Thai market where every colour, every flavour, every scent is there for the taking, or camping under the stars in Tanzania." She sounds right up my street. I've already contacted the company and I'm going in to meet her tomorrow.'

'She sounds lovely,' Laurel said.

'I hope so. It may be that on some parts of the trip I have to share a room with her. I'm just hoping she doesn't snore.'

Laurel laughed and Eva took a bite of cake.

'What are you going to do with your half of the money?' Eva asked.

'I'm going to buy a Porsche.'

'A porch? For the front of the house?' Eva asked. It seemed like an odd thing to do with the money but whatever made Laurel happy.

Laurel laughed. 'I may be the quieter sister, not like your mum who was the wild child, but I'm not that boring. A Porsche, a 911, a cherry red convertible. When I was younger,

I wanted to be an astronaut, have five kids, live on a farm with a donkey and drive round in a Porsche 911. None of those things happened for me, and I'm OK with that, but now I can at least get the Porsche, albeit a second-hand one, probably several years old. Hell, maybe I'll get a donkey as well, the garden is big enough.'

Eva smiled. 'You're getting a sports car?'

'Yes. What will old Mrs Scott from number eighty-six make of that?' Laurel laughed.

'I love it,' Eva said. 'Will you take the donkey out for a ride in it?'

'You know what, I just might.'

Eva smiled. She liked the idea of Laurel seeing at least some of her dreams come true. She just had to work on her mum's dreams now.

Chapter 3

'I think Hawaii is one of the best places to swim with dolphins,' Rebecca said, clicking through to a screen that showed photos of lush tropical islands and turquoise waters. 'You can swim with them in the wild, which is much better than some of these places that keep them captive and teach them to do tricks for food. Plus it's Hawaii – if you're going on a trip of a lifetime, Hawaii has to be on it.'

Eva nodded keenly. She had liked Rebecca immediately. She seemed sweet and kind but also completely savvy when it came to travelling around the world. She had done these sorts of tours before and knew where to go and what to see. Eva knew she would get on with her too; it looked like they could have a laugh together. Best of all, when Eva had showed Rebecca the list, not only did Rebecca think all the dreams were completely doable, she had quickly uploaded it all into a spreadsheet so they could start to come up with an itinerary around the world to tick off each of the dreams. If there was one thing that Eva liked, it was a spreadsheet. Rebecca was definitely a kindred spirit.

'Seeing the Northern Lights might be tricky at this time of year, the best time is between September and March,' Rebecca said, her fingers moving at a hundred miles an hour as she typed various things into her computer. 'But seeing as we might be going to Australia or New Zealand on this trip, we could probably go somewhere where we might see the Southern Lights, the aurora australis. Do you think that would work?'

Eva thought about this for a moment. Should she deviate from the original dreams? She guessed one aurora event was just as good as another and maybe she could be a little relaxed about things like this. She nodded.

Rebecca looked at her watch. 'Where is Thor, he should be in by now?'

Eva noticed she said Thor with a hard T as in Thomas so it sounded like Tor.

'He would know the perfect place to see the aurora australis. He has some excellent photos of it. Let me see if I can find them.'

She pressed a few buttons and then the photos of the aurora filled the screen. Green and purple swirls filling the sky over the snowy mountains. Eva gasped softly. She definitely wanted to see that.

Just then the shop door opened and the man himself strode in. God, he was even more ridiculously beautiful in real life. His photos hadn't done him justice.

She was so busy staring at his face, it took her a full five seconds to realise he was carrying a baby.

'Thor!' Rebecca said in surprise. 'You're so late, Tracy will kill you. And why have you got a baby with you?'

'He's my nephew, Felix,' Thor explained, dumping the baby bag down next to Rebecca's desk. 'I was looking after him for Pernille last night, but her car has broken down and my sister can't get to me to pick him up. She's going to get the tube but she's on the other side of the city so I thought it might be best to bring him to work, so I wasn't too late. We're closer to my sister here, so she shouldn't be too long.'

Rebecca stared at him in surprise as Felix fussed and wriggled in his arms.

'I can't believe you brought a baby to work,' Rebecca said, eyeing the back office with fear. 'Tracy was asking after you this morning but I told her you were meeting a client. She's going to hit the roof when she sees the baby.'

'What could I do? I couldn't just not come in, you know I'm down to my last chance with her,' Thor said. His eyes fell on Eva for the first time and she felt a stab of something, like a connection between friends who hadn't seen each other for years. 'I'm so sorry. We're not normally this unprofessional. Please continue with your meeting, we'll try to be as quiet as possible.'

Eva looked through to the back office where a blonde lady in her fifties was busy shopping for scarves online. She hadn't noticed Thor coming in.

Suddenly Felix let out an almighty wail and Tracy's head snapped up, looking through the glass at them all.

'Sshhh Felix, it's OK, little man, you don't want to do that, you're going to get me the sack,' Thor whispered, bouncing the little boy on his hip.

Eva looked back to the office door just as Tracy stormed through it. She seemed furious.

'What the hell is this?' Tracy said. Clearly professional tact wasn't her strong point. 'Why is there a baby in my shop?'

'He's mine,' Eva blurted out. She had no idea why she was getting involved in this drama, which had nothing whatsoever to do with her, but she suddenly felt compelled to help. 'Thor was just looking after him for me while I talked to Rebecca about my holiday.'

Thor stared at her. Tracy stared at her. Even Felix stopped crying long enough to give her a withering look.

Tracy cleared her throat. 'My apologies. When people come in to book these holidays of a lifetime, they don't normally involve babies. We don't get too many of them in here. I think it's best if you take him back. Thor has work to do.'

'Oh, erm… Thor's doing such a good job,' Eva said, back-pedalling as fast as she could. 'And Rebecca and I have so much to discuss with regards to my holiday. It would be easier without Felix grabbing at everything on the desk.'

Tracy gave her a very tight smile. 'It might be a good idea if you came back without your son if that's the case. We're not running a creche. Thor, give the lady her son and then you can come into my office and explain why you were late.'

Thor didn't move and quite rightly so. Why would he hand over his nephew to a complete stranger? Eva made no move to take him from Thor either. She was useless with babies and children. When she visited her friends who all had children of varying ages, Eva would much rather play with the cat or dog than hold their babies. What if she broke them? This was a terrible idea, but now she had interfered she had to carry it through.

Eva stood up awkwardly and offered out her hands. 'Come to Mummy,' she said, putting on her sweetest baby voice.

Felix started crying again, his wail even louder than before as he turned his face away from Eva.

'I don't think…' Thor began.

This was all kinds of awful.

'Oh, he seems to have got attached to you,' Eva said, brazening out this awfulness. 'I'm going to be here for a while, so maybe you can give Thor a nice hug before we leave.'

Thor caught on to what she was saying. 'You're not leaving?'

'I'll probably be here for an hour or two.'

'Thor, for crying out loud, give the woman her son,' Tracy said, her patience clearly wearing thin. She turned and walked back into her office.

Thor hesitated a moment longer and then shifted a crying screaming Felix into her arms. 'I swear if you hurt him—' he muttered through gritted teeth.

'Oh, you're welcome,' Eva snapped, sitting back down at the desk with a screaming baby on her lap. This was not how she envisaged today going at all.

'Don't worry, I'll watch her,' Rebecca said quietly.

What the hell? Now she was suspected to be some kind of child kidnapper. She had simply stepped in to help Thor out of a tricky situation. She should have just stayed out of it and then she could have had the pleasure of watching Tracy fire his smug ungrateful arse. He walked into Tracy's office, watching Eva like a hawk the whole time.

Eva turned back to Rebecca, who was staring at her in shock. 'I was just trying to help.'

'By taking someone else's child?'

'I didn't take him, I'm simply... maintaining him.'

Rebecca suppressed a smile. 'Maintaining him? He's not a car. Do you have much experience with babies?'

'No, but how hard can it be?' Eva said, as the baby wriggled around so much, she thought he might fall off her lap. Thor was still glaring at her through the office window as Tracy clearly berated him for his tardiness. Eva shifted Felix onto one arm as she grabbed the baby bag and rooted around inside it for something, anything that might stop Felix from screaming. She found a soft bear and waggled it in front of Felix's face, cooing and making cute noises to distract him from being lumbered with a complete stranger. Felix stopped crying for a second, reaching out for the bear with his chubby fingers.

'Not bad,' Rebecca conceded. 'Now, Niagara Falls, we can see that from the Canadian side or the US side. Do you have a preference?'

'I have no idea. I'm completely in your hands here, which do you think is best?' Eva said. She glanced over into the office and could see that Thor was still glaring at her.

'I think the view is better from the Canadian side. You also have the benefit of staying in a hotel room that has the view of the falls, you don't have that in the States.'

'Oh that sounds wonderful, I'd love to do that.'

Rebecca nodded. 'OK, we can sort that out no problem, it's also nice to be in the hotel at night as they light up the falls and it's quite spectacular. The US side does have a close-up view of Bridal Veil Falls and American Falls, the two smaller waterfalls, and we can always cross over the border and view them from the US side as well, but I honestly think that you'll be able to see all that you want to see from the Canadian side—'

Eva looked up to see Thor coming out the office looking stony-faced. He obviously wasn't fired as he sat down at his computer and turned it on.

'We can also go on a boat trip to the bottom of Horseshoe Falls,' Rebecca said.

'Oh, the *Maid of the Mist*?' Eva said as Felix threw his bear across the shop and held his hands out for Thor.

'The *Hornblower*,' Thor said, picking up the bear and bringing it back to Felix. 'The *Maid of the Mist* goes from the US, if you're going to view it from the Canadian side you'll be on the *Hornblower*.'

Felix snatched the bear off Thor and threw it back across the shop. He was clearly done being held by a stranger. Thor's lips pursed, his fingers flexing as he clearly wanted to take Felix from her. He looked back to the office and knelt down and retrieved a bottle from the baby bag. 'Try this.'

She took it off him and offered it out to Felix, whose hunger far outweighed his need for Thor. He took it greedily, his little chubby fingers wrapping around the bottle.

'Tilt him back,' Thor said, a snap to his voice that had no right to be there.

Eva bit her lip to stop herself from saying anything but did as she was told.

'Thor,' Rebecca whispered, tilting her head towards the back office.

Eva looked over to see that Tracy was watching them and Thor reluctantly went back behind his desk.

'We might as well go into the States after we've been to Niagara Falls. We wouldn't be far from Manhattan then so we can do all the touristy stuff there,' Rebecca said. 'Now, I'm not sure what your budget is like, but we can shave half off the price of your holiday if we were to stay in hostels rather than hotels for most of the trip. We'd share a room with other travellers and—'

'No,' Eva said, firmly.

Thor looked up from his computer and she couldn't help thinking he was judging her. Mr The Finer Things of Life was judging her for not wanting to stay in a hostel. She didn't care. She couldn't think of anything worse. One of her friends, Natalie, had stayed in a hostel while she backpacked around Australia and told her many horror stories of those she had shared a room with and that the *quality* of the hostels was mostly questionable. Eva liked her creature comforts and if this was going to be a trip of a lifetime then she didn't mind paying a little extra to have a hotel room with her own bathroom.

'I'm sorry but that does not sound like my idea of fun at all. I want my own room. I don't mind sharing a room with you now and again, but I'd prefer to have my own space.'

'OK, that will bump up the price of your holiday quite considerably.'

'That's OK,' Eva said, noticing that Felix had finished the bottle. She pulled it out of his mouth as he was just sucking on air now and popped it on the desk.

'He'll need winding,' Thor said.

She looked at him in horror. How was she supposed to do that?

31

'Put his head over your shoulder and rub his back,' Thor hissed.

Eva gingerly did as she was told. Felix was so chunky that he was heavy to lift and manoeuvre around. She patted him on the back just as she'd seen her friend Julie do with her daughter. Then she felt a wetness on her shoulder. She lifted Felix up to see milk dripping from his mouth. She looked down at her shoulder and saw a milky puddle. She'd just been vomited on. Wow, this day couldn't get any worse.

Just then the door was pushed open and a young girl who must have been barely twenty came running in looking stressed out. Her eyes fell on Felix and Eva saw her shoulders slump a little in relief. This must be Felix's mum. Thank God.

Thor was on his feet and round his desk to greet her in seconds. 'Are you OK?'

'Yes, I'm fine, I'm so sorry,' his sister said. She frowned at Eva holding her son. 'What's going on?'

'Don't ask,' Thor said through gritted teeth, as he all but snatched Felix from Eva's hands and gave him to his sister.

Eva had had enough.

'Look Rebecca, I'm going to go. This stuff stinks so I'm going to go home and wash it off. Why don't you come up with a rough itinerary and a rough price of how much it will cost and email me with the details?'

Rebecca nodded.

Eva grabbed her bag and, as Thor was still fussing round his younger sister and Felix, she left without another word.

She got a few steps down the street when she heard Thor behind her.

'Wait.'

She turned round to face him, crossing her arms across her chest.

He gestured back to the shop. 'Look, thank you for what you did back there.'

She shrugged. 'It's fine.'

He pushed his hand through his hair. 'Well it's not, you've got sick on your shoulder and…'

'And I've had to put up with your pissy mood for the last fifteen minutes when I was supposed to be sorting out the holiday of my dreams.'

Thor cleared his throat, awkwardly. 'Yes, sorry about that. Look, why don't I take you out for a drink to apologise properly?'

He gave her his best charming smile; clearly it was a routine that had worked with hundreds of women before.

'I don't think so,' Eva said and turned and walked away.

Chapter 4

Eva knocked on the door of Julie's house and smiled as she could hear the laughter already coming from inside. It was her friend Natalie who came to the door, a wine glass already in her hand. Natalie gave her a big hug and ushered her inside.

'Sorry I'm late, they closed the Hammersmith and City line because some idiot had dropped his phone and was stupid enough to go on the tracks to retrieve it. They got him off before he could get hurt but he wasn't exactly co-operative while he was being removed from the station and they decided to keep the line closed until he was carted away,' Eva said, dumping her jacket over the bannister where there was already a collection of coats.

'Ah, the joys of living in London,' Natalie said.

Eva nodded. Sometimes, she yearned to live somewhere a little quieter.

'Besides, you're not that late, we haven't even ordered the pizzas yet,' Natalie said as Eva followed her into the lounge.

There was a small collective cheer from her other friends

as they spotted her and they all got up to give her a hug. It made her feel warm inside. What with work and family commitments, they weren't all able to get together that often and they stayed in touch mostly through WhatsApp. But, once a month, the children were left with their dads or sent off to grandparents and the girls caught up on all the news over wine and pizza.

Julie handed her a glass of wine and Jacinda patted the sofa next to her and then plonked the bowl of nachos on Eva's lap as soon as she was sitting down.

She waved over at the laptop where Leila had been Skyped in from deepest Cornwall.

'Now we can order the pizzas,' Julie said. 'I'm starving. Shall we get our usual?'

There were nods around the room and Julie got on the phone.

'How's work going?' Lucy asked, nursing an orange juice as she shifted her large belly awkwardly. Bless her, her bump was so big now she looked like she was going to pop at any time, even though she still had another four weeks to go until her due date. She'd had her first baby much later than expected so Lucy wasn't likely to get a reprieve from the uncomfortableness any time soon.

'Good, busy as always,' Eva said. 'I designed a cover for one of my favourite authors the other day, that was a big honour, but a lot of pressure to get it right.'

'Must be so wonderful to have that opportunity to be so creative,' Jacinda said, wistfully. Jacinda and Eva had studied art and design at college and university together. Jacinda had worked in an advertising agency coming up with the most amazing concepts for adverts for all the big brands. Then she'd had a baby and then another and hadn't been back to work in over four years. She loved being a mum, but she clearly missed work too. 'The most creative I've been lately is helping Izzy to make a papier-mâché rocket. But she starts school in September and I was thinking I'd go back to work part-time. Just two days a week, Alex's mum said she's happy to have Theo those days. It will be good to get the old grey matter working again.'

'Ah, that will be lovely,' Leila said, already tucking into her slice of pizza which looked homemade. Leila always liked to cook.

'I agree,' Eva said. 'It's important to have some time just for you.'

'Pizza is on its way,' Julie said, putting the phone down. 'But I'm wishing I was in Cornwall right now to share Leila's, that looks delicious.'

Leila laughed and, to wind them all up, started eating the pizza with over-the-top moans about how delicious it was.

'I want to hear all about this wonderful holiday you have planned, Eva,' Natalie said. 'It sounds amazing, are you really going all over the world?'

Eva felt the smile erupt on her face. 'Yes. I mean it's not booked yet, but it's in the process of being finalised. I'm basically just waiting for confirmation.'

'I can't believe you're doing it,' Lucy said. 'You're so brave.'

'I'm not going alone, I'll have an escort with me.'

'Ooer! Is it that kind of holiday?' Jacinda teased.

Eva laughed. 'Not that kind of escort. A travel guide. Her name's Rebecca and she seems lovely.'

'Where are you going, tell us everything?' Julie asked.

She rattled off the big list that she had discussed with Rebecca that day and she could see her friends getting all excited for her.

'This sounds amazing,' Leila said. 'But it doesn't sound like something you would do at all.'

'I know, it really isn't. I'm a homebody, I like my flat, I like my pyjamas,' Eva laughed, knowing that some days she didn't even get out of them. 'But it's time for a change and I think my mum would have loved to see me finally going on an adventure.'

Jacinda smiled and patted her on the leg. 'I think she would have too.'

'Oh, I have to tell you what happened today at the travel agents,' Eva said, keen to get her friends on her side against the arrogant Thor. She explained about the baby and what an arse Thor was.

'You with a baby,' Natalie laughed. 'I have the photo of you holding Alfie at his christening. I'm not sure who looked more upset him or you.'

'I know, I'm not great with kids,' Eva agreed.

'Oh, it'll be different when you have your own,' Lucy said, stroking her belly lovingly.

'Maybe.' Eva hadn't ruled out having children of her own one day, but she didn't have the natural affinity with children that her friends seemed to have. 'It was safe to say Felix was not impressed with my abilities.'

'I'm not sure why Thor was being so arsey about it, you were trying to help,' Julie said.

'Ah, I wouldn't be happy about handing over my child to

a complete stranger, I understand why he was a bit overprotective,' Lucy said.

Eva sighed because she knew Lucy was right, but it did seem really unfair that Thor had been so rude when she had only done it to get him out of trouble.

'And then, after all that, he had the audacity to ask me out for a drink as if a charming smile would be enough to smooth over any bad behaviour,' Eva said.

'Did you say yes?' Julie asked.

'Of course not.'

'So this Thor, what does he look like?' Leila asked, obviously wondering why Eva was protesting so much.

'He's really unattractive,' Eva lied, not wanting his good looks to sway their opinion of him.

'What's the name of the company?' Jacinda asked, picking up her phone. 'Was it The World Is Your Oyster?'

'Yes, but I don't think his photo is on there,' Eva lied again and then decided to change the subject. 'Have you thought any more about moving house, Julie?'

'Holy hell, he's hot,' Jacinda said and they all gathered round her phone. Even Leila was looking on her own phone.

'And he's a pompous ass,' Eva tried but her friends clearly didn't hear her.

'Imagine going round the world with him – you wouldn't bother to look at the sights if he was standing next to you,' Natalie said.

'I wouldn't mind bunking with him,' Lucy said.

'Is it too late to change your escort?' Jacinda said.

'Well you wanted adventure, travelling with him would certainly give you that,' Julie said.

Leila was busy fanning herself.

'Does the fact that he's a complete knob stand for anything?' Eva said.

They all looked at each other and laughed as they shook their heads.

'I think I'd pretty much forgive this man anything,' Leila said, staring at her phone with wide eyes.

'Then you're all shallow,' Eva laughed, shaking her head in mock disgust.

'Do you really not think he's attractive?' Jacinda asked.

Eva took the phone off her and looked at him: the perfect cheekbones, the amazing turquoise eyes.

'Of course he's good-looking,' Eva said, which was a complete understatement. 'But he's a rude, arrogant ass.'

'Oh, I bet he has a lovely ass,' Jacinda said and they all laughed.

'Well thankfully, I'll never be seeing him again.' Eva said, coming out of the website and removing his photo from the screen. If she never saw him again that would suit her just fine.

Chapter 5

God, Eva was going to be sick. Maybe she was coming down with something. She really shouldn't travel if she was ill. Maybe she shouldn't go on this holiday at all.

Despite the ungodly hour, the check-in hall at Heathrow airport seemed like utter chaos with hundreds of people milling around her with their suitcases, children and grandparents in tow. She had no idea where she was supposed to go or what she was supposed to do. The last time she had been in an airport she was eight years old and travelling to Spain for a week with her mum and Laurel.

What was she doing here? This was a mistake.

It had only been four weeks since she had first met Rebecca. Surely it wasn't enough time to plan and book a holiday. But Rebecca was efficient and organised to a T. The very next day after that disastrous meeting, Rebecca had emailed Eva with a detailed plan of where they were going, all the flights, hotels they were staying in, the excursions they were going to go on and how much it would all cost. The price had left a nice lump for spending money so Eva had told her to book it, handing over thousands of pounds in one day. A few hours later, she'd received confirmation that it was all booked and a detailed list of what to pack. Eva had pretty much spoken to Rebecca every day since with her questions, fears and worries. Rebecca had dealt with it all calmly.

Eva just needed her here now to take control and calm her down.

It was going to be OK. She had worked very long hours over the last few weeks to complete all the outgoing cover projects so she was relatively free to enjoy the trip, although she would have to keep up to date with her emails and do a bit of design work here and there. She had checked her list a hundred times, she had packed everything Rebecca had told her to take and several other items Rebecca hadn't mentioned just in case. She had her passport, a small amount of foreign currency for each country she was going to visit and several travel books loaded on her Kindle for different locations. She'd even made herself a packed lunch to take on the flight today just in case she didn't like the plane food. She was ready.

So why the hell was she so nervous?

She was waiting near the ice cream stand, just like Rebecca had told her. But for someone so efficient, Rebecca was now a worryingly fifteen minutes late.

The doors from outside swept open and Eva was surprised to see Thor walking in carrying a large rucksack. He exuded this charm and confidence in his own skin and Eva noticed several women looking over at him with dreamy eyes. What the hell was he doing here? OK, so he was probably here to give Rebecca a hand. Or maybe he was going off on his own trip with another client… at the exact same time as Eva and Rebecca were flying out.

He looked around and his eyes fell on her and he started walking towards her. He was smiling, though it didn't quite meet his eyes.

'Eva, hi. We haven't been properly introduced but I'm Thor Anderson,' he said, again pronouncing it with that hard T.

'Hi,' Eva said, looking over his shoulder for Rebecca.

'I'm afraid I have some bad news. Rebecca fell down the stairs last night and ended up in hospital.'

'Oh my god, is she OK?' Eva said.

'She's fine, her ankle isn't. That's broken in three places but other than that Rebecca is fine.'

'Oh, that's why you're carrying her rucksack,' Eva said, sighing with relief.

Thor frowned, staring at her like she was stupid. 'That's why I'm here and she isn't. Obviously she can't travel with a broken ankle. I'm going to take her place.'

Eva stared at him for a full ten seconds before she spoke, her heart galloping in her chest. Her wonderful trip of a lifetime was suddenly crashing down in front of her eyes.

'Oh no you're not,' Eva said, a hot ball of emotion clogging the back of her throat.

'Excuse me?'

'I'm not going on holiday with you.'

'Why not? My boss has spent several hours changing the names on the flight tickets so that's all covered. I'm very experienced, I've probably been to every place on your itinerary more than once, I'm probably more qualified than

Rebecca is in some areas. I can carry your suitcase for you and I can almost guarantee that I can get us upgrades on most of our flights and hotels. You're in very good hands.'

'That's not the point. I don't want to go anywhere with you. You're…' she gestured to the beautiful, arrogant, overconfident package in front of her. 'Rude, obnoxious, full of yourself.'

His eyebrows shot up, his gorgeous turquoise blue eyes widening in surprise. 'You're very judgemental, aren't you? You spent fifteen minutes with me a few weeks ago when I was stressed out and a little overprotective because you were holding my nephew and you've decided I'm a horrible person. Look, I'll make this really simple: you have three choices. You can cancel the whole trip and we can go straight back to the shop now and see what we can do about getting a refund on some of your money. I presume you have travel insurance, you should be able to claim on that and get some of your money back from that too. Or you can go on this trip alone and I can see about getting a refund on my half of the trip for you. Or we can go together and I'll do my very best not to be obnoxious or rude for the whole of the trip and try to fill Rebecca's shoes.'

Eva bit her lip. She didn't want any of those choices. God, this was why she never went on holiday, because knowing her, everything that could go wrong, would. Today was a case in point. Embarrassingly, she felt tears prick her eyes. Amongst all her fears and worries, she had been looking forward to this trip. But above all else, this was her way of honouring her mum, of fulfilling all those dreams Juliette had wanted to achieve before Eva came along. There was no way she could cancel. That wasn't an option. Which left her with two choices. Go it alone or go with Thor. Being with someone she didn't like for six weeks could have the potential to ruin the whole holiday. Going it alone looked like the lesser of two evils.

'I'll go alone then,' Eva said, hating the wobble in her voice.

Thor's eyebrows shot up even further, but there was also a look of admiration there too. 'Wow. I really made a bad impression on you, didn't I? I'm really sorry about that. OK then, here is the itinerary and paperwork.' He handed her a black zip-up folder. 'I'll be in touch in a few days when I can try to sort out some kind of refund for my share. You won't get it all back, it's too late in the day for that. But your travel insurance should cover any shortfall. Have a good trip.'

He turned and made towards the doors.

Oh god, she couldn't go alone. As much as she wanted to be brave and bold and fearless like her mum was, Eva wasn't like that. She'd spent too much of her life closeted in her own house, venturing out to the shops, to friends' houses or to see her family, but never daring to go much further than that. The prospect of getting on a plane and travelling across the world alone was utterly terrifying. And now Thor was leaving and she had no idea where she had to go to check in or what she had to do.

OK, she could do this. Her mum had spent her life seeking out adventure and had loved every minute. As long as Eva avoided anything poisonous and any adrenaline-fuelled activities and walking in dodgy areas after dark, then she'd probably be fine. Probably.

She opened the itinerary with shaky fingers and stared down at a bunch of text and numbers that didn't mean anything to her. She glanced up at the departure board above her and looked for a flight to Paris around the same time as hers. She spotted one; she looked at the flight number and back at the itinerary to see if she could match it up. Sure enough the numbers were the same. The screens told her to check in at desks fifteen to twenty. OK, this was easy, she had this.

She ignored the shake in her legs as she dragged her suitcase over in that direction. She was really going to travel the world alone. She felt a little excited by this, terrified to death, but excited.

She joined a long queue and pulled out her phone to give Laurel a call. Despite the very early hour, her aunt would be up, she was always awake at this time of the morning.

'Eva, how's it going?' Laurel said as she answered the phone. Eva could imagine her sitting in her favourite chair with a cup of coffee and her favourite book.

'Well, not good,' Eva said, shuffling forward in the queue. 'Rebecca has broken her ankle and Thor turned up to escort me instead.'

There was silence from Laurel for a moment and Eva imagined she was putting her book down to give Eva her fullest attention.

'That gorgeous man that looks like he fell out of a male model catalogue?' Laurel said excitedly.

'The arrogant knob that was rude to me when I was booking my holiday, that's the one,' Eva said. 'But I sent him packing and now I'm going alone.'

'What? Eva, was that wise?'

'I'm going to be fine,' Eva said, though not quite believing her own bravado. She opened her bag and checked through her belongings once more. She fished her passport out of her bag and then rooted through the itinerary to see if she needed to hand over any paperwork or tickets when she was checking in. There didn't seem to be anything there. What if Thor still had it?

'Surely Thor can't be that bad,' Laurel said.

Eva flicked through all the paperwork again and dropped her passport on the floor in the process.

She bent down to pick it up, dropping a few sheets of paper on the floor too. A strong man's hand picked up her passport and handed it back to her.

'Thank you,' Eva said, grabbing at the papers and then looked up into the piercing blue eyes of Thor. Her heart sank. 'Laurel, I'll call you back.' She hung up. 'What are you doing here?'

'I just realised your insurance won't be valid. Your cover is for an escorted holiday, you won't be covered for anything medically, or for any theft or losses if you are on your own. So if you really want to go, you're stuck with me, I'm afraid.'

She stared at him and then stood back up. This couldn't be happening. Of all the people that worked for the travel agency, why did it have to be him? She frantically searched for some other way round this.

'I could change the insurance.'

'You could, but you might have some trouble as it's the day of departure. Or you could let me accompany you for a week. If you still think I'm obnoxious and rude after that, my colleague, Sonia, is coming back from her trip at the end of this week. If you'd prefer someone else to me, she could fly out and join you at the beginning of next week and take over from me then.'

What a complete mess. She shoved all her papers back into the folder, delaying for time while she tried to decide what to do. She looked back up at Thor and he was watching her with kind eyes, which jarred with her image of him being an obnoxious git.

He was actually being really patient, and if anyone was being obnoxious right now, it was her. She was going to blame that on the lack of coffee, the early start and the unwelcome surprise. Thor might be a bit of a knob but none of this was his fault and he was trying to make the best of a crappy situation for her. Maybe he wasn't as bad as she first thought. A week's trial wouldn't be the worst thing, with the option of swapping him for someone else if it didn't work out. Paris was their first stop and she knew from his profile that Thor spoke French. It would probably come in handy.

'OK, thank you,' Eva said. She wasn't happy about any of this but having someone coming with her did make her feel so much better about the trip.

They stood in silence as they shuffled forward in the queue.

He moved to pick up her suitcase. 'You know, most people would take a rucksack on a round-the-world trip,' he teased, obviously trying to clear the air.

She grabbed the suitcase before he could touch it. 'I might be completely inept when it comes to travelling by myself, I've never done something like this before, but I don't need you to carry my bags for me.'

'OK,' Thor said and masterfully didn't say anything else.

God, she sounded so ungrateful. And now she was being rude too. Should she have brought a rucksack? Rebecca hadn't mentioned that but it kind of made sense; there would be lots of places that weren't suitcase-friendly. She really was ill-prepared for a round-the-world trip and Thor probably thought so too.

They stood in awkward silence for a few more moments, slowly moving to the front of the line.

'I'm sorry,' Eva said. 'I've been so nervous about this whole trip. Talked myself into it, talked myself out. The only thing that has made this prospect more bearable has been having Rebecca to do it with me, she seemed nice and we got on well and now...'

'You're stuck with the arrogant knob, I get it. I wouldn't be my first choice for a travelling companion either. But I'm sure we can still have fun and enjoy the trip. I'll be on my best behaviour, I promise.'

He held up his fingers in a Boy Scout salute and she couldn't help but smile. Seeing her smile seemed to make him relax a little too.

'So, you talk about this trip as if it's something you really don't want to do,' Thor said.

'No, I do want to do it... sort of,' Eva said.

He looked at her in confusion.

'Let's say I'm pushing myself out of my comfort zone.'

'What's your comfort zone?'

'Sitting at home in my pyjamas.'

He smirked. 'Ah. Well, there's nothing wrong with sitting

around in your pyjamas, so why do you want to break the mould now?'

Eva stalled in telling him about the list of dreams – that felt too personal to share – but she knew she'd have to tell him at some point.

'Did Rebecca not tell you anything about this trip?'

'To be honest, no. We spoke a little about the places you were going and I gave her a few tips and ideas for different locations, but nothing more than that. Three hours ago, I was blissfully asleep in my bed when Tracy called, told me to get up, pack a bag for a round-the-world trip and get to the airport to meet you. I haven't even spoken to Rebecca yet.'

'OK,' Eva said, slowly, unsure of where to start. 'Why don't I explain everything over breakfast?'

'Sounds good. I need to have a closer look at this itinerary anyway. Tell you what, if I can get us an upgrade on the flight to Paris you can pay for breakfast.'

'And if you don't?' Eva asked.

He grinned. 'I will.'

She laughed. 'You're so full of yourself.'

'Well if I don't, I'll pay.'

She smiled. 'You have a deal.'

Chapter 6

Thor watched Eva as she went to get some juice. He was glad she'd agreed to him coming with her. Halfway out the door he had turned round and seen her standing there looking so completely terrified and he knew he couldn't do it. He couldn't leave her to travel the world alone. She was a bit brave and sassy but there was a vulnerability and naivety to her too, and he knew he wouldn't be able to sleep in his bed at night knowing he had left her alone. He had no idea if what he'd said about her insurance was true, though he suspected it would be, but he'd had to tell her something to get her to agree. She was wildly out of her depth with a trip like this. He was glad she had come round. Some of these places were not exactly tourist-friendly. And if they didn't get on, then Sonia would have to come out and replace him in a week's time. But at least his conscience would be clean.

He turned his attention to the itinerary as Eva returned to the table with two glasses of fruit juice. This was not like any round-the-world trip he'd done before. Some of the places they were going, even he hadn't been to. Most of the round-the-world trips seemed to hit the same places, but this one was quite unusual. His heart leapt as his eyes fell on one of the locations. Skagen. He had never been there on one of his escorted trips; it was a forgotten little town right at the top of Denmark and wasn't ever on anyone's list of must-see places to travel to. Of course he knew it well, but what was Eva doing travelling there?

'I can't believe you got us an upgrade to business class,' Eva grumbled as she sat down across from him, accidentally bumping legs with him. It wasn't her fault, he knew he was freakishly tall; he had trouble folding himself under most tables and chairs. He glanced up from the itinerary and studied her as she shook her head, a small smile on her face. Despite her grumbles about paying for breakfast he could see she was secretly impressed.

He was glad to see her smiling now. He'd honestly thought she was going to cry when he told her he was coming on the trip instead of Rebecca. He didn't cope well with crying women. But there was something about Eva that he liked. She wasn't like the other pampered princesses he escorted on holidays who were basically looking for a skivvy for the trip – either that or their rich parents wanted some kind of bodyguard. Eva was different. She had balls. He would have admired the fact that she had chosen travelling alone over going with him, if he hadn't been so offended by it. He had hurt her that day in the shop and obviously pissed her off too, so he knew he had a lot of making up to do.

'So, some of these places are not your usual touristy locations. What made you pick them?' Thor said, taking a sip of his coffee.

She delved in her bag and pulled out a slip of paper, before turning back to face him holding the paper in her hands. 'My mum died about eighteen months ago.'

Ah crap, now it was all starting to make sense. Now he knew this was somehow linked to her mum, her determination to see this trip through regardless of her fears and doubts was more understandable.

'I'm so sorry.' He meant it. He was incredibly close to his mum, he couldn't imagine losing her.

'Thank you. She was… everything I'm not. Courageous, fearless, willing to try anything. She wanted to see the world, every little corner of it.'

Eva explained about the list of dreams and the inheritance money and how she had decided to use the money to tick off as many dreams on her mum's list as possible.

She slid the piece of paper across the table towards him. 'I've put them all on here for the trip so I don't lose any of the bits of paper.'

He took it but didn't open it. This felt like something precious and he didn't want to take this lightly.

'Are you sure you want me to look at it?' he asked.

She nodded. 'The itinerary has been based on ticking off a different dream in each location, sometimes two or three in one place, but you might have other ideas about where or how we can achieve some of these.'

He opened it up, his eyes taking in forty-six different dreams. 'This is quite some list.'

'I know, my mum was very thorough,' Eva smiled. 'She had her whole life mapped out. Ultimately she wanted to be a singer on Broadway, hence number forty-four.'

He glanced down to that number. *Sing on a stage on Broadway.*

'The ones towards the end of the list I can't do now because it's the wrong time of year. Umm,' she leaned over to look at the list. 'Number thirty-seven, we're too late to see the cherry blossoms in Japan, which I'm really gutted about; I would have loved to see that. And seeing polar bears might be tricky at this time of year too. Snowmobiling, dog sledding, sleeping in an igloo and staying in the ice hotel will have to wait until winter. And the last four on the list are… well, let's say the impossible dreams. I can't do them and that's OK. But I have up to thirty-six planned for this trip, so if I can at least tick them off, I'll be happy.'

Thor immediately looked at the last four items on the list. *Sing in front of the Queen, Sing on a stage on Broadway, Be kissed in the rain, Join the Mile-High Club.* He smiled at the last two.

'I don't think these are impossible dreams,' Thor said.

Eva laughed. 'No one wants to hear me sing. I think I might be arrested for treason if I tried to sing in front of the Queen. And can you imagine anyone paying to hear me sing in a show on Broadway? I think I'd get kicked out of the States for that.'

'And what about being kissed in the rain?' Thor said, diplomatically not mentioning the last dream on the list.

Eva snorted. 'I'm not just going to kiss some random stranger in the rain just to tick that off my list. I'm not going to sleep with a stranger on a plane either so don't be getting any ideas of any business-class shenanigans.'

He laughed as he looked through the rest of the dreams on the list. *See the tulips in Amsterdam, See the midnight sun.*

Ah, that explained why they were going to the Lofoten Islands at the top of Norway. He'd never been there before. *Ride a gondola in Venice, Go in a hot air balloon, Skydiving, Hold a tarantula, Go horse riding over the Golden Gate Bridge, Ride the world's tallest rollercoaster.* This was a fun list.

'Tell me, what are you most looking forward to?'

'Swimming with dolphins, definitely.'

He smiled. 'And what are you not looking forward to?'

'Skydiving. Throwing myself out of a perfectly good plane does not seem like a good idea.'

'You'll love it.'

'You've done it?' Eva asked, her eyes wide.

'Several times in fact. It's quite addictive.'

'I'll take your word for it.'

'You're going to have the time of your life on this trip,' Thor said. 'I'm excited for you.'

'I'm excited too,' Eva said. 'But also a little scared.'

'What's there to be scared of?' Thor said.

'Oh, a million things, mostly dying a horrible and painful death.'

'You can die a horrible and painful death sitting at home in your pyjamas. If you're going to go, then it's best to go with a bang.'

Eva smiled. 'I think you and my mum would have got on like a house on fire. But you have one week to prove to me that you're someone sensible and safe to travel with.'

He smirked. 'Now I can't promise either of those things.'

She smiled as if she already knew he was neither sensible or safe and was OK with that. Maybe he could get her to open up and relax on this holiday.

She leaned across the table. 'Thor Anderson. If you get me killed, I'll come back and haunt you.'

'Duly noted.' Thor picked up his coffee mug and held it up as a toast. 'To our big, beautiful adventure, Eva Blue.'

She grinned and chinked her mug against his.

Chapter 7

'Wow, is this really us?' Eva looked around business class in awe. There were three rows of pods, each pod holding two sumptuous leather chairs and so much leg room it looked like she could lie flat if the chairs extended that far back.

She glanced over at Thor to make sure she was in the right place and he was smiling at her.

'What?'

'You. You're different to the other girls I travel with. Most of the women I escort see flying in business class as their right, wouldn't be caught dead in economy. They're normally ordering champagne before we've even taxied onto the runway. You're a refreshing change.'

'I like champagne as much as the next girl,' Eva said, finding their pod.

'You do?'

'No, I can't stand the stuff. But maybe I should drink some today to fit in with the posh knobs.' She quickly clamped a hand over her mouth as she looked around to see if anyone had heard that, but luckily their part of the cabin was empty.

'You don't need to change to fit in, just be yourself,' Thor said. 'Here, take the window seat, the view of the sunrise from up there should be quite spectacular.'

She smiled at that gentlemanly gesture and settled herself in the seat, peering out at the tarmac below as the ground crew got themselves ready for departure. They had been the last onto the plane as they had got caught up chatting and planning for the trip. Thor had some different ideas to achieve her mum's dreams than Rebecca and it had been nice to get a fresh perspective.

She had texted Laurel to briefly explain the change of plans again and said she would call her later. Laurel had simply replied with one word at the news that Thor would be accompanying her. 'Yay!'

Eva placed a postcard she had bought at the airport on the table in front of her. This one had a photo of a glorious sunrise on the front. It seemed fitting. She had decided she was going to write a postcard to her mum at every location they visited, just like Juliette had done for her when she had been on her travels. It seemed silly because of course she had nowhere to post them to, but this whole trip was for her mum and she felt like her mum would enjoy reading the postcards about her adventures if she could somehow see them. If nothing else, they would serve as a nice reminder of this trip of a lifetime, a sort of diary of the beautiful places she was going to visit. Besides, she had long ago stopped feeling silly about talking to her mum. She used to leave voice messages on Juliette's answerphone when she'd first died. It had made her feel slightly better to fool herself into thinking that her mum was not gone, but simply away somewhere, and would return soon.

Thor tossed his passport onto the seat while he took his jacket off. She looked up at him and couldn't help noticing his large muscular arms straining against the fabric of his shirt. She quickly averted her eyes, knowing it was inappropriate to look at him like that. She glanced down to his passport which had landed open on the photo page.

'So Thor is your real name?' Eva asked, being careful to pronounce it the right way. She immediately felt silly for asking that.

But Thor didn't seem bothered about the question.

'Yes. The god of thunder. It's quite a common name in Denmark. Thor is one of our Norse gods. Did you think I'd made it up?'

'No, well, yes, sort of. Not too many Thors in West London. I figured it was a name you had chosen to impress your clients.'

'It's not a name I would choose. I get too many comments about my hammer and I get into too many discussions with people on how to pronounce it. I think I'd go for something much more common, like Eric.'

Eva laughed. 'You are definitely not an Eric.'

'No?' Thor smirked.

'Thor suits you.'

'You think I look like a god?' Thor quirked an eyebrow up, his mouth twitching up into a smirk he was clearly trying to suppress.

'You're so cocky,' Eva laughed. But oddly it was an attractive feature.

Eva watched one of the air hostesses approach Thor with a wide smile on her face and those dreamy eyes she'd seen on all the women that had looked at him in the airport.

'Sir, do you need any help with your bag?'

Thor smiled back. 'I'm fine, thanks.'

'Well, if you need anything, just let me know.'

Eva waited to see if the air hostess would extend the same invite to her but she simply moved on.

'That happen to you a lot?' Eva said, checking her bag for the umpteenth time that she still had her purse, phone, passport, sweets and water.

'What?' Thor said, sitting down next to her.

Eva gestured to the air hostess. 'Women falling over themselves for you.'

'She was just being professional.' Thor stowed his bag by the side of his seat and stretched his long legs out in front of him. He was so big.

'OK, if that's what you want to call it.'

'What does that mean?'

'Oh come on, you must see it. Don't tell me you don't play up to it too. That's why we're sitting here in business class and not squashed up in economy. One look from those beautiful blue eyes and women are putty in your hands.'

'You think I have beautiful eyes?' Thor teased.

'Oh shush. As if your ego needs any more feeding. I bet the women you travel with love having you on their arm for a few weeks. Do they all try it on with you too?'

He tilted his head from side to side. 'Some of them do.'

They started taxiing onto the runway.

'So perks of the job?'

'Oh hell no. I may be an escort but I'm not that kind of escort. I would get fired on the spot if I did anything like that and I love my job too much to want to lose it.'

Eva fastened her seatbelt. 'Never been tempted?'

'Rich girls aren't my type.'

'They can't all be spoilt rich kids.'

'No, sometimes I escort older ladies, or older couples, the occasional man. Sometimes I even escort families. Mostly it's rich girls who like to have someone to carry all their bags and arrange everything for them so they don't have to lift a finger.'

'That's not why I wanted an escort.'

'No, you wanted someone to stop you dying a painful death,' Thor teased.

Eva blushed, knowing that was partly true. She decided to change the subject slightly.

'So if you don't like the people you escort on these holidays, why do you love your job?'

'I get to see the world,' Thor said. 'How many people get to go on holiday as part of their job, to fly in first class to Japan, Australia, America? I have the best job in the world.'

'Looking after people you don't like, visiting the places they want to go, you don't get a say in it. You're with them almost twenty-four hours a day, there's no escape. It doesn't sound much like a holiday to me,' Eva said.

'It's not all bad. I get to meet interesting people like you,' Thor said.

Eva smiled, feeling the warmth of that offhand comment fill her.

'So why are you so scared of travelling the world?' Thor asked.

'Not scared, just cautious,' Eva said.

'OK, and is there a reason?'

Eva weighed up what to tell him. 'I used to go on holiday a lot with my mum when I was a kid, I ended up with so many bruises, broken bones and stitches with the scrapes she got me into. One holiday, she decided she wanted to go on this private beach and dragged me in there too, we literally climbed over a fence to get in. The police were called and they sat us both in the back of the police car while they decided what to do with us. Mum was scared, I could tell that and the more anxious she became, the more scared I was. In the end they just gave my mum a good telling-off, told her that she should be more responsible as she was supposed to be looking after me. And then one of them turned to me and said, "Keep her out of trouble," as if I was the sensible one and I should be looking after her, and I just had this weird moment of clarity that it wasn't supposed to be that way.'

His face cleared with understanding. 'So you started to feel like you couldn't trust her any more.'

Eva immediately felt guilty because that was exactly it. 'She was a wonderful mum, but she had this wild, carefree streak that got us into trouble on a regular basis.' She paused, not sure if she should tell him the next bit. 'I was sort of kidnapped once.'

He stared at her incredulously. 'What?'

'It's not as bad as it sounds. I was in the back of the car and Mum got out to take photos of this sunset over a lake and this man jumped in the car and drove off. I watched Mum out the back window and she had no idea that the car had even gone, she was too busy taking pictures. I was so scared I was too afraid to say anything, I just sat in the back, watching Mum slowly disappear from view. About half a mile down the road, the man looked in the rear-view mirror and spotted me – he'd had no idea I was there. He slammed on the brakes and got me out and left me on the side of the road and drove off. The whole thing probably lasted no more than two minutes, but it was terrifying. I didn't really want to go on holiday with her after that.'

'I'm not surprised. God, that must have been so traumatic for you.'

'Well it was at the time, but no lasting scars, except of course not being overly keen on travelling and holidays any more. But I'm determined to change that.'

'Well that explains why you wanted an escort. But how come you don't have anyone else to travel with? No friends, no significant other?'

'I have friends, all happily married, most of them with children and some of them live too far away for me to see regularly, but we keep in touch. No significant other because… well, did you miss the part where I spend most of my life in my pyjamas? It's hard to meet people when you never really go out.'

'You don't work, no colleagues?'

'Oh I do, I work from home. I'm a cover designer so I just sit and play on my laptop or tablet all day. I run my own company, so it's pretty much me, but I do outsource to a few freelancers now and again. Mikael lives in Poland so I never see him. Adam is local and he comes round sometimes, but he's eighteen, listens to some very shouty music and is in that phase of wearing those ridiculously skinny spray-on jeans that are so tight I'm not sure the vital organs are still working. Not really my type, but a demon with some of the sci-fi covers.'

'What about previous boyfriends? Where did you meet them?'

'Nigel was my last boyfriend. An author of some steam-punk story. I read it, it was pretty bad, but he was local and he wanted to meet to explain his vision. So we met up and we got on pretty well and started seeing each other but it fizzled out after a few weeks. He bored me, although he said he found me pretty boring too, so safe to say we didn't set each other's worlds on fire. He did get a free cover out of it though so I'm sure he was happy. I've not had any really serious boyfriends. I like my own company too much to want to spend all my time with someone else.'

'I'd say you're with the wrong men if you don't enjoy spending time in their company. Love changes that for you.'

'You're probably right. Do you have a girlfriend, Thor?'

'No not right now. It's hard to build a relationship when I'm away with work so often.'

'But you sound like you speak from experience.'

Thor sighed. 'I was in love once. She decided she loved someone else.'

'Oh, I'm sorry.'

He shrugged, though he didn't quite pull off the nonchalance he was going for. 'It was a long time ago.'

She studied him for a moment. He had been hurt by it and she got the feeling this job allowed him to run away from that pain. Or run away from the woman.

'So, do you think you'll do this job forever, never settle down?' Eva asked, changing the subject for him.

He looked down at his phone and switched it off. 'Christel got married a few years ago, and though I no longer have any feelings for her, I do want what she has. I saw her wedding photo, how she looked at him, and while it was a bit of a kick in the teeth that she had never looked at me like that, I want that with someone one day. If I found the right person, I'd give all of this up for her, but she'd have to be someone truly special.'

'You don't have to give up travelling though, if that's what you love. You can travel the world with her. I don't know, buy a boat, see where the wind takes you,' Eva said. She caught herself and smiled at her romantic rose-tinted view. It never worked out like that.

'That sounds nice... if we were in some Hollywood romantic movie,' Thor said, teasing her.

'Ah I know, I have a foolish, romantic heart. I like the idea of people's dreams coming true and them getting their happy ending.'

'And what does your happy ending look like?'

'Oh, I've never really thought about it. Though I do like the idea of that little boat, just me, the man I love, the endless sea and the stars above us.'

He smiled at her. 'You do have a romantic heart. What about your own dreams? This holiday is all about making your mum's dreams come true, but what about yours?'

Eva thought about this for a moment. What would be on her list?

'Everyone has a list,' Thor said when she remained silent.

God, maybe she really was boring if she didn't have a list. She had become so complacent with her own life, financially secure, happy to just tick along that she had no real desires to do anything beyond that. Maybe she needed this holiday for more than just to fulfil her mum's dreams, maybe she needed this slice of adventure for herself too.

She looked over at Thor, who was still waiting for an answer. 'What were your dreams when you were younger?' he prompted.

'Well, my biggest dream was to become an artist. I love to paint, studied art at college and university. I suppose I am an artist in a way, designing covers, and I really love my job but it wasn't what I envisaged when I was growing up. I do get to be creative, which is important to me, but most of my designs are done on the computer. Occasionally I get to paint a cover and they always make me happy, but I don't get a lot of time for painting any more, certainly nothing just for me.'

'I think it's important to make that time to do something just for you. Being an artist is hard to become successful at, so the fact that you have a job that you get to be creative in is a credit to you and your skills. Maybe you'll never see your work in a gallery and maybe your name will never be held in such reverence as Picasso or Monet but if you get pleasure out of painting then you need to make sure you find time for it. Realise your dreams in your own way.'

She smiled; she liked that.

'But let's see what dreams of yours we can make come true on this trip. Is there anywhere you really wanted to visit?' Thor said.

'I've always wanted to see New York,' Eva said, eager to come up with something.

'That's a start.'

She looked around the plane for some inspiration, her eyes alighting on a brochure that had a picture of *The Lion King* musical on the back with the person dressed as the giraffe.

'Giraffes,' Eva blurted out. 'I'd quite like to stroke a giraffe.'

Giraffes were her favourite animal but she was clutching at straws here and, from the look on Thor's face, he knew it too.

'I'm sure we can do that. Look, how about a deal? You come up with your own list of dreams, preferably stuff we can do on this holiday, and I'll get us upgraded on every flight.'

'You can't promise that,' Eva laughed.

'If I don't, I'll carry your bags for you.'

'And I'm not asking you to do that,' she said firmly.

'I'll buy you dinner in every location we don't get an upgraded flight to.'

'OK...' Eva said, slowly. 'How many items do you need on this list?'

'Your mum's list is quite extensive, and we have a very full six weeks ahead of us, so let's go with ten for now.'

Eva sighed. 'OK, you have yourself a deal.'

Chapter 8

Dear Mum,

Well the trip started out as a bit of a disaster when my guide, Rebecca, didn't turn up and I got lumbered with Thor Anderson instead. But I may have misjudged him. I think we might get on quite well on this trip. He has one week to prove himself or I'm ditching his ass. OK, I just wrote that because he was reading over my shoulder. He seems nice. Damn it. He just read that too. He says he's going to try to upgrade himself from nice. I told him, nice is as good as it gets. I think you would like him, he has a bit of a wild streak but I feel safe with him.

I have stupidly agreed to come up with ten dreams of my own. No idea what to include on this list but I suppose this trip of a lifetime warrants something amazing. I have an idea for Paris to get my own back on Thor for suggesting this madness. Let's see how keen he is to continue with my crazy dreams once he hears this one.

We have just seen the most incredible sunrise from the plane, it seemed all the more magical watching it from up here above the blanket of clouds as the sun peeped out painting the sky this glorious tropical pink. A new day dawning, a new beginning. It feels like the perfect way to start this trip. I'm excited to see where the journey takes us.

Wish you were here!

Love Eva x

'It's a double bed!' Eva said, staring at the bed in the middle of the room.

Thor suppressed a smile at her shock. 'Technically it's probably a kingsize.'

'This isn't funny.'

'It is a little,' Thor said. He looked at her face and saw she wasn't remotely amused.

'Why are you not more freaked out by this? I'm not sharing a bed with you,' Eva said.

'It happens from time to time. You request a twin but a lot of foreign hotels don't have that facility or have very few twin-bedded rooms available.'

She looked at him with wide eyes. 'So this sort of thing happens a lot to you. You end up sleeping in the same bed as the rich girls you don't like?'

'No, for moral and professional reasons, when I escort a female, I and the company insist on separate rooms throughout the trip. But I know it has happened to Rebecca and my other female colleagues on several occasions. It's possible we may have this a few times throughout the trip. How many times were you sharing a room with Rebecca?'

'She persuaded me to share with her almost throughout the whole trip. There are a couple of places she said the rooms were notoriously small so we opted for separate rooms on those occasions but other than that we are sharing throughout.'

Thor sighed. This was going to be awkward. It was bad enough sharing a room with her but a bed…

'I'll contact Tracy and see what we can do about sorting out separate rooms for the rest of the trip. I know Tracy spent a few hours this morning making name changes for me for all the flights. She'll have to change this as well.'

Tracy wouldn't be happy at the added expense. An extra room at each location would be costly but the company could hardly pass the expense onto Eva. It wasn't her fault and she had specifically requested that Rebecca accompany her, not him.

'OK.' Eva seemed a bit calmer at this news. 'What are we going to do about this?'

'It's no big deal, I'll just call down to reception and see if it can be changed to a twin or see if they have an additional room.'

Although he didn't fancy their chances. There was a big rock festival in town and he imagined every hotel would be booked solid.

Eva set about making a cup of tea, clearly happy the situation would soon be resolved. He wasn't sure how to break it to her.

He phoned down to reception and in fluent French

explained the situation. But it was as he thought, the hotel was booked solid.

He put the phone down and turned back to Eva, who was humming quietly to herself. He smiled. There was something about her that he liked. In another life, they could have been good friends.

She looked up at him, smiling brightly. 'All sorted?'

'Umm, no. They're fully booked.'

Her face fell.

He looked around the room: no sofa, not even a chair. He could sleep on the floor but there wasn't much of that. The room was filled with the bed.

'Look, it's just one night, the bed is big enough that we can stretch out without touching each other and I promise to keep my eyes shut the whole time you're wandering around naked.'

'There'll be no wandering around naked,' Eva said, her voice high.

He lay down on the bed and assumed the starfish position. 'Look how much room you'll have. You won't even know I'm here.'

She looked at him, clearly not happy with this arrangement.

It made him smile. Most of the girls he had escorted throughout the years would have been more than happy to share a bed with him. She was looking at him as if the idea repulsed her.

'Look, we have one night in Paris, so we can either spend the day today exploring this beautiful city or we can spend it trying to find another hotel that has two free rooms, which might prove a little tricky with that big rock festival in town.'

Eva sighed, still clearly not convinced.

'You already said I'm nice, so you know I'm not going to jump you.'

'I snore,' Eva tried.

'So do I.'

'I talk in my sleep.'

'Which will make for an interesting night,' Thor said.

'I fidget.'

'I'm a heavy sleeper. Nothing will disturb me. Come on, give it a go.' He patted the bed encouragingly.

She sighed and gingerly lay down next to him. There was still a lot of bed between them. 'See.'

'OK, fine,' Eva said, grumpily. 'But one night only. Tomorrow night I want my own room.'

'I promise,' Thor said, with a lot more conviction than he felt. He didn't think Tracy would be that thrilled about having to change all the rooms. He would have to cross that bridge when he came to it.

Eva decided, as she tucked into a chocolate crepe, that she loved Paris. It was this buzz of cultures, people of all ages and origins, all bustling together. They had spent the day perusing all the different sights, the wonderful Louvre which she could have spent all day in and still not seen it all, the Arc de Triomphe, Notre-Dame and the Palace of Versailles. Paris was a beautiful city.

They hadn't been to the Eiffel Tower yet; she had been putting that off with dread in her stomach. She didn't want to stand at the top and sing. People would laugh at her. But in hindsight, maybe she should have got it out the way first and then she could have enjoyed Paris more.

The sun was just starting to set over the city, lending a pinky gold light to all the sights, but she had one more thing to do to put off the agony for a bit longer.

'I've been thinking about one of my dreams,' Eva said, licking chocolate off her fingers.

Thor finished his strawberry crepe and wiped the napkin across his lips. 'Shoot.'

'I'm going to need your help for this one.'

He nodded, keenly. 'Whatever you need.'

She smiled mischievously. She felt the need to get him back, for making her do her own dream list, for the double bed, for just being a smug cocky git. Although she was definitely warming to him.

'So when I was growing up, I had this big plan. I was going to marry the boy next door, Leon, who sadly for me turned out to be gay. I was going to get married in Buckingham Palace – I was a child, I didn't think about the practicalities of that one – my dad was going to fly in and give me away and I would have a hundred bridesmaids.'

Thor smiled. 'Big dreams.'

'I know. And I realise those things are never going to happen.'

'Where does your dad live?' Thor asked, focussing on the one part of that plan that would seem realistic. Little did he know.

'Oh god, Los Angeles, I think. Well, one of his homes is there. I've… never actually met him.'

'You've never met your dad?' Thor asked her in shock.

They'd spoken a little about his family and she knew they were very important to him.

'No.' She paused over what to say next. She didn't talk about her dad with many people. 'My mum had a one-night stand with a gorgeous American, and nine months later, I arrived.'

'And she never got in touch with him to tell him?'

'Oh she did. He was horrified. He... already had a wife and a child on the way. She didn't want anything from him, just thought he should know. He paid her hush money to go away.'

'Hush money? That seems a bit...'

'He was famous. Still is actually. He didn't want it to ruin his reputation. He was just starting to become known. When she met him she didn't even know who he was but then he sort of exploded in popularity overnight and—'

'You're going to have to tell me who it was.'

Eva let out a heavy sigh. 'Thomas Connor.'

He stared at her with wide eyes and with good reason. Thomas Connor had been *the* movie pinup twenty-odd years ago and was still a successful actor now, though not so much the young heartthrob any more. He had been on the cover of all the magazines, starred in all the big blockbusters and famously had been lovingly married to the same woman for the last twenty-seven years.

'You're Thomas Connor's daughter?'

Eva gave a wry smile. 'Yeah.'

'Christ, that explains the hush money.'

'Yes it does. Mum contacted him once after I was born and he paid her a ton of money to go away. She contacted him just before my seventh birthday because I kept asking about him and I asked her to invite him to my birthday party. He didn't come. As far as I'm aware, she hasn't contacted him since.'

Thor frowned. 'How do you feel about that?'

Eva shrugged. 'I've never had him in my life so it's hard to miss something you've never had. I think he's a bit of an asshole if I'm honest, but there's a tiny part of me that would still like to meet him one day, just to say hello. I'm not looking for him to sweep me into his arms and lament all these lost years, and I don't imagine he will be too pleased to see me, but now that Mum has died I kind of feel that he is this connection to my mum's past that I've never met. Beyond my aunt Laurel I don't have any other family so it would be nice to at least meet him once.'

Thor nodded. 'And if nothing else, he might give you a ton of money to go away.'

Eva looked at him in horror. 'I don't want that. I don't want to meet him because he's rich and famous. I just want to meet the man who swept my mum off her feet. His blood is in my veins, whether he wants it or not.'

He touched her arm. 'I was just joking, I know you're not the gold-digger type.'

Eva nodded to accept the apology but they were silent for a while. Is that what her dad would think too, that she only wanted to meet him for the money? It was all pie in the sky anyway – she had no contact information for him and she could hardly look him up on Twitter or Facebook and ask if he would like to meet.

'What was the dream you wanted to tick off here?' Thor asked gently.

Eva shook her head. It seemed silly now.

'Come on, whatever it is, I'll help you do it.'

She smiled at his persistence. 'OK, my mum had this painting on her wall, this man and a woman, standing in front of the Eiffel Tower, and the man was proposing to her. The look of love on both of their faces was just... beautiful. In my fancy dreams, of getting married with a hundred bridesmaids, I was always going to be proposed to in front of the Eiffel Tower.'

She looked at Thor to see what his reaction was to this. He stared at her for a moment.

'You want me to propose?'

She couldn't help the smile from spreading on her face. He kept talking about pushing her out of her comfort zone and enjoying the adventure. How would he react to this? He'd also made it very clear there were strict rules when it came to his relationship with the women he escorted. But they were already blurring that boundary with the double bed.

'Yes I do.'

She waited for him to backtrack, to redraw that line between them, but she was surprised to see the smile on his face as well.

'OK.'

Nothing fazed this man.

'OK?'

'Sure, why not. Give me your phone. We need to get someone to video this occasion. Your first dream, we need to record this for posterity. You have to act surprised though when I do it.'

She handed him her phone.

'Do you have a ring?' Thor asked.

Wow, he was really getting into this.

She'd kind of expected him to say no; she certainly hadn't been expecting that he would be so enthusiastic about the idea.

She looked down at her fingers and at the cheap dragon ring on her right hand. It would have to do.

She pulled it off and gave it to him and he laughed when he saw it. 'Not how I would imagine proposing to the woman of my dreams but OK. I think we will have to adapt quite a few times on this trip, so let's go with it.'

He looked around for a suitable tourist. He spotted an elderly couple and approached them. Spoke to them first in French and, when it became apparent they were English, he switched easily. She heard him murmur how he wanted them to record a video and to make sure the Eiffel Tower was captured in the background. He showed the lady how to use the phone and then he came back to Eva.

He took her hand and, ridiculously, her heart leapt into her mouth. It was stupid; they were both aware that this wasn't real, she didn't like Thor in that way, but something made her excited about being proposed to here in Paris, the city of love.

'Eva Blue,' Thor said, seriously. 'You have made my life complete, you make me smile and you have given me so much happiness. I love you with everything I have.' He dropped to one knee, holding the cheap-looking dragon ring aloft. 'Will you do me the honour of becoming my wife?'

The lady who was recording the video gave a little squeal

and suddenly there were several people stopping to watch this spectacle unfold.

Eva had never been proposed to before and, though the gesture was completely empty, she suddenly wanted this exact thing. When the right man came along, she wanted to come back here and recreate this for real. For now, she could ham it up just like Thor for the sake of the camera.

She gasped, bringing a hand to her mouth, partly to hide the grin that was threatening to erupt on her face. She nodded, pretending that she was too overcome by emotion to speak. The little crowd cheered.

Thor slid the ring on her finger and she dutifully admired it.

'Go on dear, give her a kiss,' the lady encouraged.

Thor's smile slipped a fraction. She hadn't thought about that. Clearly, neither had Thor.

He stood up and gave her a big hug instead. All thoughts and reason went out of her head. She'd never been held like this and there was something really sad about that. Especially when this was completely fake. He held her against him for the longest time and when he went to let her go, she stupidly held onto him for a little longer. He gallantly didn't move away, just continued to hold her.

OK, this was ridiculous. She reluctantly let him go and he smiled down at her, taking it all in his stride.

He squeezed her hand and moved over to the couple to retrieve her phone as they congratulated him, then he took her hand and led her away from their impromptu fan club.

She looked down at her hand in his. It fitted there perfectly. What the hell was she doing? She hadn't planned to feel any of this, it was all a bit of fun.

When they were suitably far enough away from any of their witnesses, he dropped her hand and turned towards her.

'How was that?' Thor asked, still smiling hugely, obviously finding the whole thing hilarious. 'Did it fulfil your dreams?'

She smiled and nodded. 'It was perfect, thank you. You know, you're not at all what I imagined you'd be like.'

'What did you imagine I was like?'

'Your profile made you sound so… stuck-up, all that stuff about enjoying the finer things in life, the secret clubs and the exclusive restaurants and you're just… you're very easy-going.'

'Well, it's a bit of an act. You get used to playing the part your clients want you to play.'

Her heart sank a little at that. Was he playing a part with her? They had spent the day chatting and laughing like they were old friends. Was that all really an act?

'Most of my clients are fairly wealthy so they want those kinds of things on their holiday, the casinos, the posh hotels, the first-class flights, so if I promise those kinds of things on my profile then they are more likely to choose me to accompany them. And I'd much rather be in St Tropez or Miami or Dubai than stuck in the office, so I'm OK playing that role.'

'So you always put on an act for your clients?'

He shrugged. 'Pretty much. Although not today, it felt like being on holiday with one of my mates today. I can definitely be myself with you.'

She smiled. She liked that

Thor cleared his throat. 'Let's look at the video?'

She played it on her phone. She couldn't help but smile when she saw it.

'My aunt Laurel will love this.' She quickly forwarded it to Laurel for her to watch it. She deliberately left off any explanation to tease her, though she didn't think Laurel would believe for one minute that her niece had got engaged in less than twenty-four hours of knowing Thor, especially when that morning she had thought he was an arrogant knob. Eva was sensible and overly cautious to a fault and Laurel would know that. She decided to send the video through their WhatsApp group to the girls too as they currently had no idea of the change in plans which now included Thor.

'You were very convincing,' Eva said, as a flurry of messages came through. She grinned at their over-the-top excitement and slipped her phone back in her bag. She would reply to their messages later.

He shrugged. 'I've had practice.'

Her heart sank for him but she was grateful for the distraction. 'You were engaged to Christel?'

'I proposed, she said no. So this one was much more successful.'

He started to walk away towards the tower and she sensed the subject had closed.

'Hey, fiancé. Shall we go somewhere to get a drink to celebrate our engagement?'

He turned to her and grinned. 'Do you need fortifying before you tick off your mum's first dream?'

Eva groaned. 'I suppose it will be better to just get it over with. But you're definitely not videoing this one.'

He smiled. 'If you're sure?'

'Absolutely certain.'

He laughed and nodded and then gestured for her to go in the direction of the tower.

She sighed and followed him.

Chapter 9

Thor watched Eva as she peered down at the city below, her hair blowing gently in the wind. She had this look of awe and wonder on her face. He had been up this tower so many times over the years that it was hard to capture the same joy of seeing Paris from up here for the first time. Seeing it through Eva's eyes made him appreciate it with a fresh perspective.

Although they had used fast-track tickets to get to the second floor of the tower, they'd had to queue for a while to get the lift to the third floor, as everyone wanted to be at the top to watch the sun disappear below the skyline. The sky was a glorious scarlet and pink, the distant gold of the sun now no more a slash on the horizon. People were busy taking photos and videos of the glorious sight.

If Eva had thought that it might be quieter at this time of day then she had been sadly mistaken.

There was a small collective murmur of excitement as the flash of burnt amber got smaller and smaller and then disappeared altogether.

Eva let out a little sigh of contentment as the colour of the city went quickly through magenta to indigo. He was happy for her to take as long as she needed. Paris was a beautiful city.

Eventually she turned back to him.

'Wow, I love it here, but I really could do with something to eat now. I'm starving.'

He grinned. 'That's fine, we can eat when we get down. But I think we have something to do first before we leave.'

She bit her lip. 'I can't do it.'

'Sure you can.'

'I'm an awful singer.'

'I'm sure you can't be that bad, considering your mum's skills.'

'I didn't inherit that from her. There was a lot that I didn't inherit from her actually. Courage being one of them.'

She let out a heavy breath. She looked so scared and he had an overwhelming urge to wrap his arms around her and hold her close. But he wasn't going to let her leave until she did this. She would regret it later and they were leaving Paris the next day so there was no second chance.

'You just need to sing one line,' Thor encouraged. 'Your mum's dream was to sing at the top of the Eiffel Tower, it doesn't specify that you have to sing a whole song.'

'Don't you think that's cheating?'

He shrugged. 'More like bending the rules.'

She nodded. 'OK.'

She looked around and saw a bit of a gap on the other side, opposite where the sun had set. She made for that direction and he followed her.

She closed her eyes, took a deep breath as she faced out onto the city and then released a very shaky first line of the chorus from R Kelly's 'I Believe I Can Fly'.

His heart soared from pride. She was doing it, she was actually doing it. And she was beyond awful. But he couldn't stop the huge grin from spreading on his face. As she sang about touching the sky and spreading her wings, her voice rose in confidence.

He looked around to see what people's reactions were. Everyone was looking in their direction, lots of people were laughing and even worse they were videoing her on their phones. A group of lads had started swaying their arms in the air and one of them had even got a lighter out of his pocket and was holding that up aloft.

Crap. He didn't want her to be ridiculed. This was such an important thing for her.

He looked back at Eva, who was still standing with her eyes closed. He took a deep breath and started singing with her. She opened her eyes in surprise and looked at him. He gestured for her to keep going. She turned back to the skyline and he quickly looked back to the crowd and gestured for them to join in too. He was banking on the group of lads complying, they seemed to be up for anything. The lads joined in seamlessly, one of them singing in a very deep tenor voice, which his friends got quite a kick out of. And then, suddenly, everyone was joining in.

Eva turned round in surprise as the singing got louder, a huge smile on her face.

Everyone got to the end of the chorus and then gave a big cheer, clapping each other, clapping Eva. The group of lads decided to carry on singing the song and Thor took Eva's hand.

'Let's get something to eat. I think we definitely have something to celebrate tonight.'

She nodded, letting out a breath of relief, and he led her back to the lift.

Eva let the bubbles of the sparkling wine dance across her tongue as she looked out at the view of the city below, lit up with millions of tiny sparkling golden lights. Thor had promised her a much more impressive view of the city by night than that from the Eiffel Tower. The view from the observation deck at the top of Tour Montparnasse was pretty spectacular because it included the view of the Eiffel Tower itself, all lit up in its glorious splendour. She imagined the colours she would use if she was to paint this – she had some fabulous glittery metallic paints that she could use for the twinkling lights although, right then, she was finding it hard to concentrate on any of that.

The terrace was packed with people, all making the most of the warmth of the day by spilling out onto the open-air terrace to take in the twinkling lights of the city below. There seemed to be a big party going on up there, and there were easily a hundred people or more filling the space. She had found a gap against the glass to take in the city but had been jostled and shoved so many times by the party-goers that she had almost smacked her head against the glass more than once. After that Thor had moved directly behind her, his hand braced on the glass beside her, effectively caging her in. She knew he had only done that to protect her from being squashed from the crowd that seemed to be getting noisier and livelier by the minute, but it seemed so… intimate. He was standing so close, she could feel his warmth all the way down her back, his soft breath on top of her head.

This felt weird and wrong and all kinds of wonderful.

They had already shared a meal three floors below as they enjoyed the views of the city over incredible food and it had felt… romantic. Which was crazy. He was her escort, nothing more. She didn't have feelings for him. She had simply got swept away with the proposal because she had hoped that one day she would really be proposed to like that. Not because she had wanted Thor to propose for real. It had been the moment she had loved, not Thor.

She placed her hand on the glass next to his; it looked tiny in comparison to his giant paw. She smiled at the *engagement ring* still on her wedding finger. It had certainly been an eventful first day and Thor had been a huge part of all of that. How different would it have been if she had shared this day with Rebecca?

He leaned in, impossibly close, but still not touching and whispered in her ear so she could hear him over the noise.

'We have to be up early tomorrow. Shall we go to bed?'

God, her heart leapt at that completely innocent suggestion. Despite knowing that they would be sleeping side by side and nothing more, he managed to make it sound so sexy. She suddenly didn't know whether to be delighted or terrified at the prospect of sharing a bed with this man.

She turned round to face him and he was right there in her space, towering over her, his eyes locked on hers. He didn't move back away from her either.

'That sounds good,' Eva said, finding her voice.

He hesitated, his eyes still on hers for a few moments, the

air almost crackling between them. This was ridiculous. She was obviously imagining this spark. The sparkling wine, the city lights, the beautiful meal, the city of love, she was just getting carried away.

'You were brave tonight,' Thor said.

'I'm not brave,' Eva said.

'You were tonight. I liked that. I think, buried deep inside, there is this bold, courageous woman ready to come out and shine.'

'Oh, I'm definitely not the shiny type.'

'You lit up the whole Eiffel Tower.'

Eva swallowed, her mouth suddenly dry.

'The women I've escorted over the years, they all fade away after the trip comes to an end. I don't really remember any of them. After this trip finishes, I don't think I'm ever going to forget about you.'

He turned and moved away slightly and she let go of a breath she didn't even know she had been holding. He looked back and offered out a hand to help her through the crowds of people. She took it and felt the spark surge between them again.

As he started to lead her from the terrace, she couldn't help smiling.

Her mum had always wanted to make her mark on the world whereas Eva had been quite happy to hide away, keep herself to herself. But it seemed that somehow she had made her mark on Thor. She was practical; she knew nothing was ever going to happen between them. But she liked that she had made an impression on him.

Eva stared at herself in the bathroom mirror, ready to give herself a really good talking to. She had been hiding in here for over ten minutes and she felt sure that Thor would soon be sending out a search party for her. She had no idea what was making her so anxious: the thought of sharing a bed with someone who was almost a complete stranger or sharing the bed with Thor.

She had texted Laurel a while before to say that due to complications with the original booking she was sharing a bed with Thor. She glanced down at the phone now to see if Laurel had any pearls of wisdom or words of warning.

Woohoo!! Go and enjoy yourself.

Eva blushed at that thought and texted back. *We're sleeping in the same bed together not sleeping with each other.*

Laurel quickly replied. *If I had a man that hot in the same bed with me, the very last thing I'd be doing would be sleeping.*

Eva smiled. This was the kind of thing her mum would say, not Laurel. Maybe, with her wild, adventurous mum missing from the picture, her aunt felt she needed to step into her shoes to ensure Eva made the most of this adventure.

Laurel sent another message. *Send me a picture.*

Eva shook her head in amusement. *I'll phone you tomorrow.*

Yes, I want all the details.

She laughed and left her phone on the side, taking a deep breath to pluck up the courage. They were just going to sleep in the same bed, nothing more, but what if he tried to kiss her – what would she do? More to the point, what *should* she do? There had been something between them up on top of the Tour Montparnasse, she was sure of it, so the possibility of a kiss wouldn't be completely crazy. But she had to keep the boundaries between them. They had six weeks travelling ahead of them, it would be awkward as hell if something happened. They could be friends but nothing more than that. She wasn't looking for a relationship and if she was it wouldn't be with someone like Thor. She didn't want Thor like that anyway. Sure, the man looked like a god, and yes he had a sweet, funny side, but she didn't have feelings for him, absolutely not, they were poles apart.

She let out a little laugh.

This was stupid. He wouldn't try to kiss her. This was just a job for him and he had always been strict about his boundaries before – she was hardly going to be the girl that tempted him out of that. He would take one look at her in her blue ice cream print pyjamas and roll over and go to sleep. If there was any spark between them, it would be vanquished on the spot. Which was absolutely for the best.

She splashed her face with water in an attempt to wash away any thought of him kissing her, took a deep breath and walked out into the bedroom.

He was sitting in bed, completely bare chested, the sheet covering his hips as he read a book. He was wearing glasses and dear god, if she'd thought he looked good before fully clothed, this was another level. It suddenly felt a lot hotter in the room. She was sorely tempted to run back into the bathroom, grab her phone and take a picture. Laurel would get such a huge kick out of this.

He looked up at her and smiled. 'Nice pyjamas.'

She tore her eyes away from him. If he had been staring at her as if he'd like to eat her, she wouldn't feel very comfortable. There was no need to make things awkward between them. Even *more* awkward.

Eva spotted the line of pillows down the middle of the bed and frowned slightly. He'd built a barricade between them. Christ, was she that obvious and needy that he was afraid she'd suddenly jump him in the middle of the night?

She moved to her side of the bed and slid between the sheets.

'I've set the alarm,' Thor said, closing his book and switching off his bedside lamp. He lay down, facing away from her.

Annoyed with his presumption, she snapped off her light, plunging the room into darkness and she lay down, staring at the ceiling as her eyes became adjusted to the dark and the faint glow of the street lights seeping in through the curtains.

If he was so keen on keeping the boundaries professional between them, why was he sleeping with no top on? Surely that was blurring the line slightly.

And what if it wasn't just his top that was missing?

'Are you naked under those sheets?' Eva blurted out and then immediately regretted it.

Thor sat back up and switched the light on again.

'Would you like to check?' he gestured to the sheet.

'Of course not,' Eva said.

'I don't mind,' Thor said.

'I bet you wouldn't.'

'Would you like me to show you?' Thor teased, not taking this remotely seriously.

She hesitated for a fraction of a second too long, causing Thor to smirk, slowly lifting the sheet.

Eva snapped her hand over her eyes. She really didn't need to see that. Hell, seeing Thor Anderson naked was galloping straight over that line that they both seemed so intent on keeping in place.

'It's fine, I don't need to see it, I mean you. I mean… I'm not interested, at all. So you don't need to worry about me clambering over those pillows in the middle of the night and taking advantage of you.'

She rolled over to face away from him.

There was silence from Thor for a moment.

'I'm wearing shorts,' he said. 'And the pillows were to make you feel safe, not to protect me.'

Oh.

Of course they were. Thor was clearly the perfect gentleman.

His light was turned off and she felt him lie down behind her. After a moment, she rolled over to find he was facing her, a smile on his face as he watched her in the darkness.

'Goodnight Eva Blue. Sweet dreams.'

'Goodnight,' Eva said, knowing that, despite her protests, they certainly would be.

Chapter 10

Dear Mum,

Paris was incredible, in so many ways, the sights, the food. I saw the Mona Lisa and some of Van Gogh's work in the Louvre, I knew you would appreciate that. And I sang on top of the Eiffel Tower, just like you wanted to all those years ago. Though I know I didn't live up to the Blue family name. I'm sure you would have done a much better job.

It was a busy day. I was proposed to and shared a bed with a handsome stranger. Not bad for the first day of my trip. I think you would have been so proud.

I know you must have been laughing at the idea of me sharing a bed with a man I barely know. If I thought this trip was going to take me out of my comfort zone, sharing a bed with Thor was in a different league. I thought it might be awkward this morning with both of us showering and getting ready, but it wasn't. Thor took all of his clothes into the bathroom to get washed and dressed and then went and sat on the balcony to have coffee, giving me privacy to get ready myself. There is an ease between us I just didn't expect. I think I got carried away last night, falling in love with the city of love. Nothing is going to happen between us, but I do think we could become good friends.

We flew, again in business class, to Belgium where we explored the beautiful gilded buildings surrounding the Grand Place. We went to the very bizarre Atomium – it looks so odd when you see it from a distance, towering above the skyline with its spheres and tubes. Up close it's quite spectacular in this wonderfully weird kind of way. I didn't know there are rooms inside the spheres, we saw them after we took a trip to the top to see the incredible view.

Belgium seems to be famous for three things – beer, waffles and chocolate – and of course we had to try them all. I know your dream was to one day eat Belgian chocolates in Belgium. One of the easier dreams on your list. Thor took me to this little chocolate shop called Frederic Blondeel. I'm glad we went there, the chocolate was heavenly, creamy and sweet. There was so much choice, each chocolate a little work of art. I stocked up on a ton of it for our trip, though I don't imagine they will last too long. You would have loved them, you always did have a sweet tooth.

Tomorrow we fly to Amsterdam where we have two nights, which I'm thankful for. This travelling malarkey is exhausting.

Wish you were here!
Love Eva x

PS Dreams ticked off:
1. Sing on top of the Eiffel Tower.
2. Eat Belgian chocolates in Belgium.

Eva looked at the tiny writing on the back of the postcard. Luckily there was no address to write on the card so she had utilised that space too. Although it was clear that she might have to buy multiple cards in the future for everything she wanted to say to her mum. She tucked the postcard inside one of the sleeves of the small photo album she'd brought with her to keep all the postcards in one place. She smiled at that. This trip might be about adventure and breaking out of her comfort zone, but that didn't stop her being organised.

She looked over at Thor, who was reading on his bed. At least this hotel had honoured the twin bed arrangement. She hadn't pushed having a separate room to him and he hadn't brought it up either. She wasn't sure who would have to pay for a separate room if they did and she wanted to save as much money as she could for other things on this holiday. Besides, as long as they had separate beds, it wasn't awkward having him here.

They had spent the day walking around, talking and laughing as if they had known each other for years. But there was an underlying spark there. She hadn't felt this kind of connection with anyone before. She wasn't sure if that connection was just great friendship or something more. And, despite trying to convince herself that it was better if nothing did happen between them and knowing it was very unlikely that anything ever would, this little bloom of hope wouldn't go away. What if he kissed her and then what if the kiss led to something more?

All kinds of fears and excitement and doubt ran through her mind at that prospect. But that prospect was also the reason why she had discreetly bought some hair removal cream at the chemist earlier that day. It had been a while since she'd had sex and her bikini line was probably looking a little unruly.

Thor was still reading so she got up and slipped into the bathroom, closing the door behind her. She undressed, picked up the tube to read the instructions only to find it was in a different language, possibly Dutch or French. These things were normally ten minutes so that would do. She smeared it on and then occupied herself by looking through the photos on her phone of her travels so far, sending a few to Laurel too. The cream tingled quite a bit but obviously it was doing its job. After a few minutes the tingling was getting worse. In actual fact it was starting to burn. Crap, it hadn't been ten minutes yet, she would just give it a tiny bit longer. But the burning quickly escalated.

'Shit,' Eva said, not bothering to try to be quiet. 'Oh God.'

Eva quickly wiped some of the cream off with toilet paper but it hurt to even touch. She stepped inside the shower, turned it on and then adjusted the temperature down to cold and used the shower head to rinse off all the rest of the cream. The burning didn't go away, in fact it just got worse.

She scrambled out the shower. She needed to sit in a bath of cold water but the room only had a shower.

'Shit, shit, shit,' Eva cried, wafting her hands over her bikini line in the hope the cool air would help. It didn't.

The sink was part of a wide shelf unit. It was quite a large sink too. She could sit in the sink and prop her legs up on the shelf.

She quickly filled the sink with cold water and then climbed up onto the unit and sat inside the sink, resting her legs up on the side.

A knock came at the bathroom door. 'Eva, are you OK?'

'I'm fine,' Eva said, the anxiety in her voice clearly betraying her words.

'Are you sure? You don't sound OK. Shall I come in?'

'God no,' she said. She looked utterly ridiculous. If there was one sure-fire way of putting a man off it would be for him to see her sitting naked in a sink. He would never be able to get that image out of his head again and definitely not in a sexy way.

What a complete disaster. The burning was easing slightly but not enough.

'I need ice,' Eva said.

'Right, like a few cubes or—'

'More like a bucket.'

There was silence for a few seconds. 'I'll be right back.' She heard him leave the bedroom.

God, what must be going through his mind right now?

A few minutes later she heard the bedroom door open and close.

'I have a bucket of ice. Shall I… leave it out here?'

'No.' Christ, she couldn't face getting out the sink, the

cool water was the only thing preventing her from climbing the walls right now. 'Bring it in, but don't look.'

'OK,' Thor said and she could hear the amusement in his voice.

The door opened and Thor came in, bucket of ice in one hand and the other hand clamped over his eyes.

'You're going to need to direct me,' he said.

'Over here,' Eva said, desperately. He moved off towards the shower in a slow kind of stumble as he felt his way forward with his feet. Was he doing this deliberately?

Frustrated, Eva grabbed a towel and laid it over herself like a blanket.

'OK, you can look.'

Thor dropped his hand from his eyes a little bit too quickly for her liking. He cocked his head as he took in where she was.

'Are you... sitting in the sink?'

'Yes, long story, just give me the bloody ice.'

'Did you fall in it, are you stuck?'

'No, it was deliberate, please just give me the ice and go.'

His mouth quirked up as he tried desperately to suppress his smile. He passed her the bucket but hovered a bit longer.

There was no way she could tip the bucket into the sink with him still standing there. He would see everything and this was definitely not her most flattering angle.

'Please go.'

He nodded and went to the door. 'By the way, there is a huge mirror right behind you so...'

She twisted round to see that he just got an eyeful of her very naked reflection.

He quickly left but she could hear him giggling in the bedroom.

Oh God, this couldn't get any worse.

She dropped the towel and poured the ice into the sink which was unbearable and soothing at the same time. She sat there in the sink for the longest time, until her nether regions had gone completely numb and the ice had melted, then she clambered out and patted herself dry. The burning had largely subsided now, but it still tingled. She got dressed into her pyjamas and took a wet towel into the bedroom with her.

Thor was sitting up in bed resolutely reading his book and not looking at her, but she could tell he was still trying not to laugh. She climbed into her bed. She kicked her pyjama bottoms off under the covers and placed the wet towel between her legs.

Well, at least that answered the question of would they be having sex at some point. There was zero chance of that happening now.

'Just so I get this story right when I retell it, may I ask what you were doing sitting in the sink?' Thor asked.

'No you may not. This is one of those things we're never going to talk about again,' Eva said, lying down and facing away from him.

There was silence from him for a moment before he turned off the light and they lay in the darkness.

'Eva Blue, if we were ever to get married, this is one of those things I would tell the grandkids.'

As she lay there, staring out the window, her cheeks burning with shame, she couldn't help smiling at that thought.

Chapter 11

'Amsterdam is a lovely, quirky little place, isn't it?' Eva said, tucking into her stroopwafel, which kind of tasted a bit like a flat, crispy doughnut with a warm caramel sauce.

They had arrived in Amsterdam at lunch after their flight was delayed so they had dumped their stuff in the hotel room and gone straight out to explore. They now were serenely drifting down one of the many canals in Amsterdam, taking in the lofty, misshapen buildings, the brightly coloured houses, the beautiful bridges, spindly tall towers and clocks. It was such a cute little city.

'It's one of my favourite places actually,' Thor said as he bit into his own stroopwafel.

'It is?'

'It's so different to any other place,' Thor said.

'It's such a colourful country, the brightly painted houses that are such weird shapes, the luminous clogs, the windmills and the Dutch penchant for cheese. It kind of feels like I've walked into a hallucinogenic dream,' Eva said.

'Well, the laws on drugs are quite relaxed here, maybe that

has something to do with it.'

Eva laughed.

'So are you going to try something while you're here?' Thor asked as the boat took them underneath yet another bridge.

'Try what?' Eva asked. He'd persuaded her to buy the stroopwafel and it was amazing, and if what Thor had in mind was anything like this, she was happy to try it. She'd heard of these delicious mini pancakes called poffertjes, she definitely wanted to try them before she left. They'd walked into several cheese shops and tried multiple samples of different flavoured cheese already. The Dutch certainly had great food.

'Drugs,' Thor said, simply.

She felt the smile fall off her face. 'What?'

He shrugged. 'Whenever I escort anyone to Amsterdam, I know we're going to end up in some coffee shop smoking cannabis or trying some other more potent high.'

She stared at him. 'Is that why you like Amsterdam so much, because of the drugs?'

'Oh god no, not my scene at all. Besides, I always like to keep a clear head whenever I'm escorting someone. It wouldn't be right to take some hallucinogenic, magic mushroom or something else while I'm looking after someone. We could end up in all sorts of trouble. But I'm happy to babysit you if you want to try that sort of thing.'

'Oh hell no,' Eva said. God, she wanted adventure but that was taking it a step too far. 'So you've never taken anything?'

They went under yet another bridge and Thor finished off

the last bite of his stroopwafel.

'I came here for my eighteenth birthday with a group of friends. We smoked a bit of cannabis, thought we were the coolest kids on the planet. I've never smoked it since and I've never tried anything stronger than that. I don't like losing control. Have you tried anything before?'

She suddenly felt so naïve. She could imagine how cool Thor was when he was younger. Hell, he was really cool now. She had somehow missed out on all that partying and rebelling when she was younger. Her studies had been important to her. She was definitely more in the nerdy camp than the party animal one. A younger Thor and a younger Eva would never have been friends.

'Of course,' Eva lied, feeling like she needed to claw back some credibility. She wouldn't go so far as to try any drugs now to impress him, but she could exaggerate her misspent youth. She just hoped he wouldn't ask for details because right then she couldn't think of a single drug. Morphine, she was pretty sure she'd been given that when she broke her leg in three places. Was that the kind of drug people took recreationally? She had no idea.

Thor laughed loudly and slung an arm round her shoulders. 'Eva Blue, you're a terrible liar. You don't have to impress me. After standing on top of the Eiffel Tower and belting your heart out, I'm already sold.'

Eva sighed. 'OK, you got me. Alcohol, chocolate, paracetamols. They're pretty much my only drugs. I think I might have had some morphine once when I was in hospital. I'm not exactly a party animal. I've never even smoked a cigarette.'

'You're so wholesome,' Thor said but he didn't say it like it was a bad thing. 'Remind me again why we are in Amsterdam?'

Eva blushed. 'To look at the tulips.'

He grinned as he looked down at her, his arm was still around her shoulders. 'I think I'm going to enjoy this trip with you.'

She smiled; he made her feel warm inside. 'So am I missing out on this cultural movement by not doing drugs while I'm here?'

He shook his head and wrinkled his nose. 'Eva, you're perfect just as you are, don't ever change. I'm sure we can find other ways to entertain ourselves while we are here.'

Her heart leapt a little. What did he mean by that?

'Like?'

'Well, cheese and clogs and windmills. There's the red-light district too.'

Her eyes widened, even though she knew he was teasing her. 'What are we going to do there, go up to one of the ladies of the night and ask if she wants a threesome?'

He laughed. 'Well I'm sure it's not the weirdest request they've heard.'

'God, I'd be nervous enough about being in bed with you without adding an extra person into the mix.'

He let his arm fall from her shoulders as if she had crossed some line by talking about them being in bed together. But he didn't move away and surprisingly he didn't change the subject either.

'Why would you be nervous about being in bed with me?'

What would sleeping with Thor be like? He struck her as

101

the sort of man that would know exactly what he was doing in the bedroom department. And, though she had been with a few men and was confident she knew which bits went where, she doubted she was as experienced or skilled as Thor was. There was also the fact the man looked like he had been expertly chiselled from marble. She had wobbly bits and, while she hadn't been overly bothered with them in the past, she certainly would be more aware of them when lying naked in bed with Thor. Christ, that was an image that was going to keep her awake at night.

'Well you're…' she gestured to his body and then gestured to her own. 'And I'm…'

He cocked his head in confusion. 'I'm not sure what that means. I've never once been disappointed with a woman in the bedroom. I think about a lot of things while I'm having sex. Where can I touch her, where can I kiss her that will give her the most pleasure? Are my hands too rough for her? How does she like to be touched? Does she like it hard and fast or soft and gentle? Is she enjoying herself? And much more than that, but I've never once wished she was more of this or less of that.'

Her mouth was suddenly dry and she cleared the lump in her throat. 'Come on, men don't really think like that.'

'Of course we do. Well I do. Don't get me wrong, I love sex. Having sex with a wonderful woman is one of my favourite things to do, but it comes with its own stresses and not one of them is about the woman being enough for me. You women are always enough. Don't ever think otherwise.'

She stared at him. She had never been so turned on in her entire life and he hadn't even touched her. His eyes were locked on hers and she knew she had to clear the air before she found herself dragging him back to the hotel and showing him how much of a woman she really was.

'And if one woman isn't enough, then you can have a threesome,' Eva said.

'I might be game for a lot of things but I think I'd draw the line at that. I like to give all my attention to the woman I'm with. I don't need any distractions.'

God, this conversation was getting more and more intense. She preferred talking about taking drugs than this.

'Oh, look at that cute windmill,' Eva said, gesturing wildly and breaking the moment. 'I've always thought it would be really cool to sleep in one.'

Thor cleared his throat and looked where she was pointing. 'You have?'

'Yeah, that would be pretty amazing.'

Thor pulled out his phone and started swiping across the screen. 'Consider it done.'

Eva let out a small sigh of relief that she had managed to divert the conversation, at least for now. He was flirting with her and she had no idea what to do with that.

Thor sat on a bench, Eva next to him as she answered a few work emails on her phone. His attention was solely on his own phone as he tried to find a windmill they could stay in for the night. It was very last minute and as this was Amsterdam's busiest time with the tulip fields in full bloom, he didn't fancy his chances, but he had contacts, many of them, and he didn't necessarily have to go down the route of a B&B or holiday home.

His phone had his full attention for another reason too. Because right now, he didn't know what to say to Eva.

What the hell had that conversation been about and why had he let it go that far? He'd talked about having sex which was not a subject for two people who had only just met properly two days before. It wasn't appropriate considering he was her escort and he was here purely in a professional capacity, but worse than that was the whole time he was talking about sex he'd been thinking about what it would be like to have sex with her. He hadn't been subtle either and he'd made her uncomfortable with the way he was staring at her and the things he'd said. He needed to apologise for it but to do that would draw attention to it, and the way she was humming softly to herself suggested she'd already moved on. She probably hadn't given it any more thought. Yet he still couldn't dispel the image of the two of them in bed together.

'I'm going to get a coffee; do you want one?' Eva said, standing up.

'Yes please,' Thor said, without looking up.

She walked across the small green to the row of shops in front of them. He watched her go, her hips swaying, her curly brown hair catching the sunlight as it cascaded down her back.

She looked back and flashed him a devastating smile and he quickly returned his attention to the phone again.

What the hell was wrong with him?

He had never done anything with any of his clients before, he hadn't even been tempted to. There was a strict line and he never crossed it. But there was something about Eva Blue that made him want to charge across that line at full speed.

He shook his head. He had to be professional about this, which was difficult when yet again that night they would be sharing a bed. Tracy had said that it was too late to change the sleeping arrangements for the first few hotels but that she would make sure she would change the rooms after that. He was more bothered by this than Eva was; she had just shrugged it off when they had checked into their hotel earlier that afternoon.

It hadn't helped that, this morning, he'd woken up a few minutes before the alarm and she had been fast asleep facing him, the sun rising behind her, breaking through the curtains and dusting her cheeks with gold. And she'd had this big smile on her face. Wherever she was in her dreams, it was obviously somewhere happy. And as he had laid there watching her, he felt the wall around his heart crumble a little. She filled him with a warmth he hadn't felt in a long time. He didn't like that.

He pushed that thought away. He was not going to lose his job over this and he most definitely wasn't going to lose his heart. He had fallen in love with Christel so hard and so fast and he'd vowed it was never going to happen again. But he'd been with Eva for just over two days and he could feel these same emotions creeping in, tugging at his heart. He didn't want any of that.

Eva came and sat down next to him again, eating a cake.

One thing was for sure, he wasn't going to ruin her holiday by making her feel uncomfortable with his inappropriate feelings.

She placed his coffee next to him on the bench along with

a small paper bag, just as an email came through on his phone. He swiped it open.

'I got you a brownie,' Eva said. 'It's really good.'

'Thank you.' He scanned the email as he reached for his coffee and took a sip. 'Ah, mission accomplished.'

He looked up at her as she took another bite of the brownie.

'What's that?' she asked.

'A friend of mine owns a windmill. She used to rent it out as a holiday let, but she stopped doing that a few years ago. It's still there though, basically at the bottom of her garden. She says we can use it if we want to. It's a bit further north from here but, as we're hiring a car tomorrow to take us to the Keukenhof tulip gardens, we can go there straight after. It's small and basic, but it has a toilet and shower and it's right on the water and the top bedroom has a glass roof so you can look out onto the stars.'

'That sounds wonderful,' Eva said, her whole face lighting up.

It also had the added benefit of having two bedrooms, so he wouldn't have the complication of sleeping in the same bed as her again tomorrow night.

'Well, I want to make your dreams come true,' Thor said.

He watched her choke on the last bite of her brownie and he frowned slightly when he realised that sounded a lot more romantic than he'd intended.

She quickly took a slug of coffee.

In need of a distraction, he grabbed his brownie and took a big bite and immediately spat it back out again into the bag. It tasted disgusting, like herbs and... He quickly sniffed the contents of the bag.

Crap.

'Did you have the same brownie as me?' Thor asked.

'Yes, it's amazing, isn't it? It's not like anything I've ever tasted before. The Dutch really have amazing food.'

His heart sank.

Shit, fuck, bollocks.

Eva had just eaten a cannabis cake.

Chapter 12

Thor looked over to the coffee shop and sure enough the little green and white licence card was in the window, showing that it was selling cannabis in all its forms.

Christ, he was supposed to look after her and he'd taken his eye off the ball for two minutes and she'd accidentally bought and eaten a cannabis cake. This had been his own fault, he'd been so wrapped up in that stupid conversation, he hadn't been paying attention.

OK, he had to do some damage limitation here. He couldn't tell her as then she'd get scared and panicky. Being on drugs and out of control was even worse if you were scared or anxious. He just had to get her back to the hotel room where she was safe. At least cannabis was one of the gentler drugs to accidentally take. She'd be giggly, silly, then relaxed and sleepy and almost definitely hungry afterwards. Her life wasn't in danger. If he thought for one second that she had taken anything harder he'd be whisking her straight off to the hospital, but as it was she was just going to have a really great night's sleep.

'OK, we have an early morning tomorrow, shall we go back to the hotel?' Thor said.

'Ah, the night's still young,' Eva said.

'I know but my back is killing me and I have a headache,' Thor lied.

'Oh you poor thing, you go on ahead of me. I'll try not to wake you when I come in.'

That was never going to happen. Even if she hadn't just eaten a cannabis cake, there was no way he was going to leave her alone in a strange city at night.

'I'm not supposed to leave you. I don't mind bending a few rules, but I'd be worried about you getting lost or falling head first into a vat of cheese.'

She laughed. 'OK, OK. Since you sorted out the windmill for me, I can hardly say no.'

'Shall we take a taxi?' Thor said, keen to get her back to the safety of the hotel as quickly as possible. They probably had an hour until the effects started kicking in but he didn't want to take any chances.

'OK,' Eva said, standing up.

Thor stood up too, making a big show of stretching his back and then holding it as if it hurt.

'Oh no, I can give you a massage when we get back if you want. I'm good at those.' She cracked her fingers mischievously, as if she was going to be ruthless with him.

Good god. What was worse, being back in the hotel room with her, where it was just the two of them with no distractions and her offer of a massage, or staying out in the dark streets of Amsterdam with a girl high on the effects of cannabis?

He was very tempted to take the latter.

Getting a taxi had proved a lot harder than he'd thought and they'd ended up walking back, which would have been fine, except the hotel was about an hour away. That was cutting it a bit fine in his eyes. They were two or three minutes away from the hotel now and the giggles had started about five minutes before. She'd laughed hysterically at someone wearing clogs, a dog weeing up a lamppost, as well as a few other times when he'd had no idea what had set her off.

Thor stopped in his tracks as she veered suddenly from his side and went into a clothes shop. He frowned – they definitely didn't need any detours. He moved quickly into the shop and found her at the till buying something red and sparkly. Wow, she was a fast mover.

She turned back to him with her purchase in her hand. She looked so excited.

'I bought us some berets,' Eva said, wielding the sequinned berets in the air like some great prize. 'You have to have berets in Amsterdam.'

He cocked his head. 'I think berets are more of a French stereotype.'

She shrugged and pulled hers on her head at a wonky angle. He suppressed a smile; she looked ridiculous. She leaned up, pressing her body against his to pull the beret onto his head. He didn't resist. If they both were wearing one, it would lessen the effect of her looking silly.

She stepped back to survey her work and burst out laughing. 'You look amazing,' Eva said, through her laughter.

He guessed he looked anything but amazing.

'Come on, we should go,' he said gently. He had no idea how much worse this was going to get for her.

She followed him back out the shop and they walked along the street in silence for a while. He glanced over at her and saw she was frowning.

'You OK?'

'I feel a bit dizzy.'

'You do?'

'Light-headed, like I'm a bit drunk.' She looked up at him and he could see the worry in her eyes.

He looped an arm round her shoulders and brought her against him as they walked. 'It's OK, you're just tired from all the travelling. It happens to me all the time.'

'I've got jet lag?' Eva asked.

'That's it. You just need a good night's sleep and you'll be fine.'

'Oh, OK,' Eva said. 'I do feel a bit tired.'

'We'll be back at the hotel in just a second,' Thor said, spotting the lights of the hotel sign, just ahead.

'Where we're going to sleep together,' Eva giggled.

'Sleep in the same bed together,' Thor clarified.

'Because you don't really want to have sex with me, do you?' Eva said.

Christ, what a question.

He cleared his throat. 'I think we should probably wait until you're not so tired for that one.'

'So I am enough for you?' Eva said as they arrived back at the sliding doors of the hotel.

Crap. He knew that conversation was going to come back

and haunt him. He ushered her inside, her warm body clamped to the side of his.

'Listen, I'm sorry about that,' he said.

'About what?'

He pressed the button for the lift.

'Talking to you about sex, it made you uncomfortable.'

'It didn't make me uncomfortable at all,' Eva said. 'If anything, it turned me on.'

Crap.

'It was unprofessional,' Thor said.

'You can talk to me about sex. We can even have the sex if you want to,' Eva said loudly.

Thor looked around the reception and saw a few people glance over with raised eyebrows.

'Go on, give her what she wants,' called an elderly lady.

Thor grinned and was relieved when the lift doors finally opened and he quickly escorted Eva inside. The doors closed, leaving them alone.

She looked up at him, her eyes slightly dazed, but she had a big smile on her face. 'Are we going to have sex?' she asked hopefully.

He smiled. She was so bloody likeable. He stroked a hair off her cheek.

'You know we can't do that. You're my client.'

'You have your arm round me, do you do that with all your clients?' she said, practically.

'No, but I think we could be friends,' Thor said, trying to let her down as nicely as he could, especially in her current state. He didn't want to do anything that upset her. 'And friends hug each other.'

She smiled. 'Yes they do. But they don't have sex?'

'No, just hugs and sleeping in the same bed together.'

She leaned her head against him and closed her eyes. 'I like that.'

The lift doors opened and when he moved forward, she stumbled a little. He scooped her up in his arms and carried her down the corridor. She wrapped her arms around his neck and nuzzled into his throat.

'I really am very sleepy.'

'It's OK, we'll have you tucked up in bed very soon.'

He put her down and leaned her against the wall outside their bedroom door while he retrieved the key. He pushed the door open just as she started sliding down the wall, then scooped her up again, walked into the room and laid her down on the bed. She seemed to drift off to sleep almost immediately. He took off her shoes and socks but decided she could keep the rest of her clothes on.

Thor grabbed his shorts and went into the bathroom to get changed. He was just cleaning his teeth when Eva walked into the bathroom in her pyjamas. Clearly not asleep then.

He raised an eyebrow at her just waltzing in but she didn't seem to think anything was amiss. She stood next to him and grabbed her own toothbrush and started cleaning her teeth. It felt like a very coupley thing to do.

'I bet you've never done this with a client before,' she waved her toothbrush in the air.

'No, cleaning teeth with a client is a first,' Thor said.

She washed out her mouth. 'You're breaking all those rules, aren't you?'

'You're a bad influence on me, Eva Blue.'

She smiled and walked back out into the bedroom and he followed her.

She got into bed and he slid into the other side and turned out the light. But he had the shock of his life when she snuggled up to him, resting her head on his chest, her arm around his stomach.

After a moment, he put his arm round her shoulders and held her tight. He had to be careful with her. He'd had it relatively easy so far and if she could sleep off the rest of the effects of the brownie, he'd be happy.

'Listen Eva, I'm not going anywhere tonight, I'm right here.'

She looked up at him, the moonlight streaming through the windows lighting up her confused face. 'OK.'

'You're safe here, but if you get scared or worried in the middle of the night, just wake me up, OK?'

She nodded and then put her head back down on his chest, snuggling in closer. 'I'm safe with you.'

He held her tighter. 'Yes you are.'

'Goodnight Thor, sweet dreams,' Eva said.

He kissed her on the forehead. 'Goodnight Eva Blue.'

He sighed as the sound of her breathing grew heavy. *Just friends.* Who was he kidding?

Chapter 13

Eva woke the next day, feeling exhausted and groggy. Her mouth was dry, her head was hurting and the memory of the night before was hazy at best. She forced her eyes open and it took a few seconds to realise she was sleeping on Thor's chest, her arms wrapped around him.

Oh, god no. What would he think of her?

She suddenly realised his arm was around her too, not just casually, but holding her tight.

She glanced up at him and saw he was wide awake, staring out the window. He looked happy and relaxed with this situation, while she was anything but.

Oh no, had they had sex?

Surely she would remember that, but she was having a hard time remembering much from the latter part of the night. She certainly had no memory of coming back to the hotel room.

She fumbled around under the covers and found she was still wearing her pyjamas. She sighed in relief but the movement had drawn Thor's attention.

'Hey,' he said gently. 'How are you feeling?'

'Tired, hungover, starving and very confused. Why are we cuddling like we spent the night having sex?'

He smirked. 'We didn't have sex.'

He sat up, releasing her from his hold.

'Did we drink last night?' Eva said.

'No, but… OK, don't freak out.'

'What does that mean? When you say something like that of course I'm going to freak out,' Eva said.

'Well there's no reason to. You're fine, you haven't died.'

'Will you just spit it out?'

He took a deep breath. 'That brownie you ate after we'd been on the canal cruise. It was a cannabis brownie.'

Her eyes widened, her heart suddenly racing. She scrambled out of bed, checking her body all over, though she didn't know what she was looking for. Everything seemed to be working OK.

'I took drugs?'

'Yes, but it's fine, it was just a bit of cannabis, no one has ever died from taking cannabis. There will be no long-term after-effects. We can go down to the restaurant now and have a big breakfast to combat your hunger pains. If you drink lots of water, you're going to be fine.'

'Oh god.' Eva sank down onto the side of the bed, with her head in her hands. 'My mum's going to kill me.'

The pain of that statement sliced into her heart. God, what she wouldn't give to call up her mum right now and tell her she'd accidentally taken some drugs and hear the lecture about how she should have been more careful. Maybe Laurel could oblige instead, though she knew it wouldn't be the same. In actual fact, knowing her mum's wild ways, she would probably be secretly impressed about the drugs and after the lecture would come the questions about what it was like.

Thor moved to her side and slid an arm round her shoulders. 'Hey, I can give you the mum lecture if that helps.'

She looked up at him and smiled, weakly. 'Go on then.'

He stood up and put his hands on his hips. 'Now you listen to me, young lady, what on earth were you doing taking drugs in Amsterdam and why did that hot bit of stuff you're with not stop you, I thought he was supposed to be looking after you.'

Eva laughed. 'She would say that too, I blame you entirely.'

He sat down by her side again. 'I know. You should. I do feel bad. I was very worried about you last night.'

She suddenly had a memory of Thor holding her in bed and telling her he was there for her and she was safe. She smiled.

'Did I do anything stupid?' Eva asked.

'No, you were fine. Bit giggly. You bought some ridiculous red sparkly berets for us and then you pretty much fell asleep as soon as you got back here.'

'I didn't say anything to embarrass myself?'

'No nothing,' Thor said. 'You were perfectly behaved.'

She sighed with relief.

'Though I'm never wearing that beret again.'

She laughed. 'Why did you wear it at all? You should have just told me to bugger off.'

'Ah no, I didn't want to do anything to upset you last

night. Consequently, when you cuddled up to me in bed, I let you do it.'

'Ah god,' Eva cringed. 'I'm so sorry.'

'Don't be. I wanted you to feel safe. Besides, I told you we were friends and that friends hug, so you were just taking that literally.'

She remembered that conversation. They had been in the lift. But they had also been talking about something else though she couldn't remember what. She sighed and shook her head.

'I can't believe I took drugs. I was always such a nerd in school. Does this mean I'm cool now?'

'You're already cool. And you've got the beret to prove it,' he nodded to the red sparkly thing on the chair.

'I shall wear it with pride,' Eva laughed.

After a shower, Eva did feel a lot better.

She walked back out into the bedroom and saw Thor was waiting for her to go to breakfast, wearing that ridiculous red beret.

She laughed at him, swiping it off his head and throwing it on the chair.

He made her feel better too. If she was going to get high on cannabis, there was no one else she would want to get high with. He had been sweet, sensitive and looked after her, made her feel safe. He was definitely not the asshole she'd thought he was.

They waited for the lift to take them down to the restaurant, and when the doors opened there was an older lady in there who looked vaguely familiar. Her face lit up as they walked in.

'So, did you have sex last night?' the lady said as the doors closed behind them.

Christ, what kind of personal question was that? What kind of person asks two perfect strangers that question? Even if she knew the lady, it still wasn't appropriate.

'That's none of your business,' Eva said.

'No we didn't,' Thor said at the same time.

'Ah, that's why she's so grouchy this morning,' the lady said. 'She was begging you for sex last night and you turned her down.'

Eva stared at Thor, aghast. 'I begged you for sex?'

'There was no begging, I can assure you of that. We were simply talking about sex.'

'And you offered yourself on a plate, dear,' the lady said, obviously loving every second of this.

Eva ignored the lady. 'You said I didn't do anything to embarrass myself.'

'There's nothing to be embarrassed about. You weren't feeling yourself, it was a silly conversation.'

'Where I begged you for sex and you turned me down,' Eva said, her cheeks burning.

Thor clearly had nothing to say to that.

The doors finally opened on the ground floor and Eva could escape this hell. She stormed out and walked straight outside the hotel into the glorious sunshine. The light hurt her eyes for a moment and she blinked and looked around. Thor was suddenly there, catching her arm.

'Why are you upset?'

Oh god, so many reasons.

'Because you lied to me when I asked you if I said anything embarrassing.'

'What would have been the point of upsetting you even more this morning, what would it have achieved?'

Eva sighed because she knew he had done it for the right reasons.

'I can't believe I asked you for sex.'

'Don't give it another thought. I certainly won't,' Thor said.

Eva cringed even more. 'Of course you won't.'

He frowned. 'What does that mean?'

'Well, you turned me down so obviously *I wasn't enough for you.*'

'Whoa, you were high on drugs, what kind of asshole would I have to be to take advantage of that? And regardless how much I wanted to, you are my client and nothing is going to happen between us. It would be unprofessional, unethical and just all kinds of wrong.'

Her heart leapt. *Regardless how much I wanted to.*

'And if you had been in the right frame of mind last night and I offered you a night of hot sex, would you have taken me up on it?' Thor asked.

She stumbled over how to answer that question.

'Of course you wouldn't,' Thor went on. 'You're not the sort of person who would have a one-night stand. Not that there's anything wrong with that, I've had a few of them myself over the years, but you strike me as the sort of person that would want a relationship rather than a meaningless fling.'

She blushed that Thor probably had higher standards and

expectations of her than she had of herself. If Thor had kissed her and asked her to spend the night with him, she wasn't confident enough in her willpower to say no. There was something about this man she found so compelling.

'Look, I like you. A lot more than what's appropriate,' Thor said.

Her throat was suddenly dry. 'You do?'

He nodded.

'I like you too.'

He stared at her and let out a heavy sigh. 'But if anything was to happen, apart from the fact I would get fired, it would make it very awkward considering we have several weeks ahead of us travelling together. There'd be all these weird feelings and regrets and emotions flying around the place. That's not going to be enjoyable for either of us. And I really don't want to ruin your holiday just for a one-night stand. So can we just agree that this is not going to happen and we're just going to stay as friends?'

She stared at him and then nodded. 'That sounds very sensible.'

He sighed and leaned his forehead against hers for a second, closing his eyes, his hands on her shoulders.

'Let's go and get some breakfast,' Thor said.

She nodded and followed him back inside.

He didn't want weird feelings, regrets and emotions between them. It was a little too late for that.

Keukenhof Gardens was beautiful, tulips stretching out in every direction as far as the eye could see. There were rows of red, blue, yellow, purple, orange and pink, there were even stunning displays of the coveted black tulip. There were little rivers and ponds that wound their way gently round the gardens, reflecting the kaleidoscope of colours perfectly. The flower beds curved and twisted around each other, seven million flowers bobbing gently in the spring sunshine. The windmill turning gently in the middle of the park made Eva smile. It was such a stereotypical image of the Netherlands but it looked perfectly at home there nestled amongst the tulips.

They had learned all about the history of the tulips and seen the tulips that had been named after different celebrities and important figures, which seemed like a cool thing to do, leave your legacy behind.

They were now waiting for the flower parade to go past. The annual parade was something that attracted tourists from all over the world. Beautiful floats made entirely of flowers, sculpted into different designs, was something she couldn't wait to see.

Eva was sitting on a bench, drawing some sketches of Amsterdam, the tulips and windmills. She didn't have any of her colours with her but she wanted to capture the quirkiness of the place. She looked around for Thor again. He had disappeared half hour before and not come back.

They had been friendly and polite to each other all day but it felt like it was forced. It had never been like that before. They had both acknowledged there was an attraction but they weren't going to do anything about it. Of course it was going to be awkward between them and she didn't see how that was going to get better now.

With still no sign of Thor, she pulled out her phone and gave Laurel a call. She had texted her a few times over the last day or so but she hadn't really gone into specifics.

'Hello, my love,' Laurel answered, cheerily. 'How's it all going?'

'Great, better than great actually,' Eva said with forced bravado. 'I'm at Keukenhof tulip gardens and it's just so beautiful. The tulips are all arranged in pretty patterns, we've been on a canal cruise and tonight we are going to stay in a windmill. I'm having an amazing time.'

There was silence from Laurel for a moment. 'OK, what's happened?'

Eva sighed. Her aunt knew her so well.

Eva moved a little out of the crowds and over to one side where she hoped people couldn't hear her.

'It's all getting a bit weird with Thor.'

'Define weird,' Laurel said.

'I like him.'

More silence from Laurel. 'A lot?'

'Yes. And it's ridiculous. You know I never do the crush thing. The men I've dated have always asked me out and I've just kind of gone along with it. The ones I've liked after a few dates we sort of progressed to a semi-casual relationship but most of them fizzled out after a few weeks. I've certainly never done the fawning over a man thing or the fancying them from afar thing and I've definitely never had these kinds of feelings for a man after such a short amount of time.'

'Why do you think that is?' Laurel asked gently.

'Because I don't need a man to make me happy, I'm happy enough on my own.'

'Or you want to protect yourself and getting involved with a man who actually means something to you would mean laying yourself open to all kinds of hurt,' Laurel said.

Eva sighed. They'd had this discussion before.

'Have you told him how you feel?' Laurel asked.

'He knows.' Eva closed her eyes for a moment, cringing as she thought about the night before. 'I got a little… drunk last night and offered to have sex with him.'

'Oh Eva.' There wasn't disappointment in her aunt's voice or any judgement, just sympathy for her predicament.

'It wasn't totally one-sided.'

'He offered to have sex with you too?'

'No, he turned me down. I'm just saying it wasn't without some encouragement from him. He has feelings for me too.'

'Then why are you holding back?'

'He doesn't want anything to happen, he's clinging to his professionalism. And it would be awkward if we did – we have several weeks ahead of us on this trip. But I think he has been hurt in the past and he's reluctant to start a relationship.'

'Like you.'

'Not like me, I'm not scared of a relationship.'

'You've never gone out of your way to have one either.'

'What shall I do, Laurel?' Eva said, trying to change the subject slightly.

'I'm not sure what you can do. If he doesn't want it to go any further and you're not convinced it's a good idea either, then I guess you have to keep it professional between you.'

'It's really awkward now.'

'Of course it is, there are all these feelings flying around. But in my experience this kind of thing can only stay professional for so long, especially when you're in such close proximity to each other for such extended periods of time. Sharing a bed together isn't going to help. It will come to a head one way or another.'

'And what should I do if it does?'

She could almost hear Laurel smile on the other end of the phone. 'I think you just have to follow your heart.'

She didn't know whether to be scared or excited by that thought.

'How are things going with you? Have you bought that Porsche yet?' Eva asked, needing to focus on something else for a while.

'I have,' Laurel said. 'It's beautiful. It's fifteen years old so was actually quite cheap. I've been driving around in it everywhere, even to the supermarket. James doesn't seem to like it though.'

'He doesn't?'

'I don't know, he seems a bit... weird lately.'

'Define weird,' Eva grinned, using Laurel's own words against her.

'Just on edge. We went out to a restaurant the other night and he was so tense he was practically buzzing. He didn't eat anything, went to the toilet a dozen times, I've never seen him like it.'

'Maybe he wasn't feeling very well,' Eva tried.

'I don't know, we ended up having a silly row over nothing and I hate that. I never row with anyone. I wonder if it's coming to an end.'

Laurel sounded so sad all of sudden, Eva immediately wanted to fly home just so she could give her a hug. After

Michael had died, Laurel swore there would never be anyone else for her. Then she had met James and she had resisted anything happening between them for a long time. Eva had finally persuaded her to give him a chance. He seemed lovely and it was clear Laurel had strong feelings for him. Eva hated the thought of her aunt losing James now just when things had been going so well between them.

'Are things OK now?'

'Well, he apologised about the fight and we're talking and it kind of feels OK, but he still seems edgy. Something's wrong but I have no idea what it is.'

'Oh Laurel, I don't know what to say. Maybe try talking to him about it? Maybe it's nothing to do with you and something else is going on.'

'Maybe. Oh, I better go, I'm meeting Jackie for coffee. Go and enjoy your holiday, don't worry about me. Call me soon and let me know how it's all going.'

'I will, I love you,' Eva said.

Eva hung up just as she saw Thor moving back through the crowds towards her, carrying a small paper bag.

'Hey,' Eva said, smiling brightly and forcing all thoughts about them and any possible relationship from her mind. If things were to get back to normal between them, then she had to carry on as normal. 'I thought you were going to miss the parade.'

'I definitely wouldn't want that.'

Eva smiled. Even though flowers were probably not his thing, he had never seen the flower parade in all his years of travelling the world, so it felt nice that they would both see it for the first time together.

'I bought a gift,' Thor said.

'Who for?'

'You.' He offered her the brown bag.

'Oh.' She peered inside and could see it was a bulb. 'Oh thanks, that's really nice.'

'It's for a tulip, this one.' He handed her a card for a beautiful sky-blue tulip. 'It's the Eva Blue tulip.'

Her eyes snapped up to his. 'What?'

'I named a tulip for you. There will be fifty of these bulbs planted in the gardens next year so you'll have to come back and see it. And you can post this one home and then plant it yourself. I've already checked, it's suitable for export to the UK.'

Eva stared at him. 'You... you named a tulip after me?'

'Well, you were talking about how cool it was to leave a legacy behind, something to mark that you were here, and I thought this one suited you. It's beautiful, isn't it...' he trailed off and pushed his hand through his hair, awkwardly. 'Shall we get a bit closer so we can see the parade?'

'That's... so lovely. No one has ever done anything like that for me. Thank you.'

He waved it away. 'It's no big deal.'

He moved away from her.

She sighed. How did he hope to keep things neutral and professional between them when he made lovely gestures like this?

There was suddenly a flurry of excitement as music drifted towards them. The parade had arrived.

She moved towards Thor and he offered out a hand, tugging her gently to his side as a brass band on bikes came cycling round the corner. She laughed as they weaved in and out of each other and miraculously managed to play their instruments at the same time. And then the first float drifted serenely past, a towering tiger that must have been about twenty feet high and probably fifty feet long. It was hiding in the long grass, ready to pounce on its prey and was made completely out of thousands of flowers. It was incredible. A brightly coloured windmill was next with sails that were actually moving round. Dancers and musicians moved between each float dressed in spectacularly colourful and elaborate costumes. A gigantic purple octopus sailed past next with some of its tentacles stretching out towards the crowd. She took pictures of a wonderful fairground carousel with splendid horses, whales jumping out of a sea of flowers, a dragon that breathed real fire, a hot air balloon, a giant saxophone that played music, a snow-capped mountain, and oversized teapot and cups.

The whole thing was a complete spectacle and Eva felt very privileged that she got to see it.

The last float came round the corner and she felt her eyes widen when she saw it. It was quite obvious that the float was displaying a couple in the throes of making love. There were no rude bits on display, as an artfully arranged sheet of flowers seemed to partly cover the couple, but as the woman's head was thrown back in ecstasy and the man was kissing her throat, it was very obvious what they were doing.

She definitely hadn't been expecting this.

Eva let out a nervous laugh and looked at Thor to see how he would react. He was laughing too. The Dutch people around them seemed to take it much more in their stride though, paying it no more attention than the octopus or the windmill that had come before it. They really were a much more liberal and open-minded bunch.

Eva hesitated to take a picture of it as it seemed invasive somehow, but she knew Laurel would enjoy seeing it. She took the photo and forwarded it to Laurel and the girls, with the message 'Taking in the sights in Amsterdam.' She smiled as Jacinda texted her straight back. 'Getting some ideas?'

She shoved her phone in her bag and, as the sex float disappeared down the lane, the crowd started to disperse.

Thor cleared his throat, awkwardly.

She laughed. She felt like she'd just watched a porno with him and clearly he felt the same.

'Well, on that note, shall we go to our windmill for the night?' he asked.

She nodded. But after that unexpected saucy surprise, she was quite glad the windmill had two bedrooms, otherwise it was going to make the awkwardness between them even worse.

Chapter 14

Zaanse Schans was like a small village of windmills. The sun had just started to set when they had arrived and the sails had still been turning on each of the six windmills that were on the edges of the lake. They kind of looked majestic, silhouetted against the tangerine sky.

Their windmill was set a little back from the main windmills but on the banks of a little inlet. The sails were no longer in use as Thor had explained they had removed the inner workings of the windmill to make way for a top bedroom that had a glass roof. But despite this, it still didn't look any less wonderful.

The doors to the windmill were embedded into a little hill, the windmill perched on top, which made Eva feel like they were entering a hobbit home. The ground floor of the windmill was a large round kitchen with a long dining table in the middle. Up one floor was the lounge, the long sofas hugging the edges of the round room. The two round bedrooms occupied the next two floors, both of which had an en-suite. Thor had claimed the room with the four-poster bed because he insisted she have the top floor, which was smaller but had a glass ceiling for watching the stars.

After a sunset walk around the lake and a delicious dinner cooked for them by Thor, they had sat together in companionable silence as he read and she did some work. She was getting wonderfully inspired on this trip for her job and she wanted to incorporate some of this splendour into her future designs. Later, he had helped her carry her suitcase up the tiny winding stairs. When she had laid down for a few minutes to appreciate the view, to her surprise, he had joined her. And that's where both of them were currently lying in the darkness, staring at the velvety canopy sparkling above them. Thor had made no move to go to his own room and she hadn't encouraged him to leave either.

'So tomorrow we're going to Legoland in Denmark. Why did your mum want to go there?' Thor asked.

'She always loved Lego when I was growing up, I used to have so many boxes of it, she would spend hours with me making great palaces and cities. I think she loved it a lot more than I did. She had a wonderful creative side and I think Lego gave her that freedom to build and create something and then take it down and do it all again. She used to tell me how much she loved Lego when she was a child. I guess that as the Legoland in Denmark was the first one, built next to the original Lego factory, she wanted to see where it all began.'

Thor smiled in the darkness. 'And we're staying in Skagen tomorrow night. Why are we going there?'

She listened to his pronunciation of the Danish town, it was just as Laurel had said. Skayne. When she spoke she made sure she said it the right way.

'Her dream simply said to go back to Skagen. I spoke to my aunt Laurel about that one and she said Mum had been seventeen when she had gone on tour with this musical production around Europe for a few weeks. I think that gave her the travelling bug. One of the stops was Skagen.'

'That surprises me. It's a tiny little town. Not really the hub of cultural events,' Thor said.

'Well I guess it has a theatre.'

'It does, though it's very small.'

'She must have performed there with her group. And from what I can gather she met a boy in Skagen and he was her first.'

Thor grinned. 'Your mum lost her virginity in Skagen. That's brilliant.'

'I guess her dream to go back to Skagen was really to go back to see him. She was eighteen when she wrote the list of dreams, so it hadn't been too long since she had left him behind. Unfortunately, I have no name for the man so I can't meet him, but I can go and see the place. From what Laurel says, Mum fell in love with the town too, though I'm sure the mystery man helped.'

'It's a beautiful place,' Thor said.

'You know it well?'

'It's where I was born and raised. I spent every day there on the beach. My parents still live there.'

'They do? Oh how lovely, you must go and visit them while we're there,' Eva said, excitedly. How wonderful it would be to see where Thor grew up.

'Well, that's what I was going to ask as we're spending the night there. It's my dad's birthday at the weekend, it would be great to see them.'

'Oh of course. I'll be fine in the hotel. I have some work to do anyway.'

He frowned slightly. 'No, you misunderstand. I thought you would want to come with me.'

Her heart stuttered in her chest. But she told herself not to be silly. So he wanted her to meet his parents, it didn't mean anything.

'You want me to meet your mum and dad?'

He nodded.

'Don't you want a night off from me?'

He looked confused again. 'Why would I want that?'

'Well, babysitting me all day can't be that much fun.'

'This trip...' Thor shook his head as he tried to find the right words. 'I'm having more fun with you than I've ever had on any escorted trip before. It doesn't seem right to leave you behind in the hotel, when I'll be eating my mum's amazing home-cooked food. You'll like her and she will make a big fuss of you and make you feel at home. Also my grandad used to work at the theatre in the town, my mum has lots of photos of all the plays that were shown there. She might even have photos of your mum's production. You should come, if only for that.'

Eva was very nearly swayed by that.

'But I don't want to intrude. I imagine you don't get to see your family very often, you should spend quality time with them. You shouldn't feel obligated to invite me along.'

'I don't feel obligated. I want you there.'

She couldn't help smiling at that. 'OK. I'll come.'

'Good.'

'So what are your parents like?'

'Dad's English, he came to Skagen with work, met Mum and fell in love. He never left. They are so completely in love with each other, they're very cute.'

Eva smiled. 'Was there a language barrier between them?'

'No, most of the Danes speak fluent English. We get English TV programmes, we listen to their songs, read books written in English.'

'They watch English TV?' Eva cringed at the thought of the Danish watching soaps like *EastEnders* and presuming the whole country was like that. 'What do they watch?'

'Right now, *Midsomer Murders* is a complete phenomenon over there, it's probably bigger there than it is in the UK. Mor, I mean my mum, is always asking me about the places they have been filming in and the villages. I managed to get Barnaby's autograph once, it's in a gold frame in her house. They love it over there.'

Eva loved the thought of the Danes getting their English fix from *Midsomer Murders* with its cute little villages and thatched cottages, the secrets, lies and affairs and of course the multiple murders. She couldn't imagine that the TV channels in England would ever show a Danish TV programme with English subtitles, which was a bit short-sighted in her view.

'I should learn a few Danish words if I'm going to meet your parents.'

'There's no need. Mor speaks perfect English.'

'Mor is Danish for Mum?'

'Yes.'

'And what's Danish for Dad?'

'Far, but I never called him that. Dad is just Dad. I actually learned English before I learned Danish as my parents were speaking in English all the time. Dad does speak fluent Danish now and we tend to speak in a mishmash of English and Danish when we're together. We seem to switch between both in one sentence.'

'Oh, I have a friend from Gibraltar who does that. I hear her on the phone to her parents and half of it is Spanish and half of it is English.'

'Yeah, the same for us. Pernille, my sister, lives in England too so I think we've developed our own way of speaking over the years, which is bits of both. But you don't need to worry about talking in Danish. My mum certainly wouldn't expect you to.'

Eva thought about this and decided she was going to learn a few words from the internet before they arrived.

He rolled onto his back to continue gazing at the stars and she watched him for a moment as a smile spread on his face.

'Mor is going to love you,' he said quietly.

She smiled and rolled onto her back too and as she shifted around her fingers grazed his.

'I can't wait to meet them.'

She was going to meet his family. It wasn't significant, of course it wasn't. So why did her heart think that it was?

They were silent for a moment as they watched the stars above them, their hands still touching. She didn't move away from him and he didn't move his hand away from hers but, after a few moments, he slid two fingers over one of hers so they were almost holding hands.

Right then, there wasn't a single part of her that didn't want this.

She didn't say anything, she didn't need to. For now, it was enough.

Thor watched a shooting star rip across the sky, leaving a tiny trail of gold in its wake, and smiled. He turned to see if Eva had noticed it and saw she was asleep.

He was still holding hands with her and he had no idea why he'd done it. And now he was taking her to meet his parents. What was he doing?

In all his years of escorting people around the world, he had never once asked for a night off or gone off to visit his parents, no matter how close he had been to them. Although admittedly, he'd never been this close before. But leaving his client was against the rules. When he was escorting people, he was with them practically twenty-four hours a day. There was no time off to go and do his own thing. And even if he had stayed in Skagen before, there was no way he would take any of his clients to meet his parents.

But he was already breaking loads of rules with Eva and, for some reason he couldn't put his finger on, he wanted her to meet them. Which was ridiculous. At the end of this trip, he and Eva would part ways and probably never see each other again. But deep down, in his heart, he knew that walking away from her wouldn't be that simple.

Nothing was going to happen between them, he knew that. He didn't do relationships and, with all his travelling, he didn't have time to ever start one. But there was a need for her, a need to be with her, that bubbled in his veins and he had no idea what he was going to do about it.

He watched her breathing softly, her eyes closed, a small smile on her face. He wanted nothing more than to snuggle under the duvet with her and stay there, wrapped around her, for the rest of the night.

And because he wanted that, he got up, covered her with the duvet and left her alone. He went downstairs back to his own room and lay down on his bed, staring up at the far more boring ceiling.

Sleep was going to be very far away that night.

Chapter 15

Dear Mum,

Legoland was so much fun. Thor was like a big kid wanting to go on all the rides, we got absolutely soaked on the Viking River Splash and the Canoe, the Polar X-plorer was brilliant and the Haunted House was really cheesy. But what I really loved was seeing all the Lego sculptures, especially in Miniland where there were little Lego versions of every big city in the world. You would have loved seeing them all.

We are now in a taxi to the car rental place. Skagen is about three hours north of here to the very top of Denmark, so we're hiring a car and Thor is going to drive us to his parents'. He hasn't told them we're coming, he wants it to be a surprise. Though I kind of wish he was preparing them. Bringing a complete stranger into their home for dinner might not be the kind of surprise they would like.

I'm excited to see the town that captured your heart.

Wish you were here!
Love Eva x

PS Dreams ticked off:
4. Go to Legoland in Denmark.
5. Go back to Skagen – we're not there yet but
we're on our way.

'It's quite a long journey up north so we need something we're going to be comfortable in,' Thor said, as he held the door open for Eva on the car rental place.

It was a quirky little place set up like a car showroom for people to choose which car they wanted to hire. Many of the vehicles were vintage classics rather than sleek modern cars with all the mod cons. He tried to decide what Eva would choose. Would she go for a flashy convertible or something more practical? He grinned to himself. She was definitely going to go for something sensible. He looked around the showroom for something that would tick that box for her and his eyes fell on a black Honda Shadow motorbike. Their hire car temporarily forgotten, he quickly crossed over to it, running his fingers over the handlebars.

Eva moved to his side.

'That doesn't look like it would be a comfortable ride,' she teased.

'Ah, but it's exciting and thrilling. The wind in your hair, the open road in front of you, there's nothing better. I used to have this exact bike when I was younger, mine was bright red though. It was my pride and joy. I'd go all over Denmark in it.

It's still in my parents' garage – I can't bear to get rid of it, even though the engine gave up and died many years ago. It has too many memories for me to chuck it out. It's been so long since I've ridden a motorbike, I do miss it. Do you fancy taking this up to Skagen?' he joked, patting the seat invitingly.

She stared at the bike, something like real fear in her eyes, and then she looked back at him and smiled.

'OK.'

The smile fell off his face. 'What?'

'Let's do it.'

'No, no, no. Don't do that for me. I was just reminiscing. Don't do something you'll hate for me.'

'I'm not. I've never been on a bike before. You make it sound so much fun. And I've always wanted to have a go on one. Consider this to be one of my dreams.'

He smiled. She was getting braver. Or at least wanted to be. 'Are you sure?'

The sales assistant came over to them. He'd obviously heard them speak English because he didn't even bother speaking to them in Danish. 'See anything you like?'

Thor watched Eva take a deep breath. 'Can we take the Shadow for one day?'

'Ah, that's a beautiful machine, an excellent choice. But only one day? You don't want it longer?' the assistant tried.

'We'd love to take it for longer but we fly to Oslo tomorrow so we just need it for the day,' Thor explained. 'We're flying from Aalborg too; do you have a store up there we can return the bike to tomorrow?'

'Yes we do, that's perfectly fine.'

'Oh, what about all our bags?' Eva said.

'That's no problem at all,' the assistant said smoothly. Clearly he'd dealt with this before. 'One of our staff is driving up to Aalborg tonight to drop off a car for one of our clients. If you can take a small rucksack of what you need tonight, then he can drop the bags off at our Aalborg office for you to collect tomorrow when you return the bike.'

Thor smiled at the Danish efficiency.

'Why don't you come over and we can fill out all the paperwork?'

Thor nodded. The assistant hurried off and Eva made to follow him but Thor caught her hand.

'Are you really sure about this? I don't want you to do anything you're scared of. We can get the Peugeot or the Ford instead.'

'No, I want to do this.'

She stared up at him and he knew what she really meant was that she wanted to do this *for him*. God, he wanted to kiss her right now. He wanted to cup her face in his hands and kiss her hard.

Christ this was a mess.

He quickly walked away from her and joined the assistant at his desk.

It didn't take long to sort out all the paperwork and details and soon the assistant was wheeling the bike out of the showroom, handing him the keys and two helmets and waving them on their way.

Thor settled himself into the seat, feeling the creak of the leather and the friction of the handlebars on his fingers. He looked up to see Eva pulling on the rucksack and fiddling with the straps of the helmet. He leaned up and tightened it for her.

'Does that feel OK?' he asked, giving the helmet an affectionate wiggle.

'It feels fine.'

He gestured to the seat behind him. She climbed on and frantically looked around for somewhere to hold onto.

'You can put your hands behind you and hold onto the handle at the back or…' he trailed off as she wrapped her arms around him and clamped her legs tightly around his thighs. 'Or you could hold onto me.'

He started the engine and smiled when she held him impossibly tighter. 'You're not going to die, I promise you that.'

'You were going to prove to me that you were a sensible and safe person to be with,' Eva yelled over the rumble of the engine. 'This doesn't feel sensible or safe.'

He grinned as he revved the engine. 'I told you, I'm neither of those things. Feel free to swap me with Sonia next week. She's far more sedate.'

'I might just do that,' Eva said.

He kicked the stand off the floor and manoeuvred slowly out of the car park. There were no other cars and he revved up the engine and roared up the road. He laughed when all he could hear were her screams. She was holding him so tight, her fingers clenched so they were almost white as she gripped around his stomach. The sun was still shining above them, the cloudless sky seemed to go on forever, so he decided to give her a break for a while. They could take their time getting to Skagen, they had several hours yet before sunset. He eased off the accelerator and she stopped screaming. After a few minutes, he even felt her start to relax around him. It felt so good to be back out on a bike again after all this time and to have Eva enjoy this with him. Christel had hated his bike. She had flatly refused to go anywhere with him on *that contraption.*

Eva shifted around to get more comfortable and her hands came to rest on the top of his belt, tucking her fingers around the belt buckle. He was suddenly hyper aware of her body pressed against his, her arms and legs wrapped around him so tightly and intimately. Her hands so inappropriately yet innocently placed. Suddenly the three-hour journey seemed agonisingly long and at the end of it he was still going to be as frustrated and turned on as he was now. He needed a break from her. Just to clear his head. Maybe tonight, after dinner, he'd take her back to the hotel and come back to his parents to spend the night alone. First thing the next day, he was going to get in touch with Tracy and insist she sort out the bedroom problem once and for all.

They had made good time into Skagen, completing the journey in a little under three hours. As Eva had relaxed and clearly started to enjoy the ride, he had slowly increased the speed so she didn't notice at first until they were flying along the roads with Eva laughing and squealing with excitement behind him.

He pulled up in his parents' driveway and cut the engine. The quiet was almost deafening for a few moments – his ears had been so used to the roar of the engine for the last three hours, it was hard to become accustomed to the gentler sounds of the birds singing and the bubble of the brook behind his parents' house.

He waited for Eva to release her grip on him and get off the bike, but she didn't.

He took his helmet off and hung it on the handlebars and looked over his shoulder at her.

'You OK?'

'Yes,' she laughed. 'I feel like I'm stuck. I've been holding onto you for so long that it feels like I can't let go.'

She had cramped up. She had been tensed up for so long, it wasn't a surprise. She would be stiff later.

He ran his hands over her fingers, stroking them and gently prising them off his belt, and she laughed as she finally unwrapped her arms from him. God, he was crossing so many boundaries with her.

She climbed down, removed her helmet and stretched her arms above her head, showing a tiny strip of belly as her t-shirt hitched up. To his embarrassment she caught him looking.

'I'm not really appropriately dressed to meet your parents, am I?'

He assessed her little denim shorts and flowery t-shirt. She looked cute.

'What do you mean? What should you be wearing to have dinner with my parents, a suit perhaps?'

'I didn't pack one of those.'

'Good job too, you'd be completely out of place amongst my dad's colourful jumpers and my mum's floaty dresses.'

She smiled but he could see she was nervous about meeting them. That was one thing that Thor was not nervous about. His parents were going to absolutely adore her.

They walked up the driveway and he rang the bell.

Normally he'd just let himself back in, but his keys to his childhood home were still sitting in the bowl by the front door at his house in London. Eva shifted nervously next to him and he found himself linking hands with her to calm her down.

He saw movement through the glass panel and then his mum answered the door. She looked stunned for a moment and then her whole face lit up into a huge smile.

'Thor! *Hvad laver du her?*'

He grinned at her surprise.

She leapt forward before he could get a word out and squeezed him tight and he inhaled her warmth and familiar scent as he held her with one arm. She stepped back, holding him at arm's length to inspect him, and that's when her eyes zeroed in on him holding Eva's hand. Impossibly, her smile seemed to get even wider. She turned her head back inside and yelled for his dad.

'Henry! Henry! *Thor er her! Og han har en pige med!*'

Thor smirked, thankful Eva wouldn't understand his mum's excitement that he'd brought a girl home with him.

'Hi Mor, lovely to see you. This is Eva,' Thor said, deliberately speaking in English for Eva's benefit. He didn't want her to feel uncomfortable around his family if they were all speaking Danish. 'Eva, this is Sofie, my mum.'

'*Det Glæder dig at møde mig,*' Eva said slowly.

It gladdens you to meet me.

Thor stared at her. Sofie stared at her. The pronunciation was slightly off and her tenses were the wrong way round but she was speaking Danish. His heart filled for her. Danish was such a hard language to learn, there were so many letters and different sounds. She must have listened to the pronunciation on the internet for her to get it right.

But clearly she wasn't finished.

'*Du har et smukt hjem,*' Eva said. *You have a beautiful home.*

Oh God. He wanted to hug her. She was trying so hard. Then he watched her glance at her hand. There was writing on the inside of her palm that he'd not noticed before. It looked a bit faded now as if it had sweated off on her long journey from Billund.

'*Mit ravn er Eva,*' Eva said, hesitantly. *My raven is Eva.*

He cocked his head and suppressed a smile. He gently took her hand and she blushed that he'd seen the words. He could see the first N of *navn* had been smudged to look like *ravn*. *My raven is Eva instead of my name is Eva.*

'Did I say it right?' Eva said.

He leaned over and pressed a kiss into her forehead. 'It was perfect.'

Sofie recovered herself well from being introduced to a fictional raven.

'Eva, how wonderful to meet you.'

Sofie threw her arms around Eva's neck and squeezed her into a big hug as his dad, Henry, came barrelling down the hall towards them, today wearing a bright green jumper with red spots. He practically barged past Sofie to hug Thor, squeezing him tight then letting him go and grabbing Eva into a hug before he'd even introduced himself.

'What a lovely surprise,' his dad said. 'Come through, come through.' He ushered Eva into the house and down towards the kitchen. He heard his dad talking to Eva as they disappeared inside.

His mum leaned up and gave him another warm hug and then linked arms with him as she brought him into the house. 'Eva's lovely, why didn't you tell us you were dating again—'

'I'm not. We're not. We're friends.'

'Oh *of course*,' Sofie said, as if she didn't believe him for one second. 'Me and Henry started out as friends too. I think it's the best way.'

'We're not starting out, this isn't...' he trailed off, not having the heart to correct her.

He moved into the kitchen where Eva was already sitting at the table with a mug of tea in one hand and a thick slice of walnut cake in the other. His dad was a fast worker.

'What are you doing here Thor, why didn't you tell us you were coming?' Henry said.

'I didn't really know, it's all been a bit last minute actually. Eva is a client for The World Is Your Oyster. She was supposed to be going on this round-the-world trip with my colleague Rebecca, but Rebecca broke her ankle the night before they were due to depart and poor Eva got stuck with me instead.'

'It's not a total hardship,' Eva said. 'You do have your good points.'

He grinned. 'Like?'

She smiled. 'Well, you're not bad at cooking.'

'That's good to know.'

'You speak French.'

'I'm glad I'm so useful for you,' he said dryly.

She shrugged. 'I don't want to blow your trumpet for you. I'm sure you are more than capable of doing that yourself.'

He realised his mum and dad were watching the exchange with interest.

'So you've only just met?' Sofie asked.

'Yes, we met briefly in the store a few weeks ago where I managed to piss her off, but we met properly for the first time on Monday and thankfully I managed to make a much more positive impression on her.'

'You've only known each other for five days?' Sofie said.

Thor nodded.

'But... you seem so at ease with each other.'

'We get on well,' Thor said, trying to play it down.

'This tea tastes amazing,' Eva said, clearly trying to change the subject as well. 'It tastes of flowers and sunshine.'

'Why don't you tell them about your list of dreams,' Thor said.

Eva explained all about her mum's list and her decision to tick off everything that her mum had wanted to do as Thor poured himself a cup of tea and sat down next to her.

'That sounds wonderful,' Sofie said. 'But why are you in Skagen?'

Eva smiled. 'One of Mum's dreams was to come back here. She didn't specify why, but I think it was because she fell in love with a boy when she was here.'

'Oh, how exciting. Do you know who?'

Eva shook her head. 'She was seventeen, so she would have been here around twenty-nine years ago. She was in a musical adaptation of *The Wizard of Oz*. She had the lead actually.'

'Oh, I remember the opening night of that show,' Sofie said.

'You do?' Eva said, leaning forward.

'Henry proposed to me that night. It was not something I'm likely to forget.'

Eva smiled and Thor got himself comfortable at the table to hear the story for the hundredth time.

'We had left the theatre and Henry was walking me home. It was a beautiful starry night and we were both talking about how much we had enjoyed the show. And then Henry pulled me into the field where we'd had a picnic on our first date. He told me he knew then, sharing our first kiss, that I was the girl he wanted forever with. He told me he loved me more every day he was with me and then he got down on one knee and asked me to marry him. He realised as soon as he touched the ground that he'd knelt in a cow pat but he didn't want to ruin the moment. Anyway, before I could say yes, this great big bull comes charging out of the darkness towards us. We ran, screaming and shouting across the field, this bull half-heartedly running after us. I lost one of my shoes, Henry lost his wallet and the ring. I fell over. We came out onto the road covered in cow poo.'

'I thought I had completely ruined my chances with her,' Henry said, picking up the story. 'Who wants to be proposed to like that?'

'I found the whole thing hilarious,' Sofie said. 'Of course I said yes. I made him go back the next day to find the ring and my shoe, and we were married two months later.'

Thor smiled as he watched the look of love his parents shared. He had never seen two people as completely and utterly in love as his parents were. There was a huge part of him that wanted that but there was a part of him that didn't. A one-sided love story was not one he wanted to be a part of again. He glanced over at Eva who was smiling at them too.

'What a wonderful story,' Eva said. 'Many people will

149

have romantic proposals, and I love hearing people's different love stories, but your proposal is one that stands out as something special.'

'It's certainly different,' Thor agreed.

'And your parents, Eva, did they have a romantic proposal too?' Sofie asked.

Thor watched the smile fall off her face slightly. 'My parents aren't married. I've never actually met my dad.'

He saw his parents immediately shift into sympathy and fussing mode. This is what they did best.

'Eva's mum was a wonderful woman,' Thor quickly rushed in. 'From what I've heard from Eva, Juliette was a fantastic mother, father and best friend. I don't think Eva was any worse off for not having a dad in her life.'

Eva smiled at him gratefully.

His dad suddenly straightened in his chair. 'Is that why you're here? Is the boy your mum fell in love with in Skagen, is he your father?'

'Oh no, definitely not,' Eva said. 'I didn't come along until at least two years later. My dad is American, not Danish.'

Henry let out a sigh of relief. 'That's good. Because I think I might know who it was.'

Thor felt his eyes widen. It was a small town, and everyone knew everyone else's business, so he wasn't surprised that his mum and dad knew, especially as the night Juliette had been in town had been so memorable for them.

Eva perked up. 'You do?'

'Do you think it was Kasper?' Sofie asked Henry.

He nodded. 'Do you remember how he was that night?'

Sofie smiled and turned back to Eva. 'I remember your mum as Dorothy, she lit up the whole stage. But my younger cousin thought she was an absolute goddess. He gave her a standing ovation that night. Kasper stood up and cheered her way before anyone else. He was only eighteen, all his mates gave him stick over it but he didn't care.'

'When we left that night, Kasper was going to try to talk to her backstage,' Henry said. 'I know he went back to watch her every night she was in town. And they were seen together around town during the day. I think he was a little bit heartbroken when she moved on.'

Eva frowned slightly and Thor knew that didn't quite fit with the version of events that Laurel had told her. 'I think *she* fell in love with him. I wonder what happened, why they never got together?'

Sofie shook her head. 'I'm not sure, maybe the distance was too far.'

Thor watched Eva carefully. 'Would you like to meet him?'

'Ah, I'm not sure that's a good idea. Kasper is happily married now. Three kids,' Henry said, protectively.

'I'm not here to cause any trouble,' Eva said. 'But it would be nice to talk to someone who has some memories of being with her. Especially of what she was like when she was young.'

'Our flight doesn't leave until tomorrow afternoon,' Thor said. 'Maybe we can give him a call and see if he's free in the morning. He can meet us down by the beach.'

Sofie nodded at Henry.

'OK, I'll phone him. It was a lifetime ago though, he might not want to relive the past,' Henry said.

'And I'll totally understand if he doesn't. I think her love of Skagen wasn't just because of Kasper. My aunt said how much she loved this place too. So I'm glad I've come here, just to see it. And of course meeting Thor's wonderful parents has been a lovely bonus.'

Thor grinned. His parents smiled, completely charmed by her already. He knew, as soon as he was alone with his mum, he was definitely going to get the lecture about not letting this one go. But right then, he didn't care.

Chapter 16

Eva's cheeks were aching from laughing so much. Of course the childhood photos had come out and Eva had been treated to a whole coming-of-age story of Thor's life. She'd seen every photo from when Thor was a tiny baby, later playing with his little sister, Pernille, right through to his teenage years and early twenties. She had loved teasing Thor about his dodgy clothes and hair. He hadn't always been the cool kid, he had been quite the dork in his childhood and teenage years. He'd even had his own miniature train set, which he seemed to be endlessly proud of in many photos growing up. He had certainly bloomed later on in life. She had listened to stories about him and his family and quite honestly she had fallen a little bit in love with his parents that night.

They had drunk several glasses of wine between them all and she had just stepped outside into the garden to cool down as she was getting a bit hot and probably a tiny bit drunk. She wasn't sure if Thor was a little drunk too. She hadn't seen him drink once on the trip so far, taking his babysitting duties very seriously, but here with his parents he seemed relaxed and happy and he clearly felt able to let his hair down a little.

She looked out over the town of Skagen. Thor's parents' house was up on a hill and the whole of the town stretched out in front of her, its lights twinkling in the darkness. She knew, in the morning, she would have a glorious view of the sea from up here too. There were plenty of places on the drive in where she'd been able to see the sea – being on a peninsula they were pretty much surrounded by it. Skagen was so quaint and picturesque, with its yellow houses tucked under red roofs, she could see why her mum had fallen in love with it. And tomorrow she was going to meet Kasper, the man who had first captured her mum's heart.

As far as she knew, there had only been two men who her mum had fallen in love with in her life: Kasper and Thomas, her dad. And neither of those relationships had worked out for her. Of course there had been other men that Juliette had dated for a few weeks here and there, but there was no one who stole her heart again. There was something quite sad about that, to live her whole life without someone to love her.

Inadvertently, Juliette had taught Eva that relationships didn't endure. Her dad's complete lack of interest in Juliette after spending that incredible night together showed her that a physical attraction was not enough to make a relationship last. Even a child was not enough.

Eva had never had any long-term relationships before and she knew in her heart it was because she had been burned by men from such an early age. Men would always let her down. Her dad had been proof of that back when she was a child and he hadn't turned up to her birthday party, even after sending him an invite. She hadn't really considered before how much damage that had caused, but she always went into a relationship waiting for it to end. She never expected a big love story because she knew it didn't exist.

Her mum and Kasper had fallen in love with each other after spending one week together, but neither of them had done anything about it when it had been time for Juliette to go. They had walked away from each other. Maybe they hadn't declared their love, maybe they had been waiting for the other to say it first. Maybe there had been a hundred other reasons why it never worked out but seemingly they never fought for each other, maybe because they knew it would never last.

Love was not the forever Eva read about in books.

Even Thor was completely anti-relationships and, judging by the conversation they'd had about sex, there had been quite a few women in his life and none of them meant anything to him. Apart from Christel.

Eva didn't really have any good role models for everlasting love.

But Henry and Sofie had that, they had been together for nearly thirty years and were clearly as in love with each other now as they were back then. Henry was not a man who would ever let his wife and children down.

It gave her hope.

She had never really wanted a long relationship before – she was quite happy in her own company. But seeing Henry and Sofie showed that the journey of life would be so much richer and colourful if you had your best friend along for the ride.

Maybe it was time she opened up her heart to the possibility of that.

The back door opened and Henry walked out. He offered out a mug of hot chocolate. She smiled and took it, wrapping her fingers around the warmth as he sat down next to her.

'You OK, dear?' Henry said, settling himself back on the seat.

'I'm fine, just cooling off.' She looked at him and his brightly coloured jumper and smiled. 'I'm so glad I came here tonight.'

'We're glad you came too. You make Thor smile and it's been a long time since we've seen that,' Henry said, getting straight to the heart of the matter.

'I think… we're going to be good friends. I hope that when this trip is done, we might stay in touch.'

Would that really happen? She tried to imagine him coming round to her house for dinner and them talking and laughing over a bottle of wine. But she couldn't envisage him in her home. Her life and his were so very different. He toured the world, having adventures every day. He had scuba-dived, skydived, climbed mountains, water-skied, been on jet skis, been to every city in the world. She sat in her flat alone every night with her books and work for company. How would he possibly fit into that? Would he even want to? There was a physical attraction between them, she knew that, but as she'd seen with her dad, that didn't mean love, marriage and a happy ever after. In reality, she knew that the trip would come to an end and, like her mum and Kasper, they would walk away and probably never see each other again.

An ache spread in her heart at that thought, which was ridiculous. She was a client to him and nothing more. He'd already made it clear that nothing was going to happen between them so why the hell was she getting so attached?

'You like him,' Henry said. It wasn't a question, he said it as a fact.

Eva smiled and shook her head. 'I'm his client, it's no more than that.'

'He's only ever brought one other girl home with him before. Christel. And, well, that ended spectacularly badly. I think it's significant that he brought you to meet us.'

'We were in Skagen, of course he would come and see you as we were so close. I just tagged along for the ride,' Eva said.

'It's more than that. You two have a beautiful connection.'

'We get on really well, but we are mountains apart.'

'I don't see that at all. I see the way he looks at you. He adores you,' Henry said.

She sighed because she had felt that connection between them, but they both seemed to be dancing around it. 'He won't do anything, he won't risk his job.'

'It's not his job he won't risk, it's his heart. After what happened with Christel he moved to England, threw himself into his work, travelled the world to try to forget the pain. We didn't think he would ever fall in love again. He guards his heart with an impenetrable fortress. It will take a special kind of lady to break his walls down. But I have a feeling you're going to be her.'

Eva smiled sadly at his optimism.

'What happened with Christel?'

Henry took a deep breath, clearly deciding whether or not to tell her. Silence filled the air and Eva felt bad for putting him in that position.

'It's OK, it's none of my business.'

'I think Thor should probably tell you himself, but maybe I can tell you some of it. I can tell you that this was way more than just a regular break-up. They were very young when they got together. She had just moved here with her family, they were both only nineteen. He fell completely and utterly in love with her straight away and they dated for about four years. They seemed very happy together. Thor thought they were forever. He spoke about marriage and children. But then Stefan arrived in town and that changed everything. I don't think Christel did anything with him, not while she was with Thor – it's a small town and you can't sneeze without someone knowing about it, and I certainly didn't hear any rumours of them sneaking around together. But everyone could see she was smitten with him. They worked together and she just came alive when she was with him. Thor could see it too and it must have been so heartbreaking for him, to watch her fall in love with someone else.'

Eva looked out over the town. She had never experienced unrequited love or had anyone fall out of love with her and in love with someone else. So she could only imagine how hard that must have been for Thor.

'She fell pregnant,' Henry said.

Eva snapped her head round to look at him. 'With Stefan's child?'

'No, with Thor's.' Henry swallowed.

'Thor has a child?'

'No.' Henry looked suddenly guilty and awkward. 'I've said too much.'

Eva's mind raced with the different possibilities. Christel had miscarried or she'd had an abortion. What would have been worse? Either way her heart broke for Thor.

'He moved away to London after that. There has been no one else for the last seven years. He says he doesn't need anyone but I think he's afraid to need someone again. I think he'll always be afraid to give his heart. But I think, when he meets the right woman, she will show him that love is worth the risk.'

Eva smiled sadly. 'I really hope he finds her one day.'

Even if it wasn't her, she wanted someone for him who would make him happy again.

'I think he already has. I think she just needs to fight for him,' Henry said.

Eva looked back over the twinkling town lights again. Maybe Henry was right.

Thor sat down with the hot chocolates he'd made for them all and passed a mug to his mum.

Sofie took a sip. 'Eva's a character, isn't she? I can see why you like her.'

Thor smiled at the not-so-subtle matchmaking. Sofie had been trading glances with his dad all night whenever Eva had teased Thor or he'd talked to her or inadvertently touched her. Knowing his parents, they'd already be booking the church or digging out their best suits for the wedding.

'I do like her. A lot. But nothing is going to happen between us.'

'Why not?' Sofie asked.

'Because she's a client, it would be unprofessional, unethical and—'

'You and I both know there's a lot more to it than that.'

He sighed. 'I'm not interested in a relationship. I don't need all the complications and stresses that come with it. I have a great life, travelling the world. I don't want to lose that.'

'Why do you have to lose that? People who are married to military partners are away from them for long periods of time, long-distance truck drivers, oil rig workers. Lots of people travel with their jobs. If it's a relationship worth fighting for, you'll find a way to make it work. You're afraid of getting hurt again and I understand that. But don't you think she's afraid too? Love is terrifying and wonderful and scary and amazing. But the good points far outweigh the bad. Life is filled with ups and downs but it's infinitely better to have someone to share those ups and downs with.'

He took a sip of his hot chocolate and felt the warmth fill him from the inside but soon the warmth faded away. The back door opened and his dad and Eva came back inside, laughing about something. He smiled when he saw how happy she was and that warmth filled him again.

Maybe Sofie was right.

They sat back down at the table and Sofie focussed her attention on Eva instead.

'So, what are your plans when you leave here tomorrow?'

'I think we are flying to Oslo about three?' Eva said, looking at Thor to confirm this. He nodded. 'And then we fly straight to the Lofoten Islands at the very top of Norway. We're going to see the midnight sun. And then we're going whale-watching the next day. That's one of *my* dreams.'

He watched her eyes light up at this prospect. God, she made him smile.

'Oh, that sounds wonderful. We went to see the midnight sun in Svalbard many years ago. It was utterly magical,' Sofie said.

'I'm really excited about it. I just can't imagine it being daylight all day. We have a cabin right on the shores of one of the beaches. It has two bedrooms so at least we won't be sharing a bed again,' Eva said.

Crap. He had successfully avoided telling his parents that little titbit of information. Straight away his parents pounced on it like a lion snatching its prey.

'You've been sharing a bed?' Sofie said.

'I thought you said you weren't dating?' Henry said.

'It's not exactly professional, is it?' Sofie said, teasing him by using his own words against him.

'We're sharing a bed, not sleeping together,' Thor said quickly before they got too carried away. He glanced at Eva and she was giggling. He scowled at her but she didn't take any notice. 'Eva and Rebecca were sharing a room and you know what the Europeans are like about twin beds, they generally don't have that facility. My boss is going to sort it out so that our sleeping accommodation is separate rooms going forward but some of the bookings were too late in the day to change, especially for places like Amsterdam where every hotel was booked up because of the flower parade.'

'Thor has been the perfect gentleman,' Eva said.

Was it his imagination or was Sofie disappointed by that?

'Is it OK if we crash here tonight?' Thor said quickly, before they could get too carried away with their excitement. 'I've drunk too much to drive us back to the hotel.'

'Of course you can and then we can all go to the beach

together tomorrow,' Sofie said.

'Is the spare room made up? Eva can sleep in my room and I'll sleep in there.'

Sofie's face fell. 'Oh, no it isn't. We've been decorating it. We've taken everything out of there. I'm afraid your room is the only one available. But as you've been sharing a bed for the last few nights, I don't think it will be any hardship for you.' She smiled mischievously.

Thor sighed. Why was the universe so against him?

'Why don't I call you a taxi to go back to the hotel?' he said to Eva. 'It seems silly to have a fully paid for hotel room just sitting there empty while we squash ourselves into my childhood bed.'

The smile fell from her face. 'Oh, OK, sure.'

'Thor! Don't be so rude. We don't kick our guests out. If you don't want to sleep in the same bed as Eva, then you can sleep on the sofa downstairs,' Sofie said.

That sofa was the most uncomfortable place in the world to sleep on. It was older than he was and his parents had never got round to changing it. They'd had it re-stuffed and covered the stains and holes with a multitude of blankets but never bothered getting a new one. They knew it was uncomfortable too. Sofie knew full well that Thor would choose the bed instead of the sofa.

Thor sighed. 'It's fine, we can share a bed again. We've done it before. And on that note, I think I'll go to sleep.'

He finished the rest of his drink, swilled his mug in the sink and left the room.

Why was he letting this get to him? They'd done this before. It was just two adults, sleeping in the same bed together, it didn't mean anything.

But in reality, he knew that was rubbish. It was becoming more than that. He'd fallen a little bit in love with Eva that night and he hated that. He didn't like losing control but there was nothing he could do to stop it.

Chapter 17

Eva lay on the sofa and stared at the ceiling. Henry and Sofie had gone off to bed a short while before. She had told them she was going to do a bit of work and then go up to join Thor, but he'd made it very clear that he was becoming increasingly uncomfortable with sharing a bed with her. He even wanted to ship her off to the hotel rather than spend another night lying next to her. She was tempted to go back to the hotel herself, but Thor had all the itinerary and travel details and she didn't know the name of where they were supposed to be staying. So, after working for half hour, she'd changed into her pyjamas, found a blanket in the ottoman and set up camp for the night on the sofa. But it was so lumpy with springs sticking in her back that there was no chance of getting any sleep that night.

She grabbed her phone and saw she had messages in the WhatsApp group from Julie and Natalie. She had been keeping them all updated with her progress on her travels and it made her smile to see they were more interested in any developments with Thor than the beautiful places she was visiting.

'How's it going?' Julie asked.

'We want more pictures,' Natalie said.

'Preferably of sexy Thor,' Julie went on.

Eva smiled. She scrolled through her phone and sent a few pictures of Legoland, which she knew their kids at least would enjoy. Then she found one of her and Thor together, eating ice creams, his arm around her as they took a selfie. He looked happy and totally at ease with her. God, he was confusing. She sent that to them too. The girls would love it, even if it wasn't exactly a true representation of where she was with Thor. She put the phone down and sighed.

Her heart hurt for what Thor had gone through several years before. She wondered if she should talk to him about it but she wasn't sure if he would want her to know any of that stuff. But at least she knew now why he was so reluctant to get involved with her. It wasn't just professionalism he was clinging to, it was a need to protect himself from getting hurt again.

She didn't know what this thing was between them and whether it was worth pushing. She had no idea what he felt for her. She knew he was attracted to her but she didn't know if it was lust or love or somewhere in between. But then she had no idea what she felt for him either. She wanted to tell him that if he let her in she would be much more careful with his heart than Christel was. But could she really offer that? She wasn't exactly a glowing example of someone who knew how to be in a relationship. She had no great track record of ever being in love.

She sighed and got up. This sofa was truly awful. She pushed the two armchairs together to make some sort of makeshift bed but as she lay down on it, it was clear it was way too short, and she had to prop her legs up on the back of the armchair. This wasn't any comfier than the sofa.

She heard a shuffling in the room with her and she looked up to see Thor standing over her, wearing no top.

'What are you doing?'

'Trying to get comfortable.'

'I meant, why are you down here?' Thor asked.

'Oh, well you made it very clear you don't want to share a bed with me. I'm trying to give you some space.'

Thor sighed. 'Come to bed.'

She hesitated but he held out a hand for her and she relented and took it. He led her upstairs without another word and into his bedroom. The bed was bigger than a single but not as big as a double. No wonder Thor hadn't been keen to share this with her. There was no way they could lie next to each other and not touch.

He climbed into the bed and held the duvet up for her to join him. She shuffled into the tiny space he had left for her but then he looped an arm round her back and pulled her onto his chest, holding her just like he had the other night when she had inadvertently taken drugs.

She didn't pull away. There was something so wonderful about lying here like this, but she was so confused by his actions.

They lay next to each other in the darkness, neither of them moving or saying a word, just staring at each other.

Feeling emboldened by the wine and this gesture, she placed a hand over his heart, tracing his heartbeat with gentle fingers. It was racing against her fingertips.

Immediately, his hand covered hers and she thought he

might snatch her fingers away but he didn't. In fact, he just held her hand there over his heart.

Their faces were centimetres apart, she could feel his breath on her lips and he bent his head down and gave her a short, sweet kiss on the lips.

God, the taste of him was amazing and she found herself reaching forward for more but he was already moving his head back, with a sad smile.

'I really bloody like you, Eva Blue, you know that. I've been giving you loads of mixed messages and it's not fair. So it's time for some honesty. I would like nothing more than to spend the rest of the night making love to you.'

Holy shit! Eva felt her heart thunder against her chest at that thought.

'But I can't do that,' Thor went on, bursting her euphoric bubble. 'And it's nothing to do with my job, although I would get fired if Tracy found out. I can't offer you what you deserve. We'd have a few nights of great sex and it would come to an end and I fear I would end up hurting you. I could really fall for you and I don't want that. I don't want a relationship. I don't want to fall in love and go through that pain again. My last relationship was devastating.'

She bit her lip, not knowing if what she was going to say was a mistake. 'Your dad told me a little about Christel and that she fell in love with Stefan.' Eva didn't mention the baby. She wondered if Thor would tell her himself.

He swallowed as he stared at her, his arm still locked round her back.

'I'm so so sorry you went through that. It must have been heartbreaking for you.'

'It was.'

He wasn't going to open up and she understood that.

'And I totally get not wanting to go through that again. Why risk getting hurt, especially with someone you've only just met?'

'That's very magnanimous,' Thor said, quietly.

'I don't know if I can offer you forever either. I've never been in a long-term relationship. And I wouldn't want you to get hurt.'

He sighed. 'This is a mess, but I'm going to fix it.'

'How? Just because you don't want to have these feelings doesn't mean you can stop them.'

He didn't seem to hear that or he chose to ignore it.

'Tomorrow, I'm going to give Tracy a call first thing in the morning and insist she sorts out separate bedrooms for the rest of the trip. I think she has been putting it off because of the added expense but it can't go on like this.'

'Right. Separate bedrooms. Of course that will sort out all this tension between us,' Eva said, dryly. 'It's more than our sleeping arrangements that's making it awkward. I'm enjoying spending time with you and every time you smile at me, this feeling for you grows in my chest. Do you not feel that too?'

'Yes. I'm enjoying being with you as well. Way too much, but what do you suggest?' Thor asked.

'I don't know.'

'We either try to put some boundaries back in place or we say to hell with it and just try to have sex in as many countries as we possibly can.'

Eva laughed. 'I like the sound of that.'

He grinned. 'I do too.'

'And we categorically promise that we absolutely will not fall in love with each other along the way.'

He held up his hand in a Boy Scout salute and she smiled. His smile faded away.

'Let me try to fix this.' He stroked his hand down her cheek. 'It will be easier to stay friends if we're not doing this every night.'

'You did this,' she laughed, gesturing to where she was lying on his chest. 'Things will definitely get confusing and frustrating if we do this every night and don't take it any further.'

'I just wanted to be clear about my feelings. I hurt you earlier when I suggested not sharing a bed and I wanted you to know why. It's not because I don't want to, it's because I really do.'

She rolled her eyes affectionately. And then because tonight seemed to be the grey area before everything supposedly went back to normal, she leaned up and kissed him briefly on the lips.

'You're a complex infuriating man, Thor Anderson. But I really bloody like you too, so I'm willing to try anything that will make you happy.'

He smiled. 'And if it doesn't work, we have a plan B.'

'Fingers crossed it doesn't work then,' Eva said.

Thor laughed. He looked away for a while over the town that twinkled through the bedroom window. After a while, his eyes started to drift closed although he showed no sign of letting her go.

'Are we going to spend the night like this after your big speech of things need to change?' Eva asked.

He smiled but he didn't open his eyes. 'What happens in Vegas…'

'We're in Denmark.'

He shrugged. 'Same thing.'

'Are you drunk?'

He held his finger and thumb up so they were a very small distance apart.

She smirked. 'Are you going to regret all this in the morning?'

His smile grew and he held her tighter. 'Not a chance.'

She grinned and snuggled in closer. She might as well make the most of this now.

Chapter 18

Eva felt Thor slip quietly from the bed the next morning. She let him go because she knew he wouldn't want to face her after what had happened the night before. He had kissed her and told her he wanted to make love to her. It was hardly the professional line he was so keen on keeping. She wondered if they would speak about it or just pretend it had never happened.

She sat up and curled her knees up to her chest. She wondered whether to give Laurel a call. Eva had sent her a few photos of the windmill they'd stayed in, Legoland and the motorbike but hadn't elaborated any more than that. So much had happened since the last time they'd spoken but, equally, she and Thor seemed to be at the same stalemate as they were before. As there was no new progress to really report, she got washed and dressed and then went downstairs to have breakfast.

Thor was standing in the kitchen, singing quietly to himself as he cooked breakfast.

'Hi,' Eva said, quietly.

He turned and grinned at her. 'Morning. Scrambled eggs and bacon OK?'

'Sure.'

He turned back to the oven. There didn't seem to be any awkwardness at all. Well, at least not from him.

'Can I help?'

'You can make the teas and coffees,' Thor said simply, as if this little domestic scene was perfectly normal.

Eva did as she was asked, making Thor's coffee black with two sugars, just as he liked it. He dished up the breakfasts and carried them to the table and she sat down opposite him.

He took a bite of his toast and chewed it, watching her carefully across the table.

'Look, last night…' Thor started.

'You don't need to apologise.'

He frowned. 'I'm not apologising.'

'Oh, what are you doing?'

'I'd drunk a few glasses of wine and—'

'It's OK. No regrets. What happens in Vegas, remember,' Eva said, trying to let him off the hook.

'Will you stop interrupting,' Thor laughed. 'I'd had a few glasses of wine but I want you to know I meant every single word.'

For once Eva was speechless.

'And I don't regret a single damned thing.'

'Oh.'

'Apart from not jumping straight into plan B, I regret that a lot,' Thor teased. 'But I meant what I said, I'm going to try to fix things today. And try to smile at you a whole lot less.'

Oh crap, he remembered everything.

Sofie swept into the kitchen then, looking very glamorous in a long floaty summer dress and large beach hat.

Thor continued staring at Eva for a few more seconds and then turned his attention to his mum.

'Morning Mor, have you guys eaten? I figured you had as you normally get up so early, but I can cook something if you haven't.'

'We have eaten, thank you.' Sofie placed a warm kiss on her son's head and then came round the table to do the same to Eva. 'Did you sleep OK?'

Eva couldn't help blushing at just how wonderfully she had slept the night before. 'Fine thanks.'

'When I woke up in the middle of the night she had a big smile on her face, so I think she slept fine,' Thor said, his eyes back on hers again.

Oh, this man was so cocky and sure of himself and she loved him a little bit for it.

'I was very comfortable,' Eva said, not taking her eyes off him.

'Hmmm, I was too.'

She glanced up at Sofie who was watching them with joy. It was clear she knew exactly what was going on between them, or at least thought she did. Sofie's mind was definitely more in the plan B zone rather than this weird in-between phase they were in now.

Eva busied herself with eating her eggs on toast as Sofie fixed herself a coffee. She glanced up at Thor who was still staring at her with a big smile on his face.

'No smiling, remember,' Eva said.

'I can't help it.'

Henry came into the room wearing shorts, a brightly coloured t-shirt and socks with sandals. Eva couldn't help but smile.

'I found this photo album of all the old theatre productions. Sofie's dad used to work there and he always took pictures of all the plays and shows. I was just looking through to see if there were any of *The Wizard of Oz* and there are,' Henry said.

He placed the album down on the table next to Eva, open on the page that showed a small programme for *The Wizard of Oz*. And directly underneath that was a picture of her mum dressed as Dorothy. Eva's heart leapt at this unexpected surprise this early in the morning.

She couldn't take her eyes off her. The photo had obviously been taken during the rehearsals or backstage as her mum was laughing at something someone had said. She was barefoot, her ruby shoes held in her hand, her head was tossed back, her smile wide and natural. She looked so young and carefree.

Thor came round to look at the photos too. 'God, she was so beautiful,' he said, quietly.

Eva smiled with pride. Her mum was a star, shining bright even when she wasn't on stage. She was born for a life in the limelight but that never happened for her.

The next photo was obviously taken from the show itself, as her mum was arm in arm with the Tinman and the Lion as they were singing. There were a few more photos of the Wicked Witch, the Wizard, the ruby shoes, the Munchkins, but no more of her mum.

'I would have loved to see her perform. She had such an

amazing voice and she always told me of her dreams to be on the stage. She had various singing jobs over the years that paid the bills, but nothing like this. This was when she was at her happiest,' Eva said.

'I'm sure that's not true,' Sofie said. 'I'm sure she was at her happiest with you.'

Her mum had adored her, that was true, but what would Juliette's life have been like if Eva hadn't come along?

'You can have those photos if you like,' Henry said. 'They're just getting dusty in this old album. You should take them home.'

'Thank you,' Eva said, slipping them from their plastic sleeve and placing them on the table. She didn't have too many photos of her mum in her younger days. She would get these blown up and framed when she got back home.

'We should probably go,' Henry said, quietly. 'Kasper will be meeting us down the beach soon.'

Eva nodded and moved out the room to get her things. She went into the dining room where they had stashed their bag the night before but Thor followed her in and closed the door behind him.

'You OK?'

'Yeah.'

Thor clearly didn't believe her as he stepped up and wrapped her in a big hug. She stood there enveloped in his arms for a second before she slid her arms round him and rested her head on his chest. She smiled as the warmth from this gesture filled her heart and soul. He held her there, not saying anything.

God, it would be impossible not to fall in love with this

man. He pulled back slightly and placed a tiny, sweet kiss on her lips. If this was Thor's attempt at fixing things then he was doing a very poor job. The tension between them sparked like a firework that was just about to explode. And something told her it would be incredible when it did.

Skagen beach was one of the most beautiful beaches Eva had ever seen, with white sands and gorgeous dunes that seemed to stretch on for miles. The sea was so blue and crystal clear, it felt like they were in some tropical paradise instead of on the most northern peninsula of Denmark. Well, it would have done if it was a bit warmer. Despite the bright sunny day, there was a definite nip in the air from the wind.

The beach was pretty busy and there was quite the queue of tourists lining up to get their photos taken at the very tip of Grenen, the sand spit which stuck out into the sea. Two seas met there and Eva could see a clear line out in the sea which frothed and bubbled as the waters joined. They had already seen dolphins and seals playing around in the waves.

Sofie waved at someone up ahead and Eva saw a tall man with dark curly hair wave back.

He came walking over. Though he had a big smile on his face, his eyes were watching Eva the whole time and they were wary.

'Kasper, good to see you,' Sofie said, embracing him in a hug. Kasper kissed her on the cheek. 'How's Erika?'

'She's fine. She's working today down at the café or she would have come.'

'And the children?'

Kasper smiled. 'Johanne is pregnant with her first.'

'Oh wow, congratulations, you're going to be grandparents.'

'I know. Erika is very excited,' Kasper said, eyeing Eva again.

'Kasper, this is Eva Blue, Juliette's daughter.'

He hesitated and then offered out his hand to shake. 'Pleased to meet you. When Sofie phoned last night and explained that you wanted to meet, I did think—'

'That I might be the long-lost daughter you never knew you had?' Eva said.

Kasper laughed nervously. 'Something like that.'

'You don't need to worry. I'm twenty-seven, I came along two years after you and my mum met. I'm not here to cause any trouble. I just wanted to talk to you about my mum.'

Kasper nodded. 'I'm so sorry to hear she died.'

Sofie, Henry and Thor started to wander a little way off, leaving her and Kasper alone to talk. Kasper gestured for her to walk alongside him and she fell in at his side.

'What did you want to know?'

'I don't know much about her time here. She had this list of dreams that she wrote the night before her eighteenth birthday, things she wanted to do with her life. One of them simply said that she wanted to come back to Skagen. I asked my aunt about it, my mum's sister, and she said when Juliette came back from her European tour she was full of excitement for this little town called Skagen and the man that she had met there. I presume you were the man she was seeing while she was here?'

He nodded. 'We had this incredible connection, right from the very first second we met. I watched her that opening night and she just... dazzled. Her voice was so incredible. I went backstage after the show and we hit it off. We spent that night together talking down here on the beach. We watched the sunrise over the sea and I think I knew then that this was the girl I wanted to marry. We spent every spare second together over the next week and, on her last night here, we made love under the stars up there in the dunes where we'd spent that first night together.'

Eva frowned. 'Then what happened?'

Kasper sighed. 'The tour of *The Wizard of Oz* was continuing through Sweden, Finland and Norway and then she was returning home to England.'

'I mean, what happened between you two? You fell in love with her, I think she felt the same way, and you just walked away from each other?'

'This was in 1990 – we didn't have mobile phones, emails or Facebook. She gave me her address and we promised to write. I wrote several letters but they came back unopened. I received a few letters from her but they all read as if I hadn't written to her and she wanted to know why. In the end I went to England to find her.'

'You did?' Eva was surprised by this. Laurel hadn't mentioned that.

'I got as far as her front door where I met her dad who told me in no uncertain terms that he would break both my legs if I didn't clear off. Well, he put it a lot more bluntly than that. He also told me to stop sending letters as he would personally make sure Juliette would never get them. I didn't know what to do. I hung around in England for a few days, lurking in the streets near her house, but I never saw her and

I went home broken-hearted.'

'Oh god,' Eva said, quietly. Her mum had never known that Kasper had fought for her. As far as she was concerned Kasper had forgotten all about her after that wonderful week but he hadn't. He'd never forgotten her.

'I suppose, looking back, I should have done more, but I didn't. I came home and a few of my friends were joining the army. It seemed like a good way to forget the girl I fell in love with. When I came out the army a few years later, I met Erika. I fell in love with her and we made a life together, but there was always a tiny little bit of my heart that belonged to your mum.'

Eva was silent for a moment as she kicked the white sand. Her grandad had ruined everything for her mum, a chance to be happy with the man she loved. Would Juliette's life have been different if she and Kasper had had a chance? Maybe it never would have lasted anyway but at least her mum would have known that she was loved.

'You don't know how happy it makes me to hear all this. I'm sad that my grandad stopped you from seeing each other and you two never really had a chance of making it work, but I'm glad you loved her as much as she loved you. That you fought for her, even if it didn't work.'

He smiled. 'Your mum was definitely worth fighting for.'

Eva looked around for Thor and, as if he had been waiting for her, he came jogging over.

'I should go,' Kasper said.

'Thank you for meeting with me today.'

He smiled and moved off to say goodbye to Sofie and Henry.

'Everything OK?' Thor asked.

'Yes.'

'Was it good to meet him?'

'Yes, it really was. It was great to hear his side of things.' Eva watched Thor for a moment. He seemed worried. 'What's wrong?'

'Nothing, it doesn't matter, I'll tell you later.'

She frowned. 'Tell me now.'

Thor looked out over the sea for a moment and when he looked back his eyes were sad.

'I phoned Tracy this morning and insisted she had to sort out the room situation, that it was unprofessional and awkward between us.'

'OK.'

He took a deep breath. 'Sonia is flying out in a few days to take over from me. When we get back to Oslo after Lofoten, she will be waiting for us. She will continue the rest of the trip with you, and I'll be flying home.'

Chapter 19

Eva stared at him in shock. 'What?'

Thor swallowed. 'I know, I'm sorry. I didn't ask for this, I didn't want it.'

'Then tell Tracy no.'

'She's my boss, what can I do? I go where she tells me to go.'

'And don't I get a say in this? This is my holiday, I don't want to share it with someone else. I don't even know Sonia,' Eva said.

'You didn't know me a few days ago.'

'But now I do, I don't want to travel the world with anyone else but you.'

'Sonia is very nice,' Thor said.

Eva wanted to cry at the unfairness of it all. 'What can I do to change this?'

He shook his head. 'There isn't anything you can do.'

'If you really didn't want to leave, you'd do something,' Eva said.

Thor let out a heavy sigh. 'Maybe it's for the best.'

Eva took a step back, feeling like she'd just been slapped.

'This thing between us isn't going to go away. It would have escalated into something so much more than either of us wanted. You know that,' Thor said.

'So the best thing is to run away from that?'

'What's the alternative, we go head first into plan B?' Thor said, exasperated.

'Why not? We're both grown adults. We can have fun without it turning into an epic love story. It doesn't have to be anything serious.'

Thor shook his head. 'It could only be something serious with you.'

Eva was lost for words for a moment because she knew he was right. But she also knew she had to fight for this. She couldn't just walk away from him.

'I'll pay for separate rooms then at every hotel. We could spend a few hours now booking rooms for you. No more cuddling or kissing or sharing a bed. We'll be friends and we'll be strict about it,' Eva said, desperately.

Thor sighed. He looked away for a moment at the sea as it merged together in two glorious shades of blue. He didn't say anything for the longest time and then he turned his attention back to her.

'Maybe we can meet up for a drink or something when you get back home,' Thor said, vaguely.

'What would be the point of that?' Eva snapped. 'You've already made it clear you don't want anything to happen between us. You'd rather run away than stay friends with me.'

Thor stared at his feet and brushed a hand through his hair. 'Come on, we need to get back so we can go to the airport. We have two more nights together, let's not ruin that time by arguing. The midnight sun is something special, I want you to enjoy that.'

He started walking away, the conversation clearly closed. Eva could only stand there and watch him leave. It was ridiculous, but she felt like her heart was breaking.

Henry and Sofie had been their normal happy, chatty selves on the way back to their house. Thor clearly hadn't told them what was going to happen – maybe he didn't think they would care or maybe he didn't want his parents to jump in with their opinions on it.

She had been made to feel so at home with their kindness and compassion, and the ache in her chest about never seeing Thor again also extended to not seeing them again as well. As crazy as it sounded, she was really going to miss them. She felt like she was leaving a tiny part of her behind here in Skagen, with her mum's love of the little town and these wonderful people who had welcomed her into their home. So before she left their house, she snuck out into their back garden and planted the Eva Blue tulip. She had no idea if it was the right time to plant it and whether it would survive and flower, but at least if it did she was leaving a very small legacy behind.

She stepped back inside just as Thor was saying goodbye to his parents.

'Don't stay away so long next time,' Sofie said, giving him a hug. 'This will always be your home. It's time you stopped hiding from your past and embraced your future.'

Eva shifted awkwardly. The fact that Sofie was saying this in English made her think she deliberately wanted Eva to hear it.

As Henry moved to hug Thor, Sofie came over to give Eva a hug. 'We'll see you soon, won't we?'

'I don't know. I'd love to see you both again but...' Eva trailed off.

'You'll come with Thor,' Sofie said, as if it was the most obvious answer in the world.

Thor clearly couldn't look at her as he deliberately took his time to wrap a few slices of his dad's cake in some napkins.

'Maybe I'll come on my own,' Eva said, and as she said it she knew that she would. Skagen was lovely and she didn't need Thor or anyone else to come back and visit it one day.

Sofie's face fell a little as she looked between the two of them and clearly picked up on the atmosphere between them. She turned back to Eva and smiled sadly. 'You'd be very welcome.'

Eva hugged her again and Sofie held her that little bit tighter. She let her go and Eva picked up her bags and followed Thor out the door.

Thor looked over at Eva as she sat next to him on the plane from Oslo to Lofoten. She had been quiet ever since they had left his parents' house. She wasn't sulking or angry, she spoke to him whenever he spoke to her, but she didn't try to make conversation. On the flight from Skagen to Oslo and at Oslo airport while they waited for the next flight, she had buried herself in her laptop claiming she had work to do. Now she was reading a travel book about Norway. It was like she was trying to avoid him. There was this huge sense of sadness emanating from her and he didn't know what to do about it.

This was all his fault. He had encouraged her feelings. Although he had been clear that nothing was going to happen between them, he had crashed across that professional line a long time ago. He had hugged her, kissed her, held her in bed, told her he wanted to make love to her. And now he had pushed her away.

He hadn't wanted it to end like this. It hadn't even occurred to him to ask Tracy to get Sonia to swap with him. He wanted to finish this trip with Eva, to spend time with her, to watch her grow in confidence and face her fears, to realise her dreams. But when Tracy had emailed him to explain that Sonia was taking over from him there was a very very tiny part of him that breathed a sigh of relief. He knew that their relationship was going to turn physical soon and he knew that, when it did, it would be way more than just sex. He didn't want that. He didn't want to fall in love. He knew it was cowardly to run away from it but he still thought that maybe it was for the best.

But he had hurt Eva and that was the very last thing he wanted.

He glanced out of Eva's window and gasped at how low they were flying over the mountains. They were in a very small propeller plane with only thirty-nine seats, and because of that they were flying at a much lower altitude than normal passenger planes, but he hadn't expected to see that.

'Eva, look,' he whispered, in awe of the beauty of Lofoten as they were coming into land.

She looked out the window and then pressed her face to the glass like a child standing outside a sweet shop. It made him smile, even though she was completely blocking the view. She must have realised this, however, as she suddenly shifted back in her seat and gestured for him to lean over her and have a look. He did, trying to ignore her scent and warmth. It was staggering to see how turquoise the water was and completely clear too. He could see all the way down to the sea bed. The mountains towered over the islands in different shapes and formations. The white sandy beaches were almost too bright to look at as they basked in the glorious bright sunshine. The sea was flat calm and the lakes were like glass, reflecting the mirror image of the mountains perfectly. He could see the bright red houses on stilts that lined the shores of the lakes and beaches. Islands curved around each other or stretched away in the opposite direction as if in some kind of dance. Out in the distance, over the glittering sea, he could even see a rainbow. It was utterly spectacular.

He turned to look at Eva and she was smiling at the beauty of it too.

He shifted back slightly so she could take another look.

'It's beautiful,' she said.

'I've never seen anything like it in my life.'

She turned to look at him and smiled.

'I'm glad I got to see it with you,' Thor said.

He knew it wasn't fair to say that. But now he was leaving there was no point hiding his feelings.

Eva smiled. 'I am too.'

They both returned their attention to the incredible view as the plane dipped lower in the sky. They were flying so close

Thor could see the colours of the flowers growing on the mountain tops, the little white boats bobbing around on the water. He could even see a small pod of whales or dolphins a little further out. He pointed them out to Eva and she laughed with joy.

He stopped staring at the view and turned to watch Eva enjoy it instead, her eyes lit up with excitement and delight, the hugest smile on her face, the angst of the day completely forgotten, at least for now.

He was definitely going to enjoy his time here over the next few days. This magnificent view with this incredible woman. If he was going home in a little under forty-eight hours, he was damned well going to make the most of the time he had left.

Eva had never seen anything like it. Standing on their decking of their red cabin, looking over the glass waters of the sea, the golden light of daylight at midnight was something she had never quite imagined when she had planned to come and see the midnight sun. It wasn't like the bright sunshine of midday, which was what she had sort of been expecting. The sun had dipped lower in the sky, leaving trails of gold and amber across the clouds, but it just grazed the top of the sea on the distant horizon as if it was taking a drink. It just seemed so magical. She wanted to paint it but she knew she'd never capture that perfect shade of rose gold no matter how hard she tried. It was a perpetual sunset and sunrise at the same time.

Her breath hitched at that thought. Her mum would have

loved to see this. Emotion clogged in her throat. Grief was a funny thing. Some days she could get on with her day with an occasional thought of her mum, a memory or something that would make her smile. But on other days something little like this could completely knock the wind out of her.

It was all well and good doing all these things that her mum wanted to do, but it didn't change the fact that Juliette would never stand on these shores and experience the rare beauty of the midnight sun. Her life had come to an end far too young. Eva felt tears in her eyes at the thought that she would never hear her mum laugh, see her smile or feel her arms around her. She never had a chance to say goodbye to her. She had left to go on holiday and never came back home.

She glanced over at Thor and felt sad that he was leaving her too. She was never going to see him again and that made her heart ache inside almost as much as it did when she thought about her mum.

He looked over at her and his face fell when he saw her crying.

'Hey, what's wrong?' Thor said, immediately pulling her into a big hug, holding her against his chest. She held him tight, breathing him in. His warmth and tenderness making her feel immediately a little better.

'I'm just thinking about my mum, thinking that she's never going to see any of this wonder that we're experiencing.'

'I don't know about that,' Thor said. 'I think our loved ones never really leave us. I'm sure your mum has seen all your travels. She would be delighted to see you experiencing these adventures.'

Eva smiled sadly. It was a lovely thought, though she

wasn't sure she believed that. If there was some kind of heaven, she was sure her mum was up there having the time of her life rather than spending her time watching Eva's every move.

'I'm sad about you leaving as well, I'm going to miss you so much,' Eva said.

Thor sighed into the top of her head. 'I know, I'm going to miss you too.'

'This is a mess, isn't it,' Eva said.

'Yes it is and I'm sorry.'

'Don't be sorry. Another life, another time, we would have been great together. But I will never regret meeting you. You've taught me so much – that life is so much more fun and colourful if you're just a little bit bold and brave.'

'I don't think I played any part in that. You were always brave, you just needed to unlock it, see the world at your own pace,' Thor said.

Eva looked out over the sea. The silence was deeper here than anything she had experienced before. There was simply no noise at all, apart from the thud of Thor's heart. The mirrored waters of the sea were liquid gold as if the sun itself had melted into the ocean. It looked so inviting.

She pulled away from Thor. 'Let's go for a swim.'

'What?'

'When I was a kid, there was a TV programme called *Duck Tales*, did you get that in Denmark?'

She started undoing her boots and kicked them off.

'Yes, it was called something different, but yes.'

'What was it called?' Eva said, unzipping her coat and tossing it over a bench.

'*Adventures of Huey, Duey and Louis.* What are you doing?'

'Ah, they missed out the main character, Scrooge McDuck,' Eva said, deliberately ignoring his question. She pulled off her jumper. 'In the opening credits, Scrooge used to swim through all his gold coins and I always thought that would be really cool to do. I mean scientifically, it would be impossible, but I always wanted to swim in gold.'

Thor looked out onto the sea, cottoning on to her intentions. 'Eva, it's going to be freezing.'

'And I'm going to be bold and brave, because that's much more fun.'

She quickly stripped off so she was completely naked, purposely not looking at Thor to see his reaction. She ran down the steps and launched herself into the water before she could change her mind.

The bitter waters were like knives to her skin as the gilded ripples engulfed her body, but she couldn't help laughing and shrieking at the exhilaration of it.

She lay on her back and stared up at the golden sky.

'Christ Eva, are you insane? It's like ice.'

She looked around to see Thor charging into the water also stark naked, which made her laugh out loud. He submerged himself and swam over to her, gathering her in his arms. She slid her hands around his neck.

'I don't think I've seen anything as spectacular in my whole life as you running naked into the golden sea,' he said. 'It was... enchanting.'

She smiled and then looked back up at the sky. It felt almost like time was standing still with no dusk and no dawn. And in this moment that seemed to last forever it felt like

THE SUMMER OF CHASING DREAMS

anything was possible, like there were no rules, no constraints, no past or future to worry about. It seemed like there was no one else in the world, just the two of them.

She looked back at him and his eyes were on her as if he was completely entranced. His fingers were gently stroking up her naked back.

He had been adamant that nothing would ever happen between them, although he had pushed that line several times. But now he was leaving. And maybe it was that that spurred her on: there would be no awkwardness, no big love story that would fail because he would be gone before they could get that far. Why not just take what they both clearly wanted, make the most of the time they had left?

Feeling beautiful and bold, she leaned forward and kissed him.

Chapter 20

Eva wasn't sure if Thor would kiss her back but he didn't hesitate, though this time it wasn't a short, sweet kiss. This one was loaded with so much passion and need. He brought her closer against him and she wrapped her legs around him. He eased her mouth open, sliding his tongue inside and the taste of him was like a punch to the gut. One hand was still round her lower back as he moved the other to cup her neck. She stroked down his spine and she heard him moan against her lips. It was like lighting a fire inside her, and suddenly she was kissing him harder, wanting more.

He moved his mouth to her throat, his hot lips kissing exactly where her pulse was hammering against her skin. She arched back against him and opened her eyes to look at the glimmering sky. He moved his mouth to her breast and a jolt of desire slammed through her. It was quite obvious that need would not be quenched here in this freezing cold lake.

She eased back away from him slightly and he lifted his head, his eyes filled with concern. There was no way in hell she was going to let him apologise and talk his way out of this.

She pressed a finger to his lips.

'I'm going for a shower, you can join me if you like.'

His mouth quirked up into a smirk. 'You know I have a shower in my room.'

She smiled and started swimming back to the shore. 'And where would be the fun in that?' she called over her shoulder.

She made it to the beach, quickly racing up the stairs to the decking as the cold night air chased across her skin. She scooped her clothes up and ran inside as she heard Thor's footsteps on the stairs too.

Eva headed upstairs to her bedroom, dumped her clothes on the bed and then changed her mind and moved them to the chair. They might need the bed to be clear later. She heard Thor thundering up the stairs but he didn't appear in her bedroom, instead she heard him run into his own bedroom, swearing and moaning as he moved things around.

She was shivering now so she quickly moved into the shower and flicked it on. The hot water burned her skin and she turned round to get her back warm, dipping her head backwards to get her hair wet. She could see the bathroom door and Thor hadn't appeared through it yet. After that incredible kiss, was he really going to have a shower in his own bathroom? Was he regretting it already?

Suddenly he was there and he was shivering. She quickly tugged him under the hot water, rubbing his arms to get him warm.

'I didn't think you were coming.'

'I had to stop to get supplies,' Thor said, his lips quivering a little, but she could feel the heat was starting to spread through him. They hadn't been in the sea that long.

'Supplies?'

He held out his hand to show her the condom and her heart thundered in her chest. Christ, they were really going to do this. He placed it on the shelf, this wonderful promise of what was to come.

She rubbed her hands down his chest on the pretext of getting him warm though she knew she wasn't fooling either of them.

'Condoms?' she teased. 'Since when does your packing list on an escorted round-the-world trip include condoms?'

'I bought them yesterday, I had a feeling I might need them.'

She frowned in confusion. 'But you said—'

'I know what I said, I just didn't want to be caught short if the moment came. You have no idea how happy I am right now for that foresight.' With his hands round her waist he swapped places with her, shifting her back under the spray.

'I am too. Are you warm enough?'

'I will be,' he said, darkly.

He bent his head and kissed her again, easing her back against the cool tiled wall. She gasped at the coldness and he captured it on his lips. He didn't take his mouth from hers as he ran his hands over her breasts, teasing her nipples with gentle fingers. She slid her hands round his back, feeling the muscles in his strong shoulders. She cupped the back of his head, kissing him with an urgency she had never felt before. He caressed his hands over her body, stroking her tenderly, and then slipped his hand between her legs. She moaned something inarticulate against his lips and she felt him smile. He was so cocky. He continued to kiss her, working his magic on her with strong, slow, confident fingers. It took mere seconds before she was shouting out a whole jumble of words, none of which made sense. It was as if the tension between them had been bubbling there just under the surface and now it was exploding out of her. He cupped her face, continuing the kiss, though she could barely catch her breath. She reached for him and his lips stilled against hers as she stroked him. He let out a noise that was somewhere between a hiss and a groan and encouraged by this she stroked him harder.

His mouth was suddenly back on hers again. Kissing her harder, he grabbed her hands and pinned them above her head, his kiss urgent, his lips burning into hers. He snatched his lips from hers long enough to tear open the condom. He quickly slid it on and kissed her hard again.

Thor lifted her and she wrapped her legs around his hips. He was right there but he seemed to hold back for a second. He pulled back slightly so he could talk.

'You're making me lose all control. Before my restraint snaps completely, are you sure you want this?'

Eva smiled and kissed him briefly. 'If I could only have one thing on my list, it would be this, you making love to me, right here, right now.'

He kissed her hard and thrust inside her. She gripped his shoulders, his hands tight around her hips, shifting her higher, taking her deeper, moving against her harder and faster. She had never had sex that was so passionate, so out of control before. She felt that feeling spiralling through her stomach, spreading out through her whole body. He kissed her with such a desperate need and it was that primal desire for her that sent her roaring over the edge. He moaned against her lips as he found his own release.

Thor held her there against him for a moment as he tried to catch his breath and then he lowered her legs to the floor. She felt shaky and she leant against the wall as he stepped back under the shower. He offered out his hand and she took it and he pulled her under the spray with him, wrapping his arms around her and holding her against him. He kissed her gently, cupping her face in his hands.

They stayed there kissing long after the golden skies outside faded away and the bright blue morning sunshine took its place.

Eva woke the next morning with a huge smile on her face but that smile soon faded away when she reached out for Thor and found the bed empty.

She sat up and looked around for him. There was no noise from the bathroom and, judging by the silence from the rest of the house, he wasn't there either. She called out for him anyway, but there was no answer.

After coming out the shower the night before, they had spent hours lying in bed kissing and stroking each other and then he'd made love to her again, slowly and gently this time, before they'd finally fallen asleep. The way he'd looked at her as he'd made love to her was with such adoration, it had made her feel so warm inside.

Surely he hadn't woken up that morning and regretted the incredible night they'd spent together?

But then, even if he didn't regret it, it didn't change

anything. He was still leaving the next day and she would never see him again.

She pulled her knees up to her chest. She was such an idiot, she'd known he was leaving when she had kissed him and invited him to have a shower with her. She'd known that sleeping with him would change everything between them and she'd done it anyway and then fallen a little bit in love with him because of it.

How had things escalated so quickly between them? She didn't do this kind of thing. When she dated a man, it took weeks before she became comfortable enough to sleep with him. It hadn't even been a week and she had not only jumped into bed with him, but probably fallen in love too.

What a complete mess.

She grabbed her phone from the drawers and called Laurel.

'Hello, my love, I've been thinking of you and how things are going between you and Thor.'

'We slept together,' Eva blurted out.

She heard Laurel let out a heavy breath. 'Well, I wasn't expecting that.'

'I know, I wasn't either. I'm so stupid. I never do one-night stands, why did I have to start with him?'

'Why does it have to be a one-night stand? He's obviously keen too. Unless... were you both drunk?'

'No, stone cold sober.'

'Well then?' Laurel said.

'He's leaving,' Eva sighed. Even saying those words hurt. It hadn't been that long since she had last updated Laurel but a lot had happened just in the last twenty-four hours. 'He wanted things to be more professional between us so he emailed his boss and insisted she do something about the room situation. Her solution was to send out a replacement. Thor flies home tomorrow and I will have some woman called Sonia instead.'

God, that thought depressed her. Not just because she wouldn't get to see Thor again, but because she couldn't imagine seeing the world with anyone but him. Even if nothing else were to happen between them, she wanted to experience these adventures with him by her side.

'But maybe you can meet up when you get back home,' Laurel tried.

'I don't think he wants that, he's not interested in a relationship.'

'So this was goodbye sex?'

'I guess it was,' Eva said sadly.

'Oh Eva, I hate this for you.'

'I'm such an idiot.'

'Well I don't know about that. If you're going to have a holiday of a lifetime and tick off all these incredible experiences, having amazing sex with a hot man is not a bad thing to add to the list.'

Eva smiled at Laurel's attempt to make her feel better.

'It *was* amazing, wasn't it?' Laurel asked. 'Please don't tell me Thor has a very small… hammer.'

Eva giggled. 'Quite the opposite. And yes it was amazing, he was very… considerate.'

Suddenly, she heard a door slam open downstairs and heavy footsteps on the stairs.

'Laurel, I have to go, I'll call you later,' Eva said.

'No wait, I need more details than that—'

Eva grinned. 'Bye Laurel.'

She hung up on a squawk of protest just as Thor came back into the room.

'Oh hey beautiful, I was hoping to get back before you woke up.'

Her heart leapt. He'd called her beautiful.

'I just ran out to get some breakfast for us so we could stay in bed for a while longer,' Thor said, stripping off his jumper and t-shirt in one swift movement. He leaned over the bed and gave her a brief kiss, plonking a paper bag on the drawers next to the bed. He sat down on the edge of the bed and quickly pulled off his boots and socks. 'I know we have our whale-watching trip later, but that's not until later this evening. We can get up and explore after breakfast if you want, or we can spend the day in bed,' he said, giving her a dark look over his shoulder.

He stood up and pulled his jeans and shorts down, quickly stepping out of them, and then he slipped back under the covers with her, kissing her deeply, his cold hands snaking over her body.

She pressed a hand to his chest to stall him. 'Wait, you want a round three?'

Although that question was somewhat redundant judging by where his hand was currently heading.

'Hell yes. To start with, then we can have breakfast and I'm sure we can fit in a few more rounds before we go out tonight.'

Was she stupid for thinking how wonderful it would be to indulge in that? Was she crazy for considering *not* doing it?

'When I woke up and you were gone, I thought you might be regretting last night,' Eva said, quietly.

She cringed. Why was she making this into a bigger deal than it was? It was just sex.

His face fell. 'No, not one bit. Last night was honestly one of the best nights of my life.'

Oh god, she loved this man. To hell with it. She would spend every spare second she had left in bed with him. She would deal with her broken heart after he had gone.

'Do *you* regret it?' he asked.

'Not for one second.'

She reached up and stroked his face, relishing the feel of his soft stubble under her fingers.

He leaned forward and kissed her, moving her gently so she was lying down and he was on top of her, his hands softly caressing her.

'I spoke to Tracy,' Thor said, in between kisses.

Through the fog of desire in her mind, she tried to concentrate on what he was saying. She really didn't want to talk about Tracy in a moment like this.

'And?'

'I told her you weren't happy about the switch and as we had already swapped your preferred escort once, that it wouldn't be professional to swap your escort again. I said this trip was really important to you and explained that you were doing it in memory of your mum.'

'Oh my god, what did she say?'

'She wasn't happy. I told her that we would sort out extra bedrooms ourselves but that I wasn't leaving you.'

'What?' Eva stared up at him in shock.

He smiled. 'I'm not leaving you.'

'You're staying?'

He nodded and, stupidly, she found tears in her eyes.

He kissed her and she slid her arms round his neck. Right then, her heart was completely full of joy. After a while he reached over to grab a condom from the drawers and then he slid carefully inside her. She wrapped her arms and legs around him, holding him close. He rested himself on his forearms as he moved deep inside her.

'You know what this means?' he said, kissing her.

'What?'

'It seems we've entered into plan B.'

She grinned. 'I love plan B.'

'I do too. No falling in love though,' he said, smiling.

She wasn't going to tell him that it might already be a little too late for that, she'd keep that bit of information to herself.

'I'll try my very best not to.'

He settled himself between her legs, gathering her close to him. 'I'm absolutely not going to fall in love with you, Eva Blue, definitely not.'

His eyes were sparkling with amusement as he spoke.

He kissed her again. 'And if I repeat that mantra every day, I might start to believe it.'

She smiled against his lips. He had feelings for her too. Maybe they were going to be OK after all.

Chapter 21

Dear Mum,

I spent the day in bed with the most incredible man. I never thought for one moment I would ever be writing that kind of thing on a postcard to you but it's true. He can't keep his hands off me. Even when we're not making love, he is stroking me, touching me or simply holding me. It feels... glorious. We did eventually get up and go for a walk around Lofoten. It's such a pretty little place, the waters are so clear, it almost feels like we're in a tropical paradise.

Whale-watching was spectacular. I'd expected to see a few tails and fins a thousand metres away if we were lucky, but a pod of five humpback whales came right up to the boat, swimming underneath it, breaching right next to us. I even got the chance to stroke one. I took the most amazing photos. They clearly weren't fazed by us and were very curious. After a while, they just swam off, seeking new adventures under the midnight sun.

We've come back to our cabin and Thor is waiting patiently or rather impatiently to make love to me again. I could definitely get used to plan B.

Wish you were here… Although not right here, there's some things a mother should never see.

Love Eva x

PS Dreams ticked off:
6. See the midnight sun.

'Venice is a funny little place, isn't it,' Eva said as they waited on the edge of one of the many canals for a gondola to come back and collect them. Now they had escaped the slightly chilly weather of northern Norway and headed south to the much warmer Italy, everyone was out enjoying the sunshine. There was quite a queue of people waiting for the gondolas, mostly couples who had come here to tick off one of the most romantic experiences. They were next in line.

They had arrived a few hours before and taken a speedboat from the airport to their hotel. It had been such a wonderful, thrilling experience – she'd felt like a movie star. They had dumped their bags in the hotel and set off to explore. They only had one evening there and they were flying out early the following morning, so Eva wanted to make the most of it.

Being in Venice felt like they were in a MC Escher painting, with all its optical illusions, there were stairs, arches and alleyways everywhere. It was such a little maze of tiny roads, some of which didn't seem to go anywhere, while others led to little courtyards that were so overgrown with beautiful flowers and vines it felt like no one had visited for many hundreds of years. They'd stumbled across little churches that had works of art inside impressive enough to rival Michelangelo's. They'd walked over magnificent ornate bridges, up twisting steps and found secret gardens and hidden alleys. They'd seen food being delivered to restaurants by boats and lots of water taxis zooming up and down the canals, some of them carrying very glamorous people. Eva felt like she could stay here for weeks and still not experience all that Venice had to offer.

Thor looped an arm round her shoulders, bringing her against his chest and kissing her nose, sweetly. Ah dear god. She had thought that going on a gondola was a bit of a romantic cliché, but it was one of her mum's dreams so she was more than happy to do it for her, but she suddenly wanted to do this for herself and to do every romantic experience with this man.

'How is it funny?' he asked.

'It's such a beautiful place, it feels like stepping back in time or into a forgotten fairy-tale kingdom, with the pretty little houses and canals. I find it so enchanting. And then in St Mark's Square, all those traders selling fake designer goods, hassling you to buy their stuff. And there is so much glamour here. I saw a couple in a tuxedo and ball gown half an hour ago, both wearing those expensive-looking Venetian masks. It's two o'clock in the afternoon, where are these people going looking so fabulous at two o'clock in the afternoon? And then there's this really tired, crumbling, broken side of the city as well and it makes me a little sad that this once great city is slowly being reclaimed by the sea.'

'Some might say that the rotten old buildings are part of its old-world charm,' Thor said.

'Oh it is, it certainly doesn't detract from the beauty of the place. It's just a shame to see it decline like this. It floods around a hundred times a year; the land is sinking. I was reading an article online before we came here and they think the whole of Venice will be gone within a hundred years.'

'I think many parts of the world will be a lot worse off in a hundred years' time. Many of the endangered species will be gone, along with forests and deserts and many coastal towns. Norfolk is slipping into the sea as well, at an alarming rate. I guess it's just important to see as much of the world as we can, to enjoy it at its finest and do our bit wherever possible with donations, beach cleans, recycling and stuff like that. We can't save it all. And a lot of the things that could save places like Venice have to be invested in at a government level. Tourism will help a little. We are bringing money into places like this and some of that can be used to build bigger and better sea defences.'

Eva smiled. 'You have a wise head on those beautiful shoulders.'

The gondolier came into view first, wearing the traditional striped shirt and large brimmed straw hat as he expertly wielded his single oar to manoeuvre the gondola through the narrow canal towards them. He pulled up alongside them and a couple got out who had obviously just got engaged judging by the giggling, kissing and admiring of the ring.

'Are you going to want me to propose to you again on a gondola?' Thor said.

Eva laughed and showed him the dragon ring still on her

wedding finger. 'I'm very happy with my Eiffel Tower proposal.'

Thor smiled when he saw the ring. 'We're still officially engaged?'

'I don't know about officially, but I'm sure there's something legally binding about any kind of proposal, real or not. Looks like you're stuck with me,' Eva teased.

Thor didn't seem fazed at all by this as he helped her down into the gondola. It was a beautiful little boat, with exquisite patterns hand-painted on the sides and front. It sat very low in the water. There was red carpet on the floor and a cute two-seater sofa at the back that looked like it belonged in the Victorian era. It really was rather grand.

'*Ciao, bonjour*, hello, *hola, namaste*,' the gondolier waved them in and gestured for them to sit down.

'Hello, *ciao*,' Eva tried, though that was the last of her Italian.

'Eeenglish?' the gondolier asked and Eva nodded. 'I am Alessandro.'

Eva sat down and Thor squeezed himself onto the seat next to her.

'You are very beautiful man,' Alessandro said.

'Thank you,' Thor said.

'Together?' Alessandro gestured between Thor and Eva.

'Very much so,' Thor said.

Eva giggled. 'We're engaged.'

'Ah congratulations. 'Tis shame. All de best men are straight. Would you like a song today or guided tour?'

'Oooh, a song please,' Eva said as Alessandro hopped up onto the back of the boat behind them. She was going to be serenaded on a gondola in Venice. Nothing could be more romantic than that.

Well, except that Alessandro suddenly launched into 'The Birdie Song'.

Eva looked at Thor and burst out laughing.

''Tis joke, little joke,' Alessandro said. 'I sing nice song now.'

He pushed them off from the side with the oar and started rowing them down the canal. Alessandro cleared his throat and suddenly launched into the most beautiful deep opera song. Eva twisted in her seat in shock to see if it really was him singing and it was. It was incredible and one of the most beautiful things she had ever heard.

She looked back at Thor and smiled in shock. 'This is amazing. Did you plan this?'

'No. I promise, I had no idea.'

She turned round to watch Alessandro again. 'I'd love to know what he's singing about.'

'It's from the opera *L'elisir D'amore*, which translates as "The Elixir of Love". It's a romantic comedy. This song is when the leading man, Nemorino, finally realises that the object of his affection, Adina, actually does love him after all,' Thor said.

Eva stared at him in shock. 'You've seen this opera?'

Thor nodded. 'Mor loves the opera. I've been with her to see various ones over the years.'

'And you understand what he is singing?'

'I know a little Italian. Let's see. "She loves me, I see it, I felt her beating heart."' He pulled a face as if he didn't quite understand the next lyrics. 'Something about her sigh is mine, my sigh is hers, I think. Yes I could die, I could ask for nothing more, yes I could die of love.'

Alessandro's hauntingly beautiful voice dragged out the last syllable of *amore* and then he fell silent. Eva clapped enthusiastically.

'Alessandro that was so beautiful, thank you so much. Thor was just telling me what the translation was. What a gorgeous song. Would you mind singing it again and, this time, we'll be quiet.'

'*Sì*. Of course.'

Alessandro launched into the song again and Eva sat back and just listened as they glided along the beautiful canals, under bridges and round narrow corners. The acoustics were amazing, echoing off the high walls and the water. People stopped and stared as they walked along the side of the canals or over the bridges. Eva wasn't surprised. The whole experience was something magical. Thor slipped an arm round her shoulders and she leaned her head against him. How was she supposed to not fall in love with this man when they were going to experience beautiful romantic things like this together?

She looked up at him and he smiled down at her. Her heart leapt. She had to admit that it wasn't Venice, or the song or any of these romantic locations that was making her fall in love with Thor – it was the man himself.

Thor watched Eva as she looked out over the view of Venice from their hotel balcony. The sun was setting and the twinkling city lights were just starting to come on. They were staying on the pretty Giudecca Island, and the view from up here over the sea and canals was beautiful, but he couldn't take his eyes off Eva.

Forcing his attention away from her, he went back inside the bedroom and pushed the twin beds together to make a double. It was kind of ironic that the hotel would give them a twin just when they no longer needed it.

He sat down on the bed and picked up the room service menu, though he wasn't really reading it.

He was in new territory here and he wasn't sure he liked it. Hell, he liked it a lot and that was the problem. He had never once in his five years of working for the company got involved with a client before – there had been no affectionate touches, no hand-holding or hugging and certainly not sex in every destination. What was he playing at? He knew he was risking his job with this behaviour but, more importantly than that, he was risking his heart.

He'd had every intention of going home. And he had been sad to go, of course he was, but he'd thought it really was for the best. But when he'd seen Eva strip naked and run into the glittering ocean under the midnight sun he had never seen anything so utterly dazzling in his entire life. And as he'd stood there staring at her in complete awe and wonder, he'd felt this acceptance settle over him. He knew he had to stop fighting the feelings that were bubbling inside him. He knew he was going to take her to bed that night and make love to her and he knew there was nothing on heaven or earth that would make him leave her.

So what happened now? And what happened when the trip was over?

She walked back into the room and he looked up at her. She was wearing a pretty, strapless sundress that was sunshine yellow and seemed to shimmer when she moved. She had caught the sun a little on her bare shoulders that day. He stood up and grabbed some aftersun from his soap bag, squeezed some onto his hands and, as she was sorting through her bag, he rubbed some into her back, neck and shoulders. She stopped what she was doing and let out a tiny moan, which was a punch to his gut. He placed a little kiss on the bottom of her neck. He just couldn't stay away from her.

She turned round and looped her arms round his neck. 'What were you thinking about when I came in? You looked very serious.'

He sighed and sat back down on the bed, pulling her onto his lap and wrapping his arms around her.

'I don't know, thinking about us, what this is, what it will be when the trip is over.'

'Oh wow, the heavy stuff.'

Maybe he should have made something up, told her he was thinking about their plan for the next day instead, but he wanted to be at least partly honest with her.

She stroked his face, clearly not deterred at all. 'Would you like this to be something when we get back home?'

'I… I don't know,' he said. So much for being honest.

He saw the flash of hurt cross her eyes and he kissed her to soften the blow slightly.

'I don't know what's going to happen in the future. I know what this is right now, incredible sex with someone I care about a great deal,' he whispered against her lips, as if saying it softly meant it didn't really count.

She smiled and kissed him back. She placed a hand over his heart. 'You protect this so fiercely. But you need to pick your battles. You're dressing yourself in a great suit of armour to do battle with an ice cream sundae.'

He smiled at that analogy. She had described herself perfectly. Delicious, sweet, lots of different flavours, definitely bad for him.

He kissed her again, enjoying that sweet taste, the scent of coconut in her hair and apples on her skin. She was the very best kind of ice cream sundae.

He pulled back to look at her. He hadn't had feelings like this for over seven years and it scared him.

'Look, I'm enjoying this plan B immensely,' Eva said. 'And if we're both still enjoying it when the trip is finished we can carry on this relationship when we get home. We can have fun and talk and have outstanding sex. It doesn't have to be more than that.'

God, she was too good to be true. Except they both knew it was already way more than that.

'Let's not worry about the future now, let's just enjoy what we have,' Eva said.

He nodded. 'OK.'

'Good.' She climbed off his lap. 'Now I'm going to write my mum's postcard and do a little work and then I may let you make love to me before we go for dinner.'

He grinned. 'I like that plan.'

'Talking of plans, what are we doing tomorrow?'

'We fly to Rome at nine, we have our cookery course first thing and then we can spend the day seeing the sights. Tomorrow evening we have a special moonlight tour of the

Colosseum, which includes the upper terraces, and the underground chambers and tunnels and we get to go into the arena as well, where you're going to complete your mum's next dream.'

Eva laughed. 'You don't need to remind me of that part.'

'What was it again?' Thor teased.

'I have to dance inside the Colosseum. Did I tell you that my dancing is worse than my singing?'

Thor laughed. 'Not possible.'

'Hey!' she took a friendly swipe at him.

'OK, so why don't we have a little practice before the big event tomorrow?'

Her eyes lit up. 'Are you dancing with me tomorrow?'

'Sure, why not.'

'Oh thank god. I had visions of me doing some dodgy robot dance on my own.'

'Now that would be entertaining. But I'm sure your mum had something a bit more traditional in mind when she wrote that particular dream. So how about a nice simple waltz?'

Her face paled. 'I think I'd rather do the dodgy robot dance.'

And to prove it, she did, turning her body and arms at different angles in clunky moves.

God this woman. How could an awful robot dance be so bloody endearing?

He cleared his throat. 'Wow! Your dancing really is worse than your singing.'

'Hey,' Eva laughed.

'Come on, the waltz is easy, I'll show you. It's just one, two, three, one, two, three,' Thor said.

'I think it's a lot more than that,' Eva grumbled.

He lined his body up next to hers so they were side by side and took her hand. 'OK, it's just a simple box step. So step forward with the left leg.'

He showed her and she copied him.

'That's one corner of the box, now slide your right leg out to make the other corner of the box.'

He demonstrated what he meant and she followed him.

'Now bring your left foot next to your right foot.'

He showed her how to complete the rest of the box and then they practised it a few times.

'OK, let's do it together. Here, take my hand and put your other hand on my shoulder,' Thor said.

Eva did as she was told and he moved his free hand to her waist.

'I am going to step forward with my left leg and you are going to be my mirror image and step back on your right leg.'

Eva nodded, concentrating on his feet.

He stepped forward slowly and she hesitantly stepped back on her right.

'Slide to your left,' Thor said. 'Now step forward.'

She trod on his foot.

'Oops sorry,' Eva giggled.

'Here, let me lead,' Thor said, bringing her warm body closer and he started swinging her round the room. But she really was terrible – she kicked him in the shins, trod on his toes, tripped over her own feet, got her legs caught between his until they both fell onto the bed, laughing, Eva on her back, Thor on top of her.

'Oh, is this part of the waltz too, I think I'd be quite good at this part,' Eva laughed. She gave her shoulders a little shimmy. 'I've got moves.'

Thor tugged her dress over her head, the dancing lesson forgotten as he layered kisses across her shoulders. He quickly removed her underwear as she wrestled him out of his shirt. They snatched desperate kisses from each other in between clothes being strewn across the room. He rolled off her for a second so he could take off his jeans and shorts. He grabbed a condom and placed it on the bed, then rolled onto his back, taking her with him so now she was on top.

'Show me what you've got.'

She sat up and stared down at him with wide eyes for a moment, then her gaze raked over his body.

'Wow, I can see why you like to be on top, the view from up here is pretty spectacular.'

'The view from down here is pretty magnificent too,' Thor said, as he took her in, caressing his hands across her hips.

She gave a little mischievous wiggle which had him nearly crawling the walls with need for her. 'Do you like these moves?'

'I'd like them a lot more if I was inside you.'

Eva laughed in shock at his bluntness and then leaned over and kissed him. 'Patience,' she murmured against his lips, but with her he had none.

She placed little kisses down his chest, causing some kind of grunt to fall from his lips. He actually felt her smile against his skin; she was enjoying this way too much.

'Eva,' he said through gritted teeth. She had barely touched him and he was already undone.

'OK, OK, I'll put you out of your misery,' Eva said.

She grabbed the condom and expertly ripped it open with her teeth, a second later she was sliding it on. Her gentle touch was enough to have him reaching for her, guiding her over him, but she affectionately batted his hands away.

'These are *my* moves.'

But thankfully she did as he wanted. God, the feel of her was out of this world. He immediately sat up and cupped her face, kissing her deeply, then he ran his fingers down her bare back. She looped her arms round his neck, kissing him hard as she started moving against him.

He slid his hands to her hips as he moved deep inside her and she arched back slightly, tilting her head so her hair tumbled down her back. She looked glorious. He placed kisses on her breasts and he heard her breath hitch.

She looked back at him, her eyes clouded with desire, and he leaned forward and kissed her, feeling her tighten around him.

'I could do this forever Eva Blue,' he whispered against her lips.

He watched her come undone, gasping against his mouth, her fingers tightening around his shoulders, and at the thought of forever with this incredible woman, he found his own release.

Chapter 22

Dear Mum,

I know one of your dreams was to eat Italian food in Italy, well we've been reliably informed that there is no such thing, that each region of Italy has its own unique dishes, recipes and styles of cooking. But we did attend an Italian cookery course this morning where we rolled, cooked and ate our own pasta and then made the sauce to go with it. The sauce was amazing, the pasta not so much but apparently we didn't roll it thin enough and it came out very thick and stodgy. But still, you can't get much more authentic than that.

Rome is wonderful, there is so much history here. On every corner there seems to be some part of an ancient ruin, an old archway that leads to nowhere, or a crumbling set of steps. We went to the Sistine Chapel and the museum at the Vatican which just had the most beautiful paintings and sculptures inside and these wonderful detailed maps that were drawn and painted in the sixteenth century. It is incredible to think that even in the 1500s there were people travelling the world, seeking out new sights and adventures, tasting new and exotic foods, just like you and me all these years later.

We saw the beautifully preserved mosaics and marble floors at the Domus Romane. We climbed to the top of the Vittoriano to see the amazing views of the city. We went to the Pantheon and the Roman Forum, we watched the street entertainers in the Piazza Navona. We visited the spectacular Trevi Fountain and Thor suggested we throw a coin in together. Apparently if you throw a coin in over your shoulder then you will return to the city and I like the idea of me and Thor coming back here together one day. Maybe I'm getting carried away.

We of course went to the Colosseum and at moonlight too to take a special guided tour of the underground chambers, the arena and the upper terraces as well. We danced the waltz for you in the middle of the arena. Your dancing was always so graceful and I know mine wasn't that but the small group of tourists that were on the guided tour with us all gave us a little clap so it can't have been that bad. Thor is a marvellous dancer.

Wish you were here to show us how it should be done.

Love Eva x

PS Dreams ticked off:

8. *Eat Italian food in Italy.*
9. *Dance inside the Colosseum.*

Dear Mum,

Egypt is nothing short of spectacular. We went to the Egyptian museum in Cairo first which literally was a walk through time. We saw all the glittering treasures of Tutankhamun and other pharaohs – I don't think I have ever seen so much gold in one place before. I know your dream was to find hidden gold in Egypt but I think every last bit of it was here in the museum. The tombs and pyramids must have been stripped bare.

At sunrise the following morning we took a trip on some camels. The camels themselves were very friendly and calm. I thought that riding on them was going to be uncomfortable but it wasn't at all. Riding them felt so exhilarating, we were up so high, easily two metres or more. We rode out to the pyramids of Giza which were pretty amazing to see from the outside and to think about how they were made all those thousands of years ago. Thor says aliens made them, which makes me laugh. He has such a sensible head on his shoulders most of the time but he has this geeky nerdy side which I'm a little bit in love with.

We flew out to Luxor this afternoon to see the Valley of the Kings and the different tombs there. The hieroglyphs and paintings on the walls are just incredible and so detailed. And as for your dream to find hidden gold in Egypt, well we did. Sort of. We were walking through the tomb of Tutankhamun and Thor spotted this necklace on the floor. It looked suspiciously like the tat you can buy from the street vendors and I'm pretty sure Thor placed it there as he was quite adamant about me going over to one section of the tomb where we found it. God, this man makes me smile so much.

Tomorrow we're flying to Kenya for our safari and I cannot tell you how excited I am.

Wish you were here!

Love Eva x

PS Dreams ticked off:
   10. Ride a camel.
   11. Find hidden gold in Egypt.
   12. Visit the pyramids.

'No!' Eva gasped.

Thor looked over to see that she was staring into her suitcase in dismay.

'What's up?'

She started sorting through her case, throwing things to one side. He sighed softly at the lack of response. He was tired, this trip was so much more fast-paced than previous trips, he felt like they were cramming everything in at a breakneck speed. He'd only done a few round-the-world trips over the years – mostly he had just done a few weeks with his clients to a handful of locations, nothing like this. He'd also almost always had his own room to escape to in the evenings if he wanted to. And, while he had no intention of having a separate bedroom from Eva for the rest of this trip as he was enjoying being with her way too much, going from being single to this full-blown relationship was going to take a little getting used to. There had been no time at the start of their relationship which could be classed as casually dating, they were with each other literally twenty-four hours a day. While this was undoubtedly the best trip he had ever been on, the holiday wasn't the only thing that seemed to be moving fast.

'My clothes, they're all gone.'

He could quite clearly see lots of clothes in the suitcase. Eva was getting tired too, he could tell that, she had seemed very stressed out when they'd arrived at Luxor airport. It was possible though that she had left some of her clothes in their last hotel.

'What do you mean, all gone?' Thor said, coming over to join her.

She held up a pair of silver glittery knee-high boots. 'Does this look like the kind of thing I would bring on a round-the-world trip?'

'Well, they certainly make a statement.'

Eva was clearly not amused.

He glanced in the suitcase at all the other brightly coloured garish patterned clothes and his heart sank a little. Eva held up a pair of brown stripy tasselled flares.

'We must have picked up the wrong suitcase at the airport,' Thor said.

'You mean you did,' Eva said, slamming the lid and checking the label.

Dorothy Jordan. Crap.

He thought back to the airport at Luxor. By the time he had got to the baggage claim, his rucksack and this suitcase were the only pieces of luggage left. He'd just picked it up because it was identical to Eva's black one and he hadn't even checked the label.

'I think Dorothy took your suitcase first. There was only this one left and I assumed it was yours.'

'Well you assumed wrong,' Eva snapped.

'Well if you hadn't taken so long in the toilet after we got off the plane, we might have got to baggage claim before Dorothy walked off with your case.'

'I'm sorry that the dodgy food you bought for me in Cairo made me have terrible... stomach issues.'

His heart sank even more. Travelling with a stomach bug was the worst and she hadn't even told him.

'That's what you were doing in there?'

'What did you think I was doing in there?'

He shrugged. 'I don't know. Girl stuff. Doing your hair and make-up.'

She stared at him. 'Do you know me at all? I didn't even bring any make-up with me on this trip.'

That was true, he hadn't seen her wear any make-up so far. She had this natural beauty – with her cute freckles on her nose and her dazzling grey eyes, she didn't need it.

'God, we're supposed to be going out tonight to that nice restaurant overlooking the Nile. And I'll either be in the shorts and t-shirt I'm wearing now or dressed as a seventies reject,' Eva said.

Thor picked up a few of the items. It was quite clear that Dorothy had been going to some kind of seventies party or had been on her way back from one as everything in the suitcase was seventies-themed. There were men's clothes in there too, a bright orange suit with flared trousers, a checked green shirt, a fake porno moustache and an afro wig.

He pulled out a turquoise sparkly catsuit. 'I think you could totally rock this.'

'You're hilarious,' Eva grumbled as she stalked off to the bathroom and slammed the door.

Thor sighed and checked the label again to see if there was a contact number for Dorothy but there wasn't. Though he knew Eva had her mobile number on her suitcase label. She was organised like that.

He sorted through the suitcase to see if there was anything remotely suitable for Eva to wear to the restaurant that night, but everything was brightly coloured and had the most hideous patterns. In actual fact, the sparkly turquoise catsuit was the best of a bad lot as at least it was plain.

After a few minutes it became apparent that Eva was not coming back out.

He approached the bathroom door. 'Are you OK?'

'Yes,' Eva sighed. 'It's not as bad as it was before.'

Thor cringed. 'Is there anything you need?'

'Yes, for you to move away from the bloody bathroom door. Christ, if there's anything guaranteed to put a man off it's listening to the woman he's with go to the toilet when she has a stomach bug.'

Thor duly stepped away and went back to the suitcase. Maybe humour would be the thing to make her feel better, at least emotionally.

He found the most hideous combination of men's clothes

– a gold shirt paired with some brown stripy tasselled flares – and though they were obviously made for a man quite a bit shorter and thinner than he was, he pulled them on and managed to squeeze into them. They were scratchy and because of the polyester or nylon in the material, he immediately started to feel hot. He even pulled on the wig and mirrored shades for good measure.

Eva came out the bathroom and stopped when she saw him. Her face broke into a huge smile and then she burst out laughing and didn't stop. Eventually she walked over to him and tugged him by his oversized lapels and kissed him.

'You're so good for me. I'm sorry for being crabby.'

'Don't be, you're tired, you're not well, and you've just lost all your clothes. I think you're entitled to be a bit fed up.'

'You're very patient.' She rested her head against his chest and he wrapped his arms around her and just held her.

After a while, he pulled back slightly. 'Now, we can go to that restaurant tonight both looking like seventies weirdos – personally I think you would look quite sexy in this catsuit – or, if you're not feeling up to it, we can stay here in the hotel and order room service. It's your call.'

Eva looked at the catsuit. He waited for her to plump for the room service option and he totally wouldn't blame her.

But then she started to smile. 'Let's do it.'

'Really?'

'Hey, if we're both looking like idiots, it's not so bad. Besides, I don't think I should keep this amazing sight all to myself,' Eva said, gesturing to his outfit.

He grinned. 'OK, but please don't make me wear this afro wig, it's really itchy.'

'I'll let you off that.'

'Thanks. Are you going to wear the glitter boots?'

'Of course.'

He smiled. He really bloody liked this woman.

'And you really think I look amazing?'

She leaned up and kissed him on the lips. 'You look shagadelic baby.'

Eva was lying with her head on Thor's bare chest as he stroked her hair. His heart was still beating from their exertions and she was sure hers was doing the same. She felt so completely happy and relaxed right now.

They had gone out to the restaurant after all and, although people did stop and stare and laugh, it had all been in good humour; people clearly knew they were dressing to a seventies theme and that their outfits were not bad attempts at high fashion. Eva definitely thought that Thor had got the raw end of the deal with his costume. She'd had more than a few wolf whistles in her catsuit and Thor had told her more than once how sexy she looked. The same could not be said for his clothes. She looked up at him, he made her so happy. Every day she could feel herself falling for this man just a little bit more.

Thor had also found her a pharmacy on the way back to the hotel, and thanks to some medicine she'd taken she was feeling a lot better.

'We need to do more work on your own dreams,' Thor said. 'We've not done too well on those so far.'

'We've done great, I've been proposed to, I've slept in a

windmill, I've ridden on the back of a motorbike—'

'That was more my dream than yours,' Thor said.

'No, I loved it. It was something I would never have done if it wasn't for you but it was still something that I wanted to do. I've swam in gold, we went whale-watching and I got to sleep with the most amazing man I've ever met. I'm doing pretty well on the dreams-coming-true part.'

He was silent for a while. Had she gone too far with that last comment? She didn't want to scare him off but she wanted to be somewhat honest about her feelings for him.

'And we're going to see the giraffes while we're on safari. Now that's going to be amazing,' Eva carried on, hoping to skate over that last dream. 'Plus we have the hot air balloon ride. I know that was one of Mum's dreams but it's always been something I've wanted to do too.'

'OK, I just don't want you to look back on this holiday with any regrets,' Thor said.

She stroked her hand down his chest. 'No matter what happens, I am never going to regret anything about this holiday.'

She looked up at him. Not one single thing. She wasn't sure what would happen between the two of them once the trip ended but she wouldn't regret this time with him.

'What about *your* dreams, is there anything you would really like to do on this holiday?' Eva asked.

He stared at her in surprise. 'No one has ever asked me that question before.'

'Well I'm guessing none of your clients have ever cared as much for you as I do.'

He smiled and kissed her head fondly. 'This is your holiday, it wouldn't be right to gatecrash it with what I want.'

'It stopped being my holiday the moment we slept together. Going forward this trip is very much ours.'

He clearly thought about it for a moment.

'Come on, let's do at least one thing on this trip that you really want to do,' Eva said.

'OK, I know this might not sit in your comfort zone, but as a kid, I always loved to go camping. Did you ever do that when you were a child?'

Eva shook her head. 'Surprisingly, when my mum was taking me on all these adventures, camping wasn't one of them.'

'There's something so wonderful about doing that. I'd love to sleep under the stars with you.'

She smiled. 'I'd love to share that with you. Where do you suggest?'

His face lit up. 'We could do it in Kenya.'

Now that definitely wasn't her ideal place to camp. 'Won't there be lots of bugs and snakes?'

'There will be, but they'll be there anyway whether we camp or not,' Thor said.

'I know but we don't have to sleep with them.'

'They have very nice, posh tents in Kenya. Some of them have proper beds and en-suite bathrooms.'

Eva grinned. 'Now that doesn't sound like camping.'

'I know, but maybe your first foray into sleeping in a tent should be a nice one. We can downgrade from there.'

'OK, sounds good.' It didn't sound good at all. Her worst nightmare was waking up next to a large hairy spider or a scorpion. But she was working on coming out of her comfort zone. She could do this.

'Thank you,' he said, seriously, and the way he was looking at her right then, she would have given him the world.

'I like being able to make your dreams come true too. What about your dreams for the rest of your life? What did you want to be when you were younger?'

He grinned. 'I don't think you can help me with that.'

'Probably not but tell me anyway.'

Thor let out a little laugh. 'I wanted to be an astronaut.'

Eva smiled with love for him; he had such a geeky side. 'I definitely can't help you with that. Was there anything else you wanted to do?'

Thor took a deep breath. 'I wanted to be an author. I had all these ideas for children's books with magical lands and amazing creatures. As a child I used to spend hours writing stories about a little boy who would go on adventures. As I got older, I never really grew out of it. I took a journalist course at my local college because there was a creative writing module as part of it. I ended up working at my local paper, writing those little fun articles about a skateboarding pig or a lady who knits clothes for her guinea pig. I really enjoyed the job. While I was there, I wrote this kids' book, well, I wrote several actually. Sent them all off to a publisher in a big brown envelope and every one got rejected. Maybe story writing wasn't really my forte.'

'So you just gave up after one rejection?'

'Multiple rejections.'

'From the same publisher, all at the same time, I'd count that as one rejection,' Eva said. 'Getting a publisher is about attracting the right person at the right time with the right story. JK Rowling famously got multiple rejections for Harry

Potter and look at how that turned out. I work in the publishing industry and many of the authors I work with had years of sending their work off to publishers and agents before they got their first publishing deal. If that was your dream, you should never give up.'

'I didn't really give up, well at least not then. I carried on writing stories with the hope I would do something with them one day. I... lost the joy for it after... after what happened with Christel.'

Eva hesitated from asking questions, although she had a ton. She wanted Thor to tell her himself, if he wanted to.

'I'm not sure how much my dad told you but I was with Christel for four years and I thought what we had was forever. I believed we would get married one day, start a family together. This new guy started at her work, Stefan, and he was all she would talk about. Of course I was jealous, but I figured, it was a blip. Maybe I hadn't been paying her enough attention. We were both saving for a house and renting this tiny little place, we worked different hours and we just didn't really see each other. Maybe along the way, we both stopped putting the effort in. I just thought we would work through it.'

He paused and Eva cringed as she waited for him to bring up the baby. She didn't want him to relive that pain but she also wanted to know what had made him so scared of having another relationship.

'She fell pregnant with my child. I was over the moon. She never told me she didn't want it. Maybe that was my fault. I was so excited, maybe I didn't see the signs. Maybe I made it impossible for her to tell me. I bought toys and clothes, cleared out the spare room and started redecorating for a nursery. I even started writing a story for my child. It was about a father and his son going on an adventure together. Although I would have been more than happy to change the little boy to a little girl in the story if I'd had a daughter.'

The pain in his voice was audible.

'Weeks went by. The nursery was finished and she came home one day and told me she'd had an abortion.'

'What?' Eva stared at him in shock. 'She let you go through all those weeks of excitement and happiness and never talked to you about how she felt? Never told you what she was planning?'

'No, not a word. Four years together and she couldn't even give me that. I was utterly heartbroken. It brought everything to a head. She thought that having that child would trap her with me forever and she didn't want that. She wasn't ready to be a mum or be tied down and she told me she didn't want my child and she didn't love me any more.'

Oh god, this was so much worse than Eva had originally thought. Her heart hurt so much for Thor. He had lost so much more than the love of his life – he had lost his child too.

'Of course it was over between us after that. I couldn't even look at her after what she'd done. I moved to London, started work at The World Is Your Oyster and tried to forget it. But, to add salt to the wound, Christel got together with Stefan straight away and she fell pregnant again, just six months after she'd had an abortion. She kept the baby. Shortly after the first child was born she got pregnant again. I think that was the final nail in the coffin. It wasn't that she didn't want children, but that she didn't want children with me.'

'Oh Thor, I'm so sorry…' She really had no words that could make this better.

'It's OK. It was a long time ago.'

She now understood so much better why Thor was so afraid of being in a relationship again. To trust a woman again after that kind of betrayal. It must have been devastating for him.

'And yeah, after that, I fell out of love with writing children's books again. I couldn't finish that book for my child and I couldn't write another. So I just let that dream fade away.'

'I hate that she took that from you as well as everything else. I'd love to read your stories one day. Do you still have them?' Eva said.

'Somewhere, probably still at my parents' house. I typed them all out and put them in ring binders. I don't think my mum would have thrown them out.' He looked at her and stroked a finger down her cheek. 'Maybe one day, I'll write a story about a girl called Eva Blue who went on an adventure around the world.'

Eva grinned. 'I would love that. I'll do the illustrations for it.'

'And I would love that.' He smiled and kissed her.

Chapter 23

'God, I'm so tired,' Eva said as they climbed the stairs to their bedroom. They had flown from Luxor back to Cairo and then south to Nairobi and it had taken most of the day to get there. She hadn't realised how vast Africa was, that flying from one country to another took so much time. The only thing good about the flight was that she'd got a ton of work done. Flight durations hadn't been so bad around Europe, a few hours at most, but for the rest of the trip she was going to lose whole days just travelling from one place to another. She hadn't fully appreciated how exhausting that was going to be when Rebecca had initially discussed the itinerary with her.

Luckily Dorothy Jordan had phoned her early that morning and they had arranged to switch suitcases again, which was a good thing as the Kenyan heat was stifling, even at this time of the day, and wearing nylon for the whole of her safari would certainly not have been pleasant.

'Well, our itinerary here in Kenya has changed a little from the original booking so we can relax and chill out here tomorrow and then we move on to the tented camp the day after. We have nothing planned for tomorrow other than breakfast,' Thor said.

Eva sighed wearily. 'I may just give breakfast a miss and sleep for the whole day.'

It had been non-stop travelling since they had started this trip and it was finally starting to catch up with her.

'Trust me, you're not going to want to miss breakfast, it's pretty spectacular,' Thor said.

He definitely had something up his sleeve. She wasn't overly keen on surprises.

'How come we're staying here anyway?' Eva said. The hotel looked like a great Scottish country house, all covered with ivy. She definitely hadn't seen this on the itinerary when they'd booked the holiday. She'd seen little wooden lodges which seemed cute, rustic but a little basic. This was something far grander.

'As I said, our plans have changed. You'll see soon enough,' Thor said, mysteriously.

Eva opened the door to the bedroom and let out a little gasp at the beauty of it. There was a four-poster kingsize bed in the middle of the room with wispy curtains billowing around it – which were presumably mosquito nets but looked far more romantic – and there was a large fireplace up one end that currently held a few flickering candles. The furniture was antique and cute, but it was the view outside that was the most startling. There were a few stairs leading up to a large balcony and the setting sun over the plains was dazzling.

'Oh,' Eva said softly.

'You haven't seen the best of it yet. Come on,' Thor said.

She dumped her bags and followed him onto the balcony

and then stopped. Walking past right outside was a giraffe.

'Oh my god, it's so close. What's it doing here?' Eva said, all exhaustion vanishing in an instant as she rushed to the railings to watch it.

'It lives here,' Thor said, looping an arm around her shoulder. 'Along with several others. Did you not see the name of the hotel when we pulled up?'

'No, I was too busy thinking about a hot bath and bed.'

'This is the world-famous Giraffe Manor. Tomorrow we will hopefully be able to have breakfast with them. They'll come into the breakfast room and eat with us.'

'Are you kidding?' Eva looked up at him.

He grinned. 'You said you wanted to get up close with a giraffe. Well, tomorrow you'll get to feed one.'

She stared at him. He was going to so much trouble to make all her dreams come true. He must have deeper feelings for her, she couldn't believe that this was just sex for him. It definitely wasn't for her.

'I can't believe you did this for me.'

He shrugged and turned away but she pulled him back, looping her arms round his neck.

'Thank you.'

He wrapped his arms around her and rested his forehead against hers, closing his eyes. She closed her own eyes and stood there in his arms for a few moments. When she opened them again he was staring at her as if he wanted to say something to her.

Suddenly there was a noise like a loud fart, which somewhat ruined the moment. When Eva looked around, there was one of the giraffes poking his nose through the wrought-iron railings, his long tongue reaching out towards them.

'Oh my god,' Eva quickly pulled away and knelt down next to the enormous head, staring into the liquid chocolate eyes. 'Hello,' she whispered as Thor knelt down next to her. 'Can we stroke it?'

'I don't see why not. If he doesn't like it, I'm sure he will move away.'

Eva reached out a tentative hand and to her surprise the giraffe stood there and let her touch him. She ran her fingers down the side of his cheek.

'He feels so soft, it's a bit like a horse's coat.'

Thor reached out his hand to stroke it too and Eva couldn't help smiling at how much Thor was obviously enjoying it. The giraffe was completely not bothered; he was obviously used to humans and kept licking out with his tongue as if trying to reach something.

'Oh, there's a nut.' Eva pointed to what looked like a small hazelnut next to where she was kneeling. 'Are giraffes allowed nuts?'

'There's actually a bag of these things in the room, I'm pretty sure this is the giraffe food they feed them here. Or part of it. Let me go and have a look.'

He got up slowly so he didn't frighten off the giraffe, which was still trying desperately to reach the nut.

Thor came back a moment later with a bag labelled giraffe food. 'Yep, it's the same thing, it's some kind of pellet.'

Eva nudged the pellet from the balcony floor closer and the giraffe licked it up while Thor opened the bag. He took a handful and passed it to Eva and then took a small handful himself.

'We hand-feed them?'

'I guess so,' Thor said. 'They did say we could when we checked in.'

Eva had completely missed that as she had been chatting to one of the porters who thought she looked like Kate Middleton. She had missed quite a bit actually, as she hadn't realised what kind of place this was or that the giraffes were so integral to it.

Eva held out a few pellets flat in her hand and the long tongue came and licked each one carefully away. She couldn't help but giggle and squeal with excitement. Thor held out his pellets and the giraffe calmly took them.

'This is incredible,' Eva said, running her hand down the giraffe's cheek again.

Thor placed his hand over hers, touching the giraffe in the gaps between her fingers and she looked up at him. He smiled at her. She wanted to take a snapshot, right now, and hold it in her heart. With the sun setting over the plains, this wonderful animal between them and his hand on hers, this was the moment she knew without a doubt that she was completely and utterly in love with this man.

Eva's phone rang just as they got out of the jeep. She quickly answered it when she saw it was Laurel. Eva had texted her several times over the last few days, telling her all the things that they had done and that Thor had stayed with her instead of going home, but she hadn't really gone into much more detail than that. Obviously her aunt wanted more.

'Hello my love,' Laurel said. 'How's it all going?'

'Oh Laurel, I am having the most amazing time. I've been to Egypt to see the pyramids and the tombs, ridden a camel, and for the last two nights we've stayed in Giraffe Manor in Kenya and yesterday morning we had breakfast with the giraffes, it was the most incredible experience. We got up really early this morning and travelled down to Masai Mara and we're just about to go on a hot air balloon safari. I'm so excited,' Eva said as she watched Thor go over and greet the pilot of the hot air balloon. The balloon was filling up nicely, the glow of the burners bright orange against the dusky light of the dawn.

'That's lovely. I'm so pleased you're having a good time. I wasn't sure if this travelling malarkey would be up your street but I can see that you're loving it.'

'I really am.'

'And would a certain sexy Dane have anything to do with your change of heart?'

Eva smiled that Laurel had got right to the important matters. 'I'm loving seeing the world with him. It's always better to have someone to enjoy these experiences with and I cannot imagine seeing and doing these things with anyone else but him.'

'And?'

Eva looked around to make sure no one was in hearing distance, but everyone including Thor was quite far away. But to be on the safe side, she lowered her voice.

'And the hot sex in every country of the world is a definite bonus.'

Laurel squealed with excitement. 'So you two are dating now?'

'I don't think we could class it as that.' Eva had no idea what to class it as.

'So just sex?' Laurel said, a note of pity in her voice.

'I think it's more than that,' Eva said, knowing she wasn't making any sense. 'I suppose we are both scared of labelling it. Neither of us came on this holiday expecting to have any kind of relationship or fall in love.'

'But that's what you've done,' Laurel said, gently.

Eva sighed. 'I have, yes, I've fallen in love with him.'

'Oh my god. I've never heard you talk about love before. Not with any of the men you've dated.'

'This is something different. Well, at least it is for me.'

'Oh Eva, he doesn't feel the same way?'

'I don't know, I... I think he does.'

'And if he doesn't?'

Eva closed her eyes for a moment and rubbed the ache in her chest at the thought of not seeing Thor again, of not kissing him, having him hold her, of not laughing or talking with him once the holiday was over.

'I'm not going to lie, if it comes to an end, of course it will hurt. But you know what, Mum had her heart broken twice and she managed to carry on and live a wonderful and exciting life. I'll be OK. I was happy in my life before Thor came along, a little bored perhaps, a lot complacent, but I was happy. And whereas I think my life will always have a little more adventure in it from now on, I don't need a man to make me happy.'

'Damn straight,' Laurel said. 'Never rely on someone else to make you happy, you have to take care of that yourself.'

Eva smiled. 'But until it does end, I'm going to enjoy every single second with this wonderful man and not worry about the future.'

'That sounds like a fabulous plan.'

'How are things going with you and James?' Eva asked.

'I don't know,' Laurel sighed heavily. 'He still seems distant somehow. Some days he seems fine and he's affectionate as always but… I feel like we're just papering over the cracks. I've asked him what's wrong and told him to talk to me but he just says everything is fine.'

Eva felt awful for her. 'It's sad, isn't it, that something as simple as talking could be the thing that could save most relationships, telling each other how you really feel. But most people don't, they bottle things up, leave things unsaid and then it's too late. Maybe you need to have it out with him once and for all.'

'Maybe you're right,' Laurel said, sadly.

Eva wondered if she should take some of her own advice and tell Thor how she felt.

'I better go, this hot air balloon looks like it's going to take off at any second,' Eva said as Thor came over to her.

'Take lots of pictures for me,' Laurel said.

'I will. I love you.'

'Love you too.'

Eva hung up and threw the phone in her bag.

'Should I be worried that you are telling someone else you love them?' Thor teased.

'Would you prefer it if I was saying those words to you?'

Thor's face fell.

'Thought not, come on.' She walked past him to talk to the balloon crew.

There were about eight others waiting for the balloon as the crew fiddled around with the burners, the loud roar of the gas and flames filling the air as the balloon expanded and billowed.

This really was beyond exciting, it was something she had always wanted to do and to do it somewhere as beautiful as Kenya just added to the thrill of it.

Thor joined her. He still looked a bit worried about her previous comment so she gave him a playful nudge and he smiled and nudged her back.

They were given a brief safety talk and told to climb into the basket. Eva quickly hurried over and clambered inside, Thor jumped in next to her.

As everyone else got in there were some last-second preparations as the crew untied ropes and prepared the basket and then suddenly they were floating off, rising gently into the warm amber sky.

It was serene and gentle and incredibly peaceful as everyone stood in awed silence as the ground drifted further away from them. They skated so close over the tops of trees that Eva could reach out and touch the branches. The occasional roar of the burners above them was the only sound.

The sun peeped above the horizon, painting the plains a beautiful gold. And that was when she saw them, these beautiful silhouettes of a small herd of elephants, two tiny ones, a slightly bigger one and three adults, all ambling slowly over the grassy slopes.

'Look, elephants,' someone squealed, pointing to the little family.

Eva looked up at Thor and couldn't help but grin at him.

She felt so privileged to be seeing this, and from this spectacular vantage point too. It felt like they were the only people in the world to witness the baby elephants playing together under the watchful eyes of their family.

They passed low over the bendy twisty river, so low they could see crocodiles sticking out of the water with only their eyes and snouts, though the large shadows of the rest of the bodies could be seen in the murky green waters. As the balloon followed the trail of the river, she saw a hippo waddling away from the noise of the balloon.

They flew on over a small forest, only to see the heads of giraffes poking out over the tops of the trees as they tried to reach the highest leaves and branches with their long tongues.

'This is incredible,' Eva said.

'It really is,' Thor said.

She wanted to remember this forever, she wanted to imprint it on her memory and pull it out and look at it every day. She wanted to paint the elephants, the crocodiles and the amazing colours. She almost wanted to stop the hot air balloon right then so she could start drawing but she would make do with taking a few photos instead.

'Look, zebra,' someone pointed.

Eva turned to see a herd of zebra running across the plains, their stripy coats shining in the early morning sun.

They carried on floating over this magnificent landscape, sometimes flying high so they could see the distant mountains, sometimes floating so low they could see the blades of long grass blowing in the wind.

'Hyena,' someone shouted and Eva turned to see three of them plodding along a little dirt track.

The sun rose higher in the sky, chasing away the night clouds and leaving behind a turquoise blue sky.

The pilot started talking about coming in to land soon and that's when they saw the male lion. On its own, it stood proudly on top of the hill line and roared to its pride. A little way off, an answering roar came and the lion ran off into the trees.

The balloon dropped lower and the pilot told them to crouch down and brace themselves for the landing.

They bumped down and the basket slid onto its side as the balloon billowed around them.

Eva lay looking up at the sky for a moment. Majestic. That was the only word to describe what she'd just experienced.

This was the adventure her mum had wanted for her, the kind that filled her heart and soul. And she knew that when she returned home, her little world would never really be the same again. She wanted adventure in her life, she wanted colour and excitement and she was going to go out and get it. She glanced over at Thor who was watching her with a big grin on his face. She only hoped this man would want to be a part of it too.

Chapter 24

Thor lay on the bed with his phone in his hand. He was scrolling through the photos he'd taken on the balloon ride that day, but also surreptitiously watching Eva with a smile as she explored their tent. He had never seen anyone get excited about a tent before. Admittedly, he hadn't been on safari many times with his work. It wasn't generally the sort of place his clients wanted to go. The occasional times he had been, he'd stayed in big hotels and only once in a tent where his client had been too horrified to touch anything. He wasn't sure how Eva would take to camping but, as he'd said to her before, this was luxury camping at its very best. It was more like a canvas house than an actual tent.

'I can't believe we have a bathroom with a shower and sink,' Eva said. 'And there's a chandelier above our bed, an actual chandelier. And a four-poster bed and we have a hot tub outside. When you said we were camping, I didn't expect this.'

'You've got the very best kind of camping here. If we were to go camping in England when we get back, it would be nothing like this. I'd make sure we'd camp somewhere with toilets and a shower on the site but that's about as luxurious as it would get.'

Eva excitedly threw herself down on the bed by his side. 'Are we going to go camping together when we get back home?'

Ah crap. He decided to quickly change the subject from this rosy coupley future where they would be going camping together.

'Ooh, look at this photo I took today of the lion,' Thor said, trying to ignore the way the smile fell from her face.

'It's a great photo,' she said, slightly more subdued now. 'Do you take many photos while you're away with clients?'

'I did, when I first started, but I stopped after a while. It felt a little weird to be taking photos of someone else's holiday.'

'But you've taken quite a lot on this holiday,' Eva said.

'This one feels different,' he kissed her on the head. 'It is different.'

He heard her sigh softly. He knew he was giving her very conflicting signals.

'I'm going for a shower, why don't you join me?' Thor said.

'I think I might go out for a little walk, take some photos of the sunset.'

'OK, we have dinner in half hour.'

'I'll be back soon,' she said as she climbed off the bed, leaving him alone inside the tent a few seconds later.

He sighed and stared up at the crystal drop chandelier above their bed which he could see through the canopy of the mosquito net.

He was an asshole. He hadn't wanted a relationship but he had got involved with her anyway. He knew she had feelings for him that went way beyond sex. He knew his feelings for her went way beyond that too, but now it felt like he was tormenting her with this unspoken promise of what would happen after they'd finished this trip. He knew what she wanted but he wasn't sure if he could give her that. And he was also scared by how much he actually wanted that. When he thought back to his last relationship, the agony of losing his child, the pain of losing the woman who he thought he was going to spend forever with, he didn't know whether he wanted to go through that again.

But he knew he had to get over this fear of being hurt again, for his sake and for Eva's. He loved being with her, talking to her, laughing with her, seeing the world through such enthusiastic fresh eyes. He needed to embrace a proper relationship with her, not this weird holiday romance where he was holding himself back. He needed to give it his best shot. He just had to find the courage to let go of his past and move forward with his future, though he had no idea how to do that.

Dear Mum,

The Seychelles is one of the most beautiful places I have ever seen. Every single picture I have seen of this tropical paradise doesn't even begin to come close to how utterly mesmerising this place is. The sea is so turquoise, I have never seen anything like it. The sand is pure white and so powder soft.

We've done a bit of island hopping while we have stayed here for the last three days. We've seen the beautiful wildlife of Bird Island, the rare birds, the coconut palm trees and the colourful coral reefs teeming with the most incredible fish. The island was so small we walked round the whole thing in less than an hour. We stayed on Praslin Island with its tiny deserted coves and cute little rainbow-coloured shops that sell the most delicious banana bread. The whole place is so tranquil. We also stayed in Alphonse and snorkelled with manta rays. I'm not sure what you imagined when you wrote that you wanted to swim with sharks, whether in your mind you envisaged a swim with a great white, but today we snorkelled with whitetip reef sharks and a scalloped hammerhead. They are the most unusual and unique creatures.

Tonight we caught fish off the end of the little jetty and then we cooked and ate them on the beach.

We stayed in a little lodge right on the sand which had its own private secluded tiny garden and a hammock. I wonder, if on your many travels, you ever attempted sex in a hammock? It was one of the most hilarious experiences of my life.

God, I am so in love with this man. It fills every fibre of my body. I want to shout it from the rooftops but I don't think he would appreciate that.

Wish you were here!

Love Eva x

PS Dreams ticked off:

15. Swim with sharks.

16. Catch, cook and eat fish on the beach.

Dear Mum,

Dubai is incredible, it really feels like it's the playground for the insanely rich. You should see the size of some of the yachts here. The shops are out of this world, every designer store you could imagine is here coupled with a ton of exclusive designers I've never even heard of. The cheapest dress I could find was three thousand pounds. I cannot imagine ever buying a dress worth that amount of money. There are so many gorgeous spas here with infinity pools overlooking the city.

We of course went to the very top of Burj Khalifa, the tallest building in the world. Standing on the observation deck, five hundred and fifty-five metres above the city is just staggering. When you walk around the city, there are many towering skyscrapers but when you are up there in Burj Khalifa those skyscrapers look like toys in a model village. From up there, the view is incredible, you can see the city and then miles of desert and the turquoise sea.

But the view from the top of the tallest skyscraper was nothing in comparison to the view while freefalling out of a plane. Thor had done it before so he wasn't scared while I was a bundle of nerves. I honestly thought my heart would explode in the plane it was banging so hard. We jumped at around ten thousand feet and had thirty seconds of freefall where the air roaring against my face made it almost impossible to breathe let alone scream in terror, but then I started to enjoy it. Ironically, in that moment when I was hurtling to my death, I had never felt so alive. When the parachute finally opened, we drifted serenely down and I could just enjoy the incredible view. It was so quiet and we could see for miles and miles. This was the dream that I was dreading the most but it was the most exhilarating, liberating, gloriously thrilling experience of my life.

Once we got back to the hotel, fuelled with adrenaline, we had the most amazing sex. As I lay looking up at the man I love, the man who has given me so much and completely changed my life, I longed to tell him how I felt and I ached inside that I couldn't. What kind of relationship is it where you can't be honest with the person you're with, where you're too scared of telling the other person how you feel for fear of their reaction? What kind of relationship is it when one person clearly feels a hell of a lot more for the other person than they feel for you? Just looking at him now and my heart is actually breaking. It's not even over but it hurts that this is never going to end the way I want it to. I thought I would just enjoy being with him and deal with the fall-out later but I'm falling deeper in love with this man every day and I know it's going to hurt even more now when it comes to an end.

I wonder if you went through this with Kasper or Thomas.

Wish you were here so much, so you could advise me on what to do, or at the very least hug me and tell me it will all be OK.

Love Eva x

PS Dreams ticked off:
*   17. Go to the top of the world's tallest building.*
*   18. Go skydiving.*

Eva slipped the postcard into the folder and sighed. She picked up the itinerary and looked through it in confusion. It clearly said they were supposed to fly from Dubai to India the following morning, but Thor had said they were now not flying out until late tomorrow night.

'How come our plans changed?' Eva asked, as she got into bed beside Thor.

He wrapped his arm around her and pulled her onto his chest, stroking her hair.

'Well, something is happening in Dubai tomorrow and I thought you might want to go.'

She looked up at him. 'What's happening?'

'We don't have to go if you don't want to, there are lots of things we could do with our day. We could take a boat trip or take a day out a little further afield. Or there's the Miracle Garden or the aquarium, Jumeirah beach is supposed to be nice. I just thought I would give you the choice and if you don't want to do it, that's absolutely fine.'

She frowned in confusion. 'OK, you're being all weird. What did you think I might want to do?'

He took a big breath. 'Thomas Connor is doing a book signing tomorrow in Dubai from twelve till three. I figured as we were in the same place, you might like to go along.'

Eva sat up in shock. 'Thomas is going to be here?'

'Yeah.'

'My dad?'

Thor nodded.

'Oh my god, why didn't you tell me?' Eva didn't know whether to be excited or terrified by this news. Right now she was settling for terrified with a side order of not even wanting to meet him.

'Because I didn't want you to spend days freaking out about it. This way you can follow your gut tomorrow without too much overthinking. You did say you wanted to meet him one day so I thought this might be a good way to do it.'

'At a book signing? What do you expect me to do, buy his book and go up to him and say, "Can you sign it from Dad?" I don't think he will be over the moon.'

'I thought this might be an easy way to get access to him. We don't have a telephone number or email address. How else would you ever be able to contact him unless it was at an event like this? And I'm not suggesting you walk up to the table and out him in front of everyone, you could go completely incognito if you like, just get him to sign the book and leave. Or even go up and say something like, "I'm Eva Blue, Juliette's daughter," and see what he does.'

'And what if his reaction is to have me thrown out?'

'From what you've told me, you don't have the greatest opinion of him. According to you, he abandoned your mum and you after a one-night stand and wanted nothing else to do with you. If he has you kicked out, as upsetting as that will be, it's not going to ruin your image of him being a great dad,' Thor said.

Eva nodded to concede this. 'But I don't know if I want to meet him. What good can possibly come of this?'

'You get closure. You've always wondered about him. He is this huge link to your and your mum's past that you've never met. If you get the chance to properly talk to him, you can tell him exactly how you feel about him and if you don't meet him you'll always be wondering about his side of the story.'

Eva groaned and lay down, staring at the ceiling.

'Look, you don't need to think about it now. You can wake up tomorrow and decide what you want to do. I'm easy either way, I'm very happy to spend a lazy day on the beach. I'm not going to pressure you to do this. It's entirely up to you.'

She rolled over onto her side, facing away from him, not sure whether to be angry with him or not.

He wrapped himself around her back, pressing a kiss to her neck.

'Go to sleep, Eva Blue. We can worry about this tomorrow.'

Eva sighed. They both knew that she was going to see her dad tomorrow and they both knew she would spend the rest of the night worrying about it.

Chapter 25

'I can't believe we're here,' Eva grumbled, looking at the autobiography of Thomas Connor in her hand that she had been forced to buy in order to join the queue to meet her dad. 'I can't believe you did this.'

Thor wrapped an arm around her shoulders and kissed her on the forehead, not fazed at all over her moaning at him. They both knew she had made the decision to come here that day. Thor hadn't even mentioned it that morning as she had gone through every outfit change possible trying to decide what to wear.

She'd told Thor several times that she didn't want to go and he had simply shrugged and started suggesting other places they could visit that day instead. But they'd both known she was going to come here.

They moved forward in the queue and, for a fleeting few seconds, she got a glimpse of her dad. He was still a good-looking man, his eyes sparkling with affection for the fan standing in front of him, an easy smile on his face as he chatted easily with the people who had queued up to see him.

Then someone moved in front of her and he vanished from view.

'God, what am I going to say to him?' Eva said, flicking through the pages of the book without even looking at them.

'Just tell him your name and see if that gets a response.'

She sighed. 'This is going to be so embarrassing when we get kicked out.'

The queue moved forward again, she was now next in line.

'I feel sick,' Eva muttered.

'Look, we stay here for a few seconds, you don't even need to tell him who you are if you don't want to. And then we'll go and get a big stiff drink or a large slice of cake, or both.'

Eva stared at her feet, a hundred different conversations she wanted to have with her dad flying through her head.

Then suddenly the person in front moved away and she looked up into the smiling grey eyes of her dad.

She stood frozen to the spot for a second before Thor gently nudged her forward.

'Hi, thanks for coming today,' Thomas said, easily. 'Hope you haven't been waiting too long?'

'Hello,' Eva said, quietly. 'Not too long, only half hour or so.'

'Ah you're English,' his smile broadened. 'I love the English.'

She cleared her throat, wanting to say so much to him, but she probably had about thirty seconds before he signed her book and she was ushered away. There was an assistant standing nearby and she was already holding her hand out for the book so she could open it at the right page for Thomas to sign.

'What are you doing out here in Dubai?' Thomas prompted when Eva still said nothing.

'I'm on holiday, a round-the-world trip. My mum died about eighteen months ago and she had this bucket list of dreams she wanted to achieve in her lifetime which she never got round to doing. So I thought I would try to tick these things off for her.'

'I'm so sorry about your mum, but that trip sounds wonderful. What kind of things are on the list?' Thomas asked as the assistant almost prised the book from her fingers.

'Well, she wanted to go up the tallest building in the world, which is why we are here in Dubai, she wanted to swim with sharks, jump out of a plane, see the midnight sun. We're going to New Zealand in the hope of seeing the aurora australis and we're going to swim with dolphins in Hawaii.'

'That sounds like a lot of fun,' Thomas said, as the assistant passed him the book and he looked down at the blank space just below the title. Her time was almost up. 'Who should I make this out to?'

She swallowed. 'Eva Blue.'

His head snapped up to look at her, all amusement in his eyes suddenly gone. 'Blue is an interesting surname. Not too many of them about.'

And here was the way in she had been hoping for. 'My mum was a singer; her stage name was Juliette Blue. She had it legally changed to that before I was born and then I became Eva Blue too.'

He stared at her. 'You're Juliette's daughter?'

She nodded as she tried to read his face. There was no fear or horror there, but there certainly wasn't any happiness at meeting her either.

He turned his attention back to the book, stared at the blank page for a second and then turned over to the dedication page instead. He scrawled a message underneath the dedication and then signed it in big loopy writing. He snapped the book closed and passed it back to her.

'Well, thanks for coming, it was good to meet you.' His eyes held hers for a moment longer before his gaze shifted to the next person in line.

She stood there in shock for a few moments. That was it? The assistant gestured for her to move away and she shuffled out of the queue.

Thor put his arm around her and escorted her out of the shop. 'I'm sorry Eva, this was a terrible idea. I didn't know what his reaction was going to be to meeting you but I didn't think he would just dismiss you like that.'

Eva stared at the book and then opened the page to where he'd signed it.

'Oh!' she said softly.

'What is it?' Thor said.

She stared at the hotel name and his room number and a time of four o'clock. 'He wants to meet me.'

She passed him the book so he could see. 'Well, that's something. Wait, Eva, have you seen this?'

He passed the book back to her and pointed to the printed dedication.

Her heart missed a beat as she read it.

For my beautiful wife Alexandra and my children Phoebe and Florence, I love you all.
For EB, I think about you every day.

She looked up at Thor. 'Is that... Is that me?'

'I think it's pretty significant that he deliberately chose to sign the dedication page instead and I don't think he just turned to that page for the extra room,' Thor said.

Eva stared at the note again. There was nothing else there to say what the meeting would involve but, coupled with the dedication, she couldn't help but have a glimmer of hope.

She knew her father wasn't going to suddenly decide he wanted to be a part of her life, give her a big hug and start playing dad of the year. It was too late for that. But she hoped at least she might be able to talk with him.

Eva walked into her dad's hotel a while later. It was a very posh place with marble floors and chandeliers and gold inlaid flowers climbing the walls. Of course someone as successful as Thomas Connor would stay somewhere like this.

Thor gave her hand a squeeze. She had considered going to meet her dad alone but abandoned that thought pretty much as soon as she had it. She needed Thor with her for this.

She was even more nervous now than she had been before in the bookshop because this was going to be a proper conversation, away from prying ears and eyes. They would be free to talk honestly and she had no idea what he was going to say. He had paid her mum hush money to go away. She hoped he wouldn't think that she was here for that.

They walked up to reception and the receptionist smiled brightly. Eva was sure she was nowhere near as glamorous as most of the hotel's other clients.

'I'm here to see Thomas Connor. My name's Eva Blue,

he's expecting me,' Eva said, realising how surreal that sounded in her head.

But the receptionist didn't even bat an eye. 'He just phoned down to tell us of your arrival. Go on up. He's on floor twenty-three, in the Jupiter suite.'

Eva went up to the lifts, stepped inside and pressed the button. She wondered what Juliette would make of this meeting, whether she'd be happy or angry that they'd finally met after all this time.

The lift doors pinged open and she and Thor stepped out. There were only six doors along this corridor and they found the Jupiter suite tucked up in the corner.

Eva took a deep breath and knocked on the door.

A few seconds later, Thomas answered it. He actually smiled when he saw Eva standing there, which wasn't what she was expecting at all.

'Hi Eva, I'm so glad you came,' Thomas said and then his eyes flicked to Thor.

'This is Thor, my boyfriend,' Eva said.

She hoped Thor wouldn't mind being labelled as such. But it was easier than saying that Thor was just some guy she was sleeping with and she hoped Thor understood that.

Thomas shook his hand and then gestured for them both to come in.

'Can I get you both a drink?' he said.

'Just a water for me please,' Eva said.

'I'm fine,' Thor said.

Thomas went to the fridge and pulled out a bottle of chilled water, passing it to her as she sat down on the sofa. He looked casual now, wearing shorts and a shirt with the sleeves rolled up, and as he sat down on the sofa opposite her, he actually seemed relaxed.

'I was so sorry to hear that Juliette died,' Thomas said. 'It came as quite a shock when I heard the news last year. She was so full of life, this... vivacious firework. It's so sad that her light went out too soon.'

Eva frowned. 'How did you hear that she died?'

'Because of the house in Clementine Avenue. It was in my name and Juliette's. Well, I bought it for her but it was in her name as well. Tenants in common, I think my English solicitor called it. He contacted me shortly after her death to say that her half had been bequeathed to you and asked what I wanted to do about my half. Of course I signed it over to you as well.'

'What? That's not... I didn't know.'

Juliette had never told her that. Surely that should have come up in all the paperwork and proceedings that followed her death. For a brief time Eva had owned the house in Clementine Avenue jointly with her dad and she'd never known.

'I made sure that you were kept out of it. I'm guessing there are quite a few things that Juliette never told you... Maybe I can fill in a few gaps?'

Eva stared at him in confusion. She suddenly had no idea what to say to him.

Thor cleared his throat. 'Maybe you could start by telling us how you and Juliette met.'

Thomas smiled as if he was remembering her fondly. 'We met in a bar in London one Friday night. She was an incredible woman. She was singing on stage, strutting her stuff, and I think I fell in love with her right there and then. She came off stage and we started chatting and stayed in the bar until the early hours in the morning, talking. When we were kicked out we went back to my hotel and... well, we were already very drunk by that point. We spent the rest of the weekend in bed, kissing, cuddling, talking, making love.'

'Wait, the whole weekend? Mum always said it was one night.'

'No, it was definitely a weekend, one of the most spectacular weekends of my life. I think I would have asked her to marry me right there but on Monday morning when I told her I was going back to America the following day, she started getting all weird, muttering stuff about how she always picked the wrong ones and she wasn't going to let it happen again. Anyway, I went for a shower and when I came out she had gone. She didn't leave a number or any way of getting in touch so I had no idea how to find her. I went to the club where she had sung but of course they wouldn't give me her address. I left her my number but I never heard from her, well at least not for the next nine months.'

Eva's heart sank. Her poor mum had been so broken-hearted over what happened with Kasper that she had pushed Thomas away from fear of it happening all over again, of falling in love and not having it reciprocated.

'So she called you to tell you she was pregnant?' Eva said.

'She phoned to tell me I had a daughter called Eva. You were a week old at that point. I had just got married. I met Alexandra on a film I was working on a few months after I'd met your mum. She was my leading lady and we just fell in love. We married six months after we'd met, it was a total whirlwind romance. The public loved our story, people couldn't get enough of us. We were invited on all the chat shows together, cast in several films. Our career took off because of our relationship. And suddenly your mum was there with my baby. My agent was furious. I had this very wholesome on-screen image and having a secret lovechild didn't fit in with that.'

'And you panicked and paid her hush money to go away.'

Thomas frowned slightly. 'No, that wasn't what happened at all. Is that what she told you?'

'Yes, and that she used that money to buy the house.'

'I bought her the house as I wanted to provide for you and her but it wasn't hush money. She would never have gone to the press, I knew that. Did your mum ever tell you that I flew over to meet you after you were born?'

Eva let her face drop into her hands as she stared at him. 'No, she never told me that.'

He dug his phone out of his pocket and scrolled through it and then passed it to her. There was a picture of an old crinkled photograph that clearly showed a much younger Thomas standing in the kitchen of Clementine Avenue, cradling a baby Eva. His whole face was lit up with a huge smile.

Eva swallowed down the huge lump in her throat. None of this made sense.

'You were such a beautiful baby.'

'Stop it. Just stop!' Eva suddenly snapped. 'Don't act like the doting father. You were never there. I never saw you, I never heard from you, I never even received a Christmas card.'

'Eva, when I came over to see you for the first time, your

mum told me that she didn't want me to come by again. She didn't want a part-time dad for you. I was just about to start filming a trilogy in Australia for the next two years with very limited time off. She didn't want me swanning into your life every few months or years. She said it would confuse you. I was heartbroken but I understood. Beyond money, what could I really offer you? Your mum wanted to be a family, but I couldn't offer that to her. Me and Alexandra were already a family, she was pregnant with Phoebe, I wasn't going to walk out on her and I didn't want to. I loved your mum, Eva, she was so utterly lovely, but when she didn't call I put it down to a glorious fling and moved on. What I had with Alexandra was something significant. Maybe I would have had that with your mum or maybe not, but your mum never gave us the chance to find out.'

Eva felt a lump in the back of her throat. She'd never had a dad in her life because Juliette had pushed him away. Anger, disappointment and hurt flooded through her.

'I still wanted to be part of your life in some small way, even if it was from a distance. The first few years of your life I sent you birthday and Christmas presents but your mum just sent them straight back so eventually I stopped. I suppose it was easier to give Juliette what she wanted. A week before your seventh birthday, she got in touch and asked me to come to your party. She said you had asked for me to be there. But I was working on a film and we were already weeks behind schedule, I couldn't get the time off to fly over. But I called her on your birthday, asked to speak to you and she wouldn't let me. She said I'd let you down and it was never going to happen again. After that she changed her numbers, blocked my messages. I never heard from her again but I never stopped thinking about you, about both of you.'

Eva took a drink of her water and stared at the floor. She had no words. She felt like she'd stepped into a weird parallel dimension where everything was not as it should be. The image she had built up of her father over the years was suddenly crumbling in front of her eyes.

'I'm sorry Eva, I really am.'

She sighed heavily. 'Well, this has been... enlightening.'

'Look, I understand if you never want to see me again, I've been a crap dad and I suppose it's way too late to try to change that now, but how would you feel about keeping in touch?'

Eva stared at him. 'We don't know each other. You've missed out on twenty-seven years of my life.'

'And while some of that was my fault, a lot of it wasn't. I'd really like to not miss out on the next twenty-seven years,' Thomas said.

'I don't know. This has all been so much to take in.'

'Well, you can have my number and email and if you want to drop me a line occasionally, that would be great. You could keep me updated about your trip, if you want. Maybe send me pictures of the aurora if you get to see it. I've never seen it myself.'

'Maybe,' Eva said.

'And I'm in England in a month. If you're back, we could meet up?'

She smiled slightly. 'Maybe.'

He grinned. 'Well I'll take that.'

He fished a business card out of his wallet and passed it to her.

Eva took it and slipped it into her pocket. 'We should go.'

Thor stood up and Thomas escorted them to the door.

'Thanks for coming, it was really great to finally meet you properly.'

'Thanks for inviting me,' Eva said, wondering if he was expecting her to give him a hug. It was a bit too soon for that and a handshake seemed way too formal. He settled for a pat on the shoulder and she couldn't help but smile slightly at that.

Once they were out in the corridor, Thor hugged her close and she felt all the tension leave her body as he held her. She felt exhausted just trying to process it all. Her dad did care about her after all and after years of resenting him for abandoning her and her mum, she had no idea what to do with this new version of him.

She pulled the business card out of her pocket. Maybe she didn't need to decide what to do now. She had his number and that at least was a start.

Eva sat on the beach staring out at the sea, a large cupcake Thor had bought her sitting on her lap.

She picked an iced flower from the top and popped it in her mouth and then phoned Laurel. She answered on the second ring.

'Hello my lovely, how are you?'

Eva had no idea how to answer that so she decided to cut straight to the point.

'I've just met my dad.'

There was silence from the other end for so long, Eva thought they'd been cut off.

'Oh Eva,' Laurel said. 'How did it go?'

'Well, it was quite... surprising. His version of events didn't exactly match my mum's.'

Her aunt sighed, heavily.

'You knew, didn't you?' It wasn't really a question. She remembered Laurel defending Thomas the last time they'd talked about him before Eva left on her trip. Now it suddenly made sense.

'Yes I did. That was the one thing your mum regretted more than anything. She told me often that she had no right to deprive you of a dad, even if he would have been part time. She was proud and fiercely independent and, after our dad kicked her out, I think she felt abandoned and alone. She put all these walls up to protect herself. When she found out that Thomas was married she pushed him away and wanted nothing more to do with him. When he let you down on your seventh birthday and she saw how hurt and upset you were, she thought she'd done the right thing in severing all contact but it wasn't really his fault. He was working and couldn't get the time off. But years later she wished she had done it differently. She had no idea how to rectify the situation at that point though, she had no contact details for him and she didn't know how to tell you what she'd done. She knew you'd be angry and quite rightly so.'

'She should have told me the truth,' Eva said, bitterly.

'Yes she should have,' Laurel said.

'You should have told me,' Eva said, which she knew was very unfair.

'It wasn't my place to say. Your mum didn't want you to know and I wasn't going to go against her wishes.'

Eva shook her head angrily, still trying to process it all.

'How was he with you?' Laurel asked after a while.

'He was nice, he seems... lovely. He asked if I'd like to keep in touch.'

'And do you want that?'

Eva looked at the business card in her hand, turning it over so the gold mirror foil glinted in the sunshine. Over twenty-seven years ago, when her mum met Thomas, she had his number and fear had stopped her using it. Fear of getting hurt again, fear of being let down. Juliette had never given Thomas a chance. Eva wasn't going to make the same mistake her mum made. Thomas deserved a chance now. And maybe she would only see him once a year or less, maybe they'd never be close, but she owed it to herself and to him to give it a go.

'Yes I do.'

'That's good. I've never met him but I've followed his career over the years – no one ever has a bad word to say about him. I think it will do you good to get to know the real him and make your own mind up about him.'

'I think you're right.'

Eva sighed. It was so much to take in.

'How's it going out there?' Laurel asked, gently.

'Good, really well. I did a skydive yesterday, it was incredible,' Eva said, deciding to let it go for now. None of this was Laurel's fault.

'Oh, how amazing,' Laurel said.

'How are things with you?' Eva asked.

'Well, I actually have some news. James proposed.'

'Oh my god, Laurel,' Eva said, her own worries momentarily forgotten. Thor glanced up next to her in concern and she waved away his worries. 'Did you say yes?'

'Yes I did. That's what's been bothering him for the last week or so. He was trying to pluck up the courage to propose to me, but then he got scared that it was too soon and I'd say no. It's crazy, he's been so worked up about proposing to me, it drove a wedge between us.'

'Oh god, I can't believe it was that. You two really needed to talk.'

'I know. A lot of problems could be solved if people just talked about their feelings,' Laurel said, echoing what Eva had said to her before.

Eva smiled, sadly. 'I'm happy for you. You won't be getting married just yet, will you?'

'Oh no, I definitely want you there.'

'That's good. I better go, we have to go back to the hotel to pick up our bags and leave for the airport shortly. I'll speak to you soon.'

She ended the call and rested her head on Thor's shoulder. 'Are you OK?'

She nodded. 'I will be.'

Dear Mum,

I'm so angry at you. You had no right to do what you did. I grew up without a dad because you were afraid of getting hurt and in the process you hurt me too. What was worse, you lied about it, you told me lies about what Thomas did to turn me against him and I'm so heartbroken that you would do that.

He seems really nice and I hate that I never got the

chance to know him properly.

I do understand why you did it. Kasper broke your heart and I can only imagine how you must have felt when things came to an end with him. I know you were trying to protect yourself and me from getting hurt like that again. You were trying to do what you thought was best for me.

I know you regretted it but how I wish we had talked about this before you left me. If you were here, we'd shout and cry and then probably hug it out and cry some more. But I can't even do that.

God I wish you were here right now.

Love Eva x

Chapter 26

'This place is something else, isn't it?' Eva said quietly, as she took in the towering arches of the Taj Mahal. They were standing in the great chamber where the king, Shah Jahan, lay next to his favourite queen, Arjumand Banu Begum, or as she later became known, Mumtaz Mahal, which meant the Exalted One of the Palace. Eva had read all about it in her guide book. Mumtaz Mahal had died giving birth to their fourteenth child and he had spent the next fifteen years building this magnificent mausoleum as a tribute to his love for her. The whole place was made out of ivory white marble and the walls, ceilings and floors were covered in exquisite intricate patterns and carvings made from precious stones. The colourful walls seemed to glow with the sun streaming through in different places.

They walked outside and slipped off their shoe covers. Eva looked out on the view as they walked down the stairs and into the beautiful gardens. She was tired but the quiet beauty and tranquillity of the place was enough to wake her up.

They had arrived in New Delhi in the very early hours of

the morning and then travelled to their hotel where they had pretty much fallen straight into bed. All the mess surrounding her dad was still playing on her mind, but there was no point being angry with her mum forever. While she didn't agree with what Juliette had done, Eva did understand why she'd done it. Eva still had a ton of unanswered questions but with her mum no longer around, she was never going to get any answers. All she could do was try to make the best of a bad situation and that meant that she would keep in touch with her dad. He had offered the olive branch and she had to carry on with her holiday, not let this mess ruin it.

'Over twenty thousand architects, stonemasons, carvers and artists from all over the world were employed to make this monument and a thousand elephants were used too,' Eva said as she returned her attention to the guide book.

'The world's most expensive gravestone,' Thor said.

'Thor! This is a testament to undying love.'

'Oh don't get me wrong, this place is spectacular, but it is just an oversized gravestone at the end of the day. And the kind of money that he spent building this place in the 1600s is the equivalent to several hundred million pounds in today's money. India has always been such a poor country and whenever I come here I always think about how that money could have been put to better use.'

'You're so unromantic,' Eva said as they walked alongside the reflecting pool. Grey clouds swirled overhead. They weren't quite in monsoon season yet but in the taxi on the way to the hotel earlier they'd experienced a small shower and it looked like they might get another. The heat was so stifling that she wouldn't have minded a good downpour. Her

THE SUMMER OF CHASING DREAMS

clothes were sticking to her and sweat seemed to be seeping from every single part of her body.

'I'm plenty romantic.'

'This was a symbol of the king's love for his wife. I cannot imagine anyone ever loving me that much that they wanted to build a magnificent... *palace* in my memory,' Eva said.

'If it's wealthy over-the-top extravagant gestures you're after, then you're probably with the wrong man. You should see the size of my flat back home, I think you'd be very disappointed.'

She looked at Thor in surprise. 'What's wrong with you today? You've been grumpy since we got here.'

'You've been going on about how romantic this place is. Well, if romance is measured in marble and jewels and extravagance then I have nothing to offer you.'

She pulled him to a stop as they reached the end of the reflecting pool and looped her arms round his neck. 'You're so silly, I don't want any of those things from you. What makes you think I want that?'

'Isn't that what all women want, to be looked after and spoiled?'

'I'm quite capable of looking after myself, I have done for most of my life, and the most extravagant thing I have in my house is a memory foam pillow, which I bought, used once, and it now sits at the bottom of my wardrobe.'

She saw a small smile on Thor's lips.

'And by all women, do you mean Christel?' Eva asked.

Thor sighed. 'Stefan was rich, he had a big house with a swimming pool and an expensive car. When Christel and I were living together we just about managed to make ends meet. We never went hungry but the food we ate was very much on the budget end of the spectrum. We had one car between us which always inevitably broke down. I don't think it was the luxury life she'd imagined. I always wondered if Stefan's wealth was one of the reasons she fell for him.'

'I would never get married to someone because they were rich. I would marry someone because they made me laugh, because they were kind and easy to talk to, because they made my heart soar whenever I looked at them and obviously because they were great in bed,' Eva teased.

He dipped his head and leaned his forehead against hers.

'There is only one thing I want from you and it's not precious jewels or an expensive car.'

He pulled back to look at her. 'What do you want Eva? If I can, I'll give it to you.'

She smiled sadly. 'Well you won't give me this. You protect it so fiercely it might as well be precious jewels.'

She trailed her hand down his chest and laid it over his heart.

His face softened. 'Eva…'

'It's OK.' She pulled away from him to take a photo of the Taj Mahal reflected in the long pool. With the dark clouds behind it, it looked quite dramatic.

Suddenly, it started to rain, great big heavy splats hitting her, bouncing off the pavement and creating giant ripples in the pool. Eva quickly stashed her camera out of the way and then lifted her arms and face to the sky. The rain grew heavier and, while everyone around them darted for cover, Eva couldn't help giggling and laughing as the rain cooled her and soaked into her clothes. She danced around with her arms in the air, shrieking as the rain pelted down on her.

She turned to look at Thor and realised he was staring at her like she was a goddess. She stopped dancing and in two large strides he was in front of her, cupping her face and kissing her hard. She slipped her arms round his neck, and he gathered her close as the kiss continued. The rain continued to fall around them, soaking them both to the skin, and she couldn't care less.

Eventually he pulled back slightly. 'There's your kiss in the rain, Eva Blue.'

She grinned against his lips as she kissed him again. 'You make all my dreams come true.'

'Come on, let's go back to the hotel.'

She nodded and he grabbed her hand and marched back down towards where they could catch a taxi. Every few yards he would stop and kiss her again and she couldn't help but giggle over his need for her.

They climbed into the back of the taxi and Thor gave the driver the address of their hotel before he started kissing her again, his arm round her shoulders as she rested on his chest. They couldn't get back to the hotel fast enough as far as she was concerned. Thankfully they weren't too far away and soon Thor was thrusting some money at the driver and almost dragging her back into the hotel.

No sooner had they closed their bedroom door behind them, Thor was stripping her out of her clothes as she fought to get him out of his. He scooped her up and she giggled against his lips as he laid her down on the bed and then lay down next to her.

'You've cast a spell on me,' Thor said, his hands exploring her body, bringing her very quickly to the edge of insanity.

He grabbed a condom and kissed her as he moved inside her. He pulled back slightly and just stared down at her. 'I didn't want any of this. You. Us. This incredible connection. But you got inside me and filled my entire being with this warmth and happiness and now I can't escape and I don't even know if I want to. I want to give you everything you want but I'm scared, I fear it won't be enough.'

He kissed her again and she wrapped her arms and legs around him as he moved against her, taking her deeper, taking her back to the very edge again.

He pulled back to look at her and she reached up to stroke his face. 'You are enough for me, exactly as you are. I love you,' she said.

He stilled for a moment, a frown forming on his face before he kissed her again and this time he didn't stop. She got the impression it was so she couldn't say the words he didn't want to hear again. He moved against her harder and as that feeling exploded inside her, he collapsed on top of her, trying to catch his breath. She stroked the hair at the back of his neck. After a few moments he rolled off her and onto his back. He brought her with him so she was now on top and he stroked a finger up and down her spine.

They lay there like that for the longest time, not saying a word. But she knew, no matter how long they lay there, he wouldn't say the words back.

Dear Mum,

The Great Wall of China was incredible, we took a helicopter ride over the top of it and it was just amazing to see it stretching on for miles and miles, undulating over hills and mountains, into valleys curving like a silvery river. The helicopter flew in so close hugging the steps and slopes of the wall. It was incredible to see how well preserved the wall is in some sections, while other sections are completely overgrown with trees and bushes, the walls and towers collapsing and crumbling away. You would have loved to see this, although I imagine you'd have loved riding in the helicopter more – it was fast, exciting and more than a little scary as it swooped and soared across the wall.

Things are still going well with Thor. Well, I say going well, both of us haven't mentioned that I told Thor I love him. It's like this great big elephant in the room. We both know I said it. I keep waiting for him to bring it up, even if it's just to apologise that he doesn't feel that way or at least acknowledge it in some way. Everything else seems to have carried on as normal, he's still tactile, hugging me, kissing me, making love to me. He's been teasing me that on this long-haul flight from Beijing to Australia we're going to join the Mile-High Club. That side of things couldn't be better. I just don't know how you can do all those things and not feel anything for the other person. I know I've had relationships before where I've not loved the men I was with, and I never felt that was wrong at the time. But this feels so different to my previous relationships. But maybe that's because I love him. It might not be any different for him. I can't even be angry at him for not having those feelings. But I do feel disappointed.

Wish you were here!

Love Eva x

PS I cannot believe I'm writing this, but we have just joined the Mile-High Club. We are travelling in first class again and our seats can be laid flat into beds as it was an overnight flight. The pods have screens around them so no one can see. The air hostesses turned off all the lights so everyone could get some sleep and I lay there in the semi-darkness for a while as I could hear Thor trying to get comfortable in the pod next to me. The next thing he had snuck into my pod and was climbing into my bed. The beds are made for one person, not one person and one extra-large Dane, but somehow we made it work. We kind of spooned while we were doing it as Thor said if anyone looked in, it would just look like we were cuddling. He kept saying we had to be quiet but I couldn't help giggling at the prospect of getting caught. God, this man, he makes me feel so alive.

PPS Dreams ticked off:

20. See the Great Wall of China.

21. Go on a helicopter ride.

46. Join the Mile-High Club.

Chapter 27

Eva let out a sigh of contentment as she looked out over the sparkling blue waters of the Coral Sea near the Whitsunday Islands. Australia was a different pace of life; the locals were laidback and so completely chilled out that it didn't take long for that mentality to seep into her bones. Nothing seemed worth worrying about here. The stresses of everyday life seemed to fade away. Even in the busy city of Sydney, where they'd spent a night, it seemed a slower way of life than London, maybe because everyone seemed so much happier here. They'd spent the night before on Hamilton Island which felt like they were staying on some kind of utopia with its palm trees, long white beaches and crystal-clear waters. They had been picked up that morning by a catamaran and they'd sailed out to the pontoon where they were going to scuba-dive the Great Barrier Reef and spend the night under the stars. She'd already had an hour's basic training in the shallow pool-type area of the pontoon, which didn't seem anywhere near enough preparation to be ready to go into the depths of the sea and survive.

'You ready?' Thor said from behind her.

She turned to survey him in his shortie wetsuit. He looked like he'd just stepped out of a James Bond film with Thor in the title role. He looked sexy and dynamic, as if he was just about to go and save the world. Eva knew she looked less than appealing, having had to squeeze her curves into her hired wetsuit. But the way that Thor was looking at her he didn't seem to mind.

She nodded. 'If I die, I'm coming back to haunt you.'

He grinned. 'You're not going to die. We're only going a few metres deep.'

'You only need a few inches to drown,' Eva grumbled.

Thor held out his hand and she took it. He led her down to the equipment deck where everyone else was kitting up with dive gear. Their guide, Amelia, handed them a weight belt each and then helped them on with their air tanks. Eva tested the regulator in her mouth, making sure she could breathe through it, and gave Amelia the OK signal. Amelia helped Eva and Thor fit their masks and then they made their way down the steps into the water. There was an underwater platform there where they could stand and put on their fins. Amelia gave them an OK signal and then the thumbs-down signal and she disappeared under the water.

'Ready?' Thor said.

Eva pressed the button on the back of the regulator to make sure the air was still coming through. She looked up at him and nodded and he moved to put his regulator in his own mouth.

'Wait,' Eva stopped him. She leaned up and kissed him. 'If I die, I want you to know that I love you.'

His regulator was frozen halfway to his mouth. There, she'd said the unmentionable word again. This time not in the throes of passion or under the influence of drugs or alcohol, but in the cold light of day where he couldn't mistake it.

Grinning to herself, she put her own regulator in her mouth and knelt down on the platform so she was under the water. After a few moments of making sure she could still breathe, she pushed out into the deep blue sea where Amelia was waiting. She gave a little giggle into the regulator at Thor's reaction, which made her cough on the air. Focussing on the task in hand, she looked around and saw hundreds of fish, some drifting close by, many more further off, all different sizes and colours. And there was the reef right underneath them, swirling gently with the ebb of the sea, some of it looking as soft as carpet, other parts looking sharp like thorns, but all of it looked so beautiful and so full of life, little fish darting in and out of the plants and blooms.

A few moments later, Thor joined them. He gave her the OK signal to check she was all right but it made her giggle again to see that he was frowning slightly underneath his mask. She returned the signal and then Amelia gestured for them to move off over the reef. Eva kicked out, feeling the muscles in her legs working as she moved her fins up and down.

The surface of the water shimmered a few metres above them, the sunlight streaming through and picking out the beautiful colours of the fish and the coral. Right beneath her she could see a tiny little Nemo, a clownfish, darting amongst the soft fronds of the coral. Up ahead she could see the large looming shape of the gold and blue Māori wrasse with its oversized lips. Thor tapped her on the arm and pointed and she looked over towards where the reef nearly reached the surface to see a large turtle swimming along the reef, seemingly flying through the water with its flapping motion. Eva squealed through her mouthpiece. They had been told they might see them there, and as swimming with turtles was another one of her mum's dreams, Eva couldn't be happier that they'd managed to tick that one off the list. Far down the wall of the reef, they saw a whitetip reef shark disappearing into the shadows near the ocean floor.

It was so pretty down there, just like swimming in a giant aquarium. The visibility was astounding too, the view of the reef seeming to stretch on forever.

All too soon, Amelia was gesturing for them to return to the pontoon. They surfaced in a different place from where they'd entered, inflated their dive jackets and bobbed around in the water for a minute or two while they waited for the ladder to become free.

'How was that?' Amelia said, raising her mask onto her forehead.

Eva did the same. 'That was incredible.'

Amelia grinned. 'I've been working out here on the pontoon for about five years and I never get tired of seeing it.'

She turned to help another of the divers aboard the pontoon, and as they trod water to keep themselves afloat, Eva looped her arms around Thor's neck. 'And I'm glad I got to see it with you.'

He leaned his forehead against hers. 'I am too.'

He didn't say anything more, but in true Australian fashion she was going to let it go for now.

Thor stared up at the stars above them as they lay on the top deck of the pontoon. The day guests had left the pontoon earlier that afternoon, leaving only a tiny handful of people who were staying the night too. They had snorkelled together, enjoying the quiet of the reef without the rest of the tourists, and as the sun sank into the sea they had gone on another dive, seeing the reef come to life with a whole load of nocturnal fish that had been hidden away on their previous dive. And now they were camping out under the stars. They had been given a swag, which was a kind of tent with a mattress inside to sleep on, with pillows and blankets to make them more comfortable. And although they were snuggled under the blankets as the night on the reef had become a bit chilly, they hadn't yet zipped up their tent as the view of the starlit canopy above them was hard to beat.

'This is pretty spectacular, isn't it,' Thor said, quietly so not to wake up the other guests who were all sleeping in nearby swags.

There was silence from Eva and he could hear her breathing was quite heavy as she lay snuggled against his chest. He stroked a hand down her hair but she didn't stir.

She really was the most incredible woman he had ever met. So many of these things on her mum's list would never have made it onto Eva's list; skydiving, holding a tarantula at Sydney Zoo, scuba-diving, singing on top of the Eiffel Tower had all been things that she had been scared of but she'd done them anyway. She was so brave and determined and he loved that about her. He wasn't brave at all. He could jump out of a plane, dive the deepest oceans, ride the fastest motorbike, go on the biggest rollercoaster and would laugh at the thrill of it all but, when it came to matters of the heart, he was a complete coward.

She had been brave enough to hand her heart to him on a plate. Twice. And he just couldn't do it. He had never had feelings like this before and the intensity of them scared him to death. Because having feelings like this meant that if it ended the pain would be even worse than it had been before. He wanted to push Eva away before these feelings got too much but he knew it was too late for that and he couldn't push her away even if he wanted to. They were intrinsically linked now and that scared him too.

But hiding away from those feelings, not admitting them even to himself, didn't change the way he felt about her. And now he was hurting Eva by not returning those feelings. She didn't deserve that. She needed to know that this meant as much to him as it did to her.

He just had to say the words and if Eva could throw herself out of a plane or into the deepest seas when she was petrified of doing so, then he could damn well say a few words.

He opened his mouth but nothing came out. This was ridiculous.

Thor dipped his head a little lower and took a deep breath. 'Eva, I love you,' he whispered and the words seemed to dance in the air above them for a moment before being chased away by the sea breeze over the waves.

There, he'd said it. No one had heard him, especially not

the woman in question, but he'd said it. That would have to be good enough for now.

Eva couldn't help but smile as she walked into the little café to pick up coffee for her and Thor. They had dived together that morning as the sun rose over the reef and then had breakfast right there on the water's edge, their feet dipping into the sea before they returned to Hamilton Island. They were due to spend the night there before they flew to Sydney and then on to Christchurch and Stewart Island the following day. Another long day of travelling ahead of them, although she could catch up with some work on the flight. They were now just over halfway through their trip, although it seemed a lifetime since she had been in her flat in London.

Thor had been sweet and attentive all day, even more so than he had been before, holding her hand, kissing her constantly. She couldn't put her finger on it, but there seemed to have been a shift in him.

Everything couldn't be more perfect right now.

She placed her order for two coffees and picked up two slices of cake with gooey icing on the top. While she was waiting she switched on her phone. She'd kept it off over the last day and night to conserve the battery as she'd known there would be nowhere to charge it out on the pontoon.

Eva walked out of the coffee shop and her phone lit up with a flurry of texts, WhatsApp messages and phone calls from all her friends as everything that had been sent over the last twenty-four hours or so suddenly came through. Christ, had someone died? She scrolled through her messages and got the sense it was something exciting, certainly not bad news, though she would need to read them all properly once they got back to the hotel to get the gist of what was going on. She glanced up at Thor and could see him pacing as he spoke to someone on the phone. As she approached she could see he was clearly angry. His whole body seemed tense, his jaw was clenched as he listened to the other person, and he didn't even say goodbye before he hung up.

'What's wrong?' Eva asked, the smile falling off her face.

Thor stared down at his phone and then up at her in shock. 'I've just been fired.'

Chapter 28

'What?' Eva said.

'I don't know. Tracy said she'd seen us kissing and she just fired me.'

Eva stared at him. 'How could she possibly have seen us kissing? I know we've been far from discreet but unless she's here spying on us, she couldn't possibly have seen us.'

Thor shook his head in confusion, as he started pacing again, then he groaned. 'Rebecca texted me yesterday to say I'd gone viral and she sent me this YouTube link. I never opened it at the time because I didn't have internet access and then I completely forgot. I thought she was just winding me up.' He quickly scrolled through his phone and found the text. Eva moved closer to him as he pressed the link.

YouTube took an agonisingly long time to load and when it did the opening shot was of the Taj Mahal in the rain. Eva's stomach sank as she guessed what was going to happen next. As the camera panned round, text came up on the screen. *Find a man that will kiss you like this.*

The next second Eva and Thor came into view, Eva

dancing and laughing in the rain, Thor staring at her as if she was the only woman in the world. Then he stepped forward and kissed her, hauling her close, kissing her with such passion and need. It was smoking hot and incredibly sexy to watch and the kiss went on and on with the rain lashing down on them both, before he grabbed her hand and marched off with her. It was very clear what they were going to do next as they ran and kissed and giggled in the rain.

Eva looked down at the number of views and her heart leapt. 'What the hell, six and a half million people have seen us kiss in the rain? I know it was hot and everything but—'

'This is what Tracy must have seen. This is what has cost me my job.'

Eva had to admit, it didn't look good. Suddenly the texts and messages from all her friends made sense. She hadn't told them anything about her relationship with Thor – they would want all the details and she wasn't willing to share everything. Besides which, she had no idea how to describe what she and Thor had. They would be all excited about marriage and babies and happy ever afters when it clearly wasn't that. But now it seemed they had found out too.

'Maybe we can explain—'

'Explain what?' Thor snapped. 'There is nothing we can say to make this look better than it is. There is no excuse in the world that we can use for why I was kissing a client and then clearly dragged her off to have sex with her. Christ, if I'd seen that, I'd be firing my ass too.'

'Well, maybe we can tell her that this is not just some fling but that it's serious between us and that it's been going on for a while.'

'I'm getting paid to fly around the world and have sex with my client. How is telling her that I've been doing this for the last few weeks going to help?' Thor said.

'I… I don't know. I'm sorry.'

'I need to go home.'

Her heart sank. 'You're leaving?'

'I need to try to sort this out with her or try to find myself another job. I can't afford to lose my house as well.'

'Well if it comes to that you can always stay at my house until you can sort yourself out,' Eva suggested. 'You won't be on the streets.'

'No, I'm not doing that. I'm not going to be beholden to you, or to anyone.' He pushed his hands through his hair. 'I'm such an idiot. I should never have got involved with you. This was not worth losing my job over.'

Eva took a step back, feeling like he'd just slapped her round the face. *She* was not worth losing his job over.

Tears smarted her eyes and she took another step back.

'Wait, I didn't mean that,' Thor said, reaching out for her but she flinched away from him.

'You know what, you should go. There's definitely nothing *worth* staying here for,' Eva said.

She turned and walked away and when he called after her she refused to look back.

Thor returned to the hotel a while later and made his way slowly up to the bedroom. He felt horribly guilty for what he'd said; he had been angry over losing his job and he had lashed out at her. She didn't deserve that.

He pushed the bedroom door open to find Eva packing their belongings into their separate bags. It was quite evident she had been crying.

'What are you doing?' Thor said, and then cringed because he should have opened with an apology.

'I have a flight to catch tomorrow, I'm going to New Zealand to try to see the Southern Lights. And you're going home. So I'm packing everything up. A lot of our belongings have just got thrown together over the last few weeks so I'm separating everything. It's quite cathartic really. Removing you from my life just like it will be once you've gone.'

Thor sighed. 'I'm sorry for what I said, I didn't mean it.'

Eva carried on packing and he knew he had to give her more than that.

'I was upset with Tracy and I took it out on you and I'm sorry. I never want to hurt you. The last few weeks have been the best weeks of my life.'

Crap, that was probably way too much.

She paused in what she was doing and looked at him.

'I don't regret a single second of it.' He pulled a face. 'I regret getting caught. I loved my job and now I have the hassle of trying to find something else. But if I was to do it all over again, I wouldn't change a single thing.'

She gave a little sigh. She still seemed angry and hurt, and understandably so, but some of the fight had gone from her.

'I'm sorry I lost you your job.'

He shook his head. 'Don't be. It's not your fault.'

He watched her as she carried on packing. 'So I take it, if I was to leave, you'd be carrying on without me?'

Eva sighed. 'Yes, I would. I need to finish my mum's list,

I want to swim with dolphins in Hawaii, I can't tell you how excited I am about that. I want to see New York and Niagara Falls and go to Canada. I want to do these things for me now, not just my mum.'

He couldn't help but smile at her. A few weeks before she had been terrified about going travelling on her own, but she had grown in confidence and was now actually excited about doing it.

'But also… I don't know what I'd be coming home for if I was to leave now,' Eva said. 'You've not given me any indication that this thing between us is more than a holiday romance, so why would I come home just to have you end things between us? If it's going to end, I'd rather you said goodbye here and leave me to carry on my holiday on my own.'

And there it was, the opening he needed to tell her what he wanted. Except he had no idea what that was. He could not imagine her living in his house or him living with her, he could not imagine marriage and happy ever afters with her, because he had no idea what that looked like. He'd thought he had that with Christel and that had ended spectacularly badly. But he couldn't imagine walking away from Eva either – he simply could not imagine leaving her and then never seeing her again. He wanted her in his life, he needed her, and that scared him.

'Look, I don't need to leave straight away, but I will need to spend some time each day looking and applying for jobs. Hopefully interviews won't be for another few weeks and maybe they might even agree to a Skype interview, but if something good comes up and the interview is sooner rather than later then I'm going to have to go. And you should stay here. I don't want you to miss out on the rest of your holiday. This is important to you and you should do it, you should tick all those boxes on your mum's list.'

'OK,' she said, quietly, clearly willing him to offer her something more.

'But maybe, when you get back home, and you've unpacked and caught up on your sleep, maybe we can meet for a drink and you can show me the photos of the rest of your trip?'

Eva broke into a slow smile. 'I'd like that.'

'I'm not making any promises,' Thor said, which made him feel like a complete shit.

'What you're offering is enough,' Eva said.

Thor pushed his hands through his hair because it really wasn't. He had lost Christel because what he was offering her was not enough for her and he couldn't lose Eva in the same way. But maybe what he was offering was enough *for now.*

Dear Mum,

Stewart Island, at the very bottom of New Zealand, is such a beautiful rugged place. It feels like we've stepped into the wilds of Canada with its lakes and snow-capped mountains. I've always thought Australia and New Zealand were so close to each other so it seems weird that a few days before we were in northern Australia and swimming in some kind of tropical paradise and here it's definitely winter – it's cold during the day and even worse at night. But still the colder it is, the more chance we have of seeing the aurora australis. We have this aurora app which tells us when it's likely that we will see it. I think it might be broken as it has told us we should have seen it last night when we arrived and tonight but we haven't seen a single flicker of colour so far. Tomorrow afternoon we start the long journey to Hawaii, so if we don't see it tonight I'm afraid this particular dream will have to be put on hold for now.

Thor has been distracted since we got here. He has spent several hours looking for a new job while I've gone out and explored the island. I know the loss of his job is weighing on his mind and with over two weeks of our trip still ahead of us, the money that he'll be spending on food and other incidentals is obviously making him worry. But there is a distance between us that wasn't there before. I feel like I'm losing him and he's right here next to me.

Wish you were here!

Love Eva x

It was the early hours in the morning and Eva couldn't sleep as she lay looking at the way the reflection of the sea danced off the ceiling of their bedroom. Thor was lying next to her on his back fast asleep.

He'd made love to her that night but there was a sadness to it, as if he sensed they were drifting apart too.

She wasn't sure if this distance was coming from her or from him.

She was so confused. She had been so sure he felt the same way, the way he looked at her when they made love, the way he smiled at her when they talked. There was a connection there but she had told him she loved him twice now and he hadn't said it back.

Truth be told, when he'd agreed to meet her in London so she could show him the photos from the rest of her trip, she'd been over the moon that he was throwing her a tiny nugget, a possible sliver of a chance that they had a future together. But in reality it wasn't enough. She had tried to convince herself that if she loved him and he cared about her and they got on well then it didn't matter that he didn't love her, but of course it did. What kind of future did they really have if he didn't share the same feelings as her? What kind of relationship was it if one person loved the other person more?

God, her heart hurt at the thought of losing him but she wasn't sure what she could do to stop it. If he didn't feel the same way then there was no point pursuing it once they got home. Maybe they should put it down to a wonderful holiday romance and draw a line under it. She felt tears well up in her eyes at that thought and the reflections on the ceiling shimmered even more.

She wiped her eyes and realised that the shimmering now had a slight green tinge to it. She frowned in confusion and looked out the window to see that outside there was a definite green glow.

She shot out of bed and ran to the window, barely noticing how cold the wooden floor was on her bare feet as she pressed her hands and nose to the glass. There out in the bay a green smudge hung low in the sky.

Eva gasped and quickly ran back to the bed, shaking Thor awake. 'Thor, it's here.'

His eyes shot open and he looked at her blearily.

'What's here?'

'The aurora, quick,' Eva said, as she threw some clothes on, grabbed her coat, hat and scarf and shoved her feet into her shoes. A few seconds later, she rushed out onto their balcony to watch the display. The green smudge moved across the sky like someone running their finger up the keys of a piano really fast. As Thor arrived next to her, pulling on his jumper over his jeans, a slight tinge of purple shimmered underneath the green too.

'I can't believe this,' Eva said as Thor wrapped a blanket round her. 'This is… like magic.'

She quickly fired off a few photos with her phone and then, because Thomas had specifically asked to see photos of the aurora australis, she sent him a quick text with one of the pictures and a short message that simply said, *We saw it, Eva x.* It was a start.

She shoved her phone in her pocket and leaned into Thor as he hugged her against him. They stood in silence for the longest time watching the green turn to yellow and the purple turn to pink as the lights danced and rippled across the bay. It really was magnificent. She wanted to paint it to capture the different shades and tones, the arcs and twists and turns. This trip had given her so many dazzling sights; she knew her cover designs would be so much more beautiful because of it. She was well and truly inspired.

Eventually the colour faded away completely and they were left staring at the starry sky. Silence dragged on between them, neither of them keen to break the spell.

Eva finally spoke. 'You need to go home, don't you?'

Thor sighed. 'Yes I do. I was going to talk to you tomorrow about it. I have a big decision to make and I'm not sure what I'm going to do next. If I go home I can get agency work until something else turns up or I decide what to do. Or if I need to I can move out of my flat and go somewhere cheaper. There's just a lot to sort out now and I can do it better if I'm there.'

She swallowed down the lump in her throat. 'I understand.'

She pulled away from him and went back inside. After a moment he followed her and closed the door behind him.

'Are you going to be OK on your own?'

'I'll be fine,' Eva said and knew she would be.

'I'm sorry if this ruins your holiday.'

'You leaving isn't going to ruin my holiday. You ripping my heart out and taking it with you when you leave, that certainly puts a dampener on things.'

He stared at her in shock. She was quite surprised herself. She'd had no intention of bringing that up. But now the can was open and there were worms crawling down the sides. There was still time to scoop them back in and close the lid, she could make a joke of it, change the subject.

'What?' Thor asked.

But suddenly she didn't want to dismiss it. They both knew when he left tomorrow, they'd probably never see each other again. So she was damned well going to let him know exactly what she felt.

'I love you.'

She watched him visibly flinch, which made the anger bubble through her veins.

'I LOVE YOU!' Eva shouted, so there could be no mistake. 'I know you said it was just sex and nothing more, I know you told me not to fall in love with you and I stupidly went ahead and did it anyway. But the worst thing is I'm pretty sure you fell in love with me too.'

Thor started shaking his head.

His phone began to ring on the other side of the room. Tracy had been ringing fairly regularly since he was fired – the first time had been to tell him he would need to pay back any expenses he had paid for on the company credit card on this trip. Since then Thor hadn't taken any more of her calls. She was probably ringing to rant again. Thor ignored this call too and thankfully the phone finally fell silent.

'You can't deny the connection we have,' Eva said, trying to pick up from before the phone disturbed them. 'You and I both know this is way more than just sex. But you're a coward. You're too scared to take a risk with your heart. Love is a risk but something as special as this doesn't come around very often and you're prepared to just let it slip away because your heart was broken in the past. I know what happened was devastating for you, to lose a child in any circumstances is heartbreaking and in your case it was particularly horrible. You had your trust broken by the woman you loved. I know how hard that must have been for you but you can't let it ruin the rest of your life.'

He pushed his hands through his hair.

'Do you love me?' Eva asked.

'It's not as simple as that.'

'Of course it is. It's a yes or no question.'

He stared at her but it wasn't the look of someone who

was going to fall into her arms and confess his love for her. It was the look of someone who wanted to let her down as gently as possible. Had she really misread all the signs?

'Look, this is a really bad time to have this conversation,' Thor tried.

'When is it a good time?'

'I have no job and if I don't get one soon, I won't have a home either,' he snapped. 'This *really* isn't the right time.'

'What does that matter?' Eva said. 'Do you think I care about any of that?'

His eyebrows shot up. 'You don't care that I lost my job and could be homeless?'

'Of course I do. That's not what I meant and you know it. I meant that none of that impacts on us, on what we have, on our feelings for each other. You could never have a job for the rest of your life and I would still love you. If I lost my job would that change the way you felt about me?'

'Of course not.'

'Then why is this an issue? And if you start spouting some sexist crap about how it's a man's job to look after the woman, I swear to god, I will pin you to the ground and shave off your eyebrows.'

He stared at her and for the briefest of seconds she thought she saw his mouth twitch into a smirk before it was gone.

'I've been offered a job in Denmark,' Thor said.

That took the wind out of her sails because, no matter how much they loved each other – if he actually did feel that way for her– long-distance relationships rarely worked.

'And you're going to take it?' Eva asked.

'It's a job at my old newspaper. I enjoyed working there.

This would be a bit of a promotion too and the money is good.'

'So that's a yes.'

'It's not a yes,' Thor said.

'But it's not a no?'

'It depends.'

'On what?'

'I have to decide what's the best thing to do.'

'Best for you?' Eva snapped.

His eyes flashed furiously. 'If you think that then you don't know me at all.'

Thor's phone rang again.

He sighed in frustration. 'Let me just turn it off.'

He moved towards his phone and picked it up. He stared at the screen in confusion and then quickly answered it.

'Mor, are you OK?'

Eva watched him as he sat down on the bed, his face visibly paling. He looked at his watch and listened some more. She watched him swallow as if he was trying to find the words. When he did speak it was in Danish and he rattled off several questions and Eva had no idea what he was saying. Eventually he hung up. He stared at the phone for a few seconds and when he looked up he had tears in his eyes.

'What's happened?' Eva asked.

His voice was broken when he spoke. 'It's my dad. He's had a heart attack. He's at the hospital but they don't think it looks good.'

Eva's heart leapt, fear erupting in goosebumps across her body. Shit.

'Oh god Thor, I'm so sorry.'

Thor stood up and started grabbing his things and throwing them in his rucksack. 'I need to go.'

'Of course, right,' Eva said, hurrying around and gathering her things together. She ran into the bathroom and gathered up all her toiletries, stuffing them back into her soap bag before racing back into the bedroom and throwing it into the suitcase.

'What are you doing?' Thor said, his voice cool, as he zipped up his rucksack and pulled on his coat.

'I'm packing, just give me a few minutes.'

'Why?'

She looked up at him and his eyes were blazing.

'I'm coming with you.'

'I don't want you to come. I don't need you there. I don't... need you.'

She stared at him in shock, tears welling in her eyes as his words cut like broken glass.

He rubbed his hand down his cheek, dragging his skin with his fingers. 'I'm sorry. I have to go.'

He picked up his rucksack and walked out the door.

What the hell had just happened?

Eva waited for him to come back but he didn't. She wrapped her arms round herself feeling so cold, she rubbed the ache in her chest but it wouldn't go away. His words echoed in her heart. *I don't want you to come. I don't need you.*

She sat down on the bed and cried.

Chapter 29

Thor stared out the plane window as it took off from Singapore airport. He'd managed to get the first flight of the day from Stewart Island back to the South Island and then another flight from Invercargill to Christchurch and from there a flight to Singapore. It had already been fifteen hours since he'd received the call. It couldn't have happened at a worse time, being on Stewart Island – he was at the furthest possible point away from his parents and he knew he was still a long way from being with them. At least the flight from Singapore was direct but it would be another thirteen hours before he arrived in Copenhagen and then he had to try to get a flight to Aalborg at the very top of Denmark.

He'd been in touch with his mum, who had told him that there had been no change with his dad, which Thor could only hope was a good thing. Henry was no better but he was no worse either.

He sighed and as he did he caught a waft of Eva's scent on his skin. God, if he closed his eyes he could picture her there, feel the softness of her skin against his, taste her, touch her.

He'd tried to call her numerous times but got no answer every time and he couldn't blame her. He'd cocked up spectacularly. And the pain on her face as he'd walked out the door stabbed him in the heart every time he thought about it. When he'd said he didn't want her to come he'd meant that he didn't want her to abandon her holiday because of him. It was so important to her to finish her mum's list, and swimming with dolphins in Hawaii – the next place on their itinerary – was the thing she had been looking forward to the most. When he'd said he didn't need her he'd meant he didn't need the stress of taking that stupid row with them, he didn't want that when he needed to be there for his parents, for his dad.

But he hadn't said any of those things because his only thought had been his dad and getting to him as quickly as possible. When things went wrong he always pushed people away, preferring to deal with things on his own. He'd been the same when it had ended with Christel, he'd run away to London. But in pushing Eva away he had hurt her and now he had ruined everything.

Because he did need her. Not just because he needed someone here with him to hold his hand as he went through this hell, but he needed her in his life, he needed to be with her always.

And it had been a stupid row because of course he loved her and why had he not grabbed her and told her so when she had first told him she loved him? He *was* a coward. He'd been through hell with his last relationship but that didn't mean it would happen again. And even if it did he would survive. He would move on and rebuild his life just like he had last time.

Losing his job had thrown a spanner in the works because he felt like, with no job and probably soon no home, he had nothing to offer her. But of course he did. She loved him for him, not for what he could give her. She'd said as much at the Taj Mahal – that the only thing she wanted was his heart, and he couldn't even give her that.

He needed to speak to her but right then he just had to get to his dad and make sure both he and his mum were OK.

Eva staggered out of Aalborg airport and looked around for a taxi. She had been travelling for around thirty hours and she was beyond exhausted. It had taken her half hour to decide that she needed to be there for Thor. He was lashing out because he was scared and she wanted to help him in any way she could. Regardless of what happened between them, this was the man she loved and she couldn't let him face this agony of possibly losing his dad on his own. She had caught a plane to Invercargill but missed the plane to Christchurch and had to wait two hours for the next one. Then she'd caught several planes from Christchurch to Sydney, to Dubai, to Copenhagen and to Aalborg.

She had no idea what day it was, what time of day it was, other than it was dark outside and chilly and her coat was stuffed inside her suitcase and she couldn't be bothered to get it out.

She flagged down a taxi and the driver immediately got out and helped put her suitcase in the boot. They both got in the car.

'To the hospital please,' Eva said.

'Which one?' the driver asked.

Eva wanted to cry. She had circumnavigated the world, caught six planes and was practically within touching distance of Thor and now she had fallen at the last hurdle. She had no idea which hospital Henry might be at. And what if she was too late anyway? No, that didn't bear thinking about.

'My boyfriend's dad lives in Skagen and he had a heart attack. Which hospital do you think he would have been taken to?'

'Hjørring Hospital,' the driver said.

Eva blinked at the pronunciation which was heavy on the *H* and had that rolling *R* in the middle that she had never managed to master.

She shrugged. 'Let's try that one then.'

Eva sat back in her seat as the driver pulled out onto the road. She had no idea what Thor's reaction was going to be to her turning up. What if he pushed her away again? But she hadn't just come for him, she also wanted to be there for Sofie and Henry too, to help them in any way she could.

She must have dropped off because the next thing she knew the taxi driver was pulling up outside a hospital and calling her to let her know they had arrived. She looked out the window blearily, wondering if she'd got the right place. But then she saw Sofie, standing outside one of the doors. She was on the phone. Eva quickly paid the driver and scrambled out. She was vaguely aware that the driver was getting her suitcase out the boot.

Sofie looked up as she approached and her whole face lit up. She quickly finished the conversation she was having and hung up.

'Eva my darling, what are you doing here?' Sofie said, embracing her in a big hug.

Eva's throat ached with supressed emotion as she held Sofie tight.

'I came to see if Henry is OK,' Eva said, her voice muffled by Sofie's shoulder.

Sofie pulled back. 'Oh my love, he's fine, he's stable now. He came round a short while ago and the doctors are happy with his progress. I mean, we have to talk about the future at some point, he might need to be on some medications for a while and we have to try to figure out what caused it and what we can do to prevent it happening again, but he is out of the woods for now. He's resting.'

'Oh I'm so pleased.' Eva said, feeling the relief rush through her. After the last thirty or more hours, this was the best news.

'Did you fly all the way from New Zealand too?' Sofie said.

Eva nodded. 'I wanted to be here for Thor, for all of you.'

Sofie smiled. 'Thor's at home resting. As soon as Henry was given the all-clear, I sent Thor home, he was dead on his feet. Pernille will be here soon so I won't be on my own. Why don't you go home and rest too? You look exhausted.'

'Oh, but is there anything you need?' Eva said. Sleep did sound tempting right then but she hadn't flown across the world to go to bed as soon as she got there. She felt like she should at least check in on Henry but if he was sleeping there really would be no point.

'I need you to go and be with Thor,' Sofie said, flagging down Eva's taxi just as it was pulling away. 'Take my key.'

Sofie opened the taxi door and bundled her inside. The driver didn't seem to mind that he had to get her suitcase back into the boot again. She saw Sofie give him some money and Eva made a mental note to pay her back later. Sofie poked her head back into the taxi, rattled off the address in Danish and then turned to Eva. 'I'll see you tomorrow.'

Eva gave her a little wave as the taxi pulled away and then watched the street lights whizz past as the car took her closer and closer to Thor. She didn't know if she had the energy to face him right now, and she had no idea what she was going to say to him. She couldn't shout at him any more but if he tried to push her away she might actually lose it and burst into tears again.

It took a lot longer than she would have liked to reach the house, which was in complete darkness. She thanked the taxi driver and climbed out. He pulled her suitcase out of the boot and carried it to the front door before leaving her alone. With a deep breath she let herself into the house. There was silence inside as she made her way upstairs to Thor's room. She slipped inside the room and could see Thor, topless, lying with his back to the door, a duvet slung over his waist. He was fast asleep.

She stared at him for a moment and then undressed. She found a t-shirt of his in one of the drawers and put that on, then slipped into the bed behind him.

He didn't even stir.

She snuggled into his back and wrapped an arm round his stomach. She pressed a gentle kiss to his shoulder and then felt herself drifting off to sleep with a smile on her face. She had no idea what would happen when he woke up but right now she was home.

Chapter 30

Thor woke up with the dawn. He opened his eyes as the sun reached through the window and grazed across his face. He closed his eyes again. Eva was wrapped around his back. He sighed happily. Everything was right with the world.

But as clarity seeped into his waking mind, he realised he was back in his childhood bedroom and he remembered the last horrendous forty-eight hours: abandoning Eva in New Zealand and the long and tortuous journey home to see his dad. There was no way Eva could be in his bed with him. She would probably be in Hawaii by now.

He opened his eyes because there was definitely a warmth behind him and wrapped around him. He peered down and saw an arm slung over his waist.

He quickly rolled over to see Eva fast asleep. Eva was here, in his bed. She had travelled halfway round the world to be with him. He ran his hands over her shoulders, down her arms – she was warm to the touch and very much real.

Her eyes fluttered open and she looked at him and smiled. Oh god that smile. He leaned forward and cupped her face and kissed her, the taste of her slamming into his gut.

'Christ, you're really here,' Thor said against her lips, before kissing her again.

He tore his lips from hers long enough to pull her t-shirt off and fling it across the room. He rolled on top of her and she wrapped her arms round his neck, stroking round his shoulders. He moved his hand to her breast, running a thumb over her nipple. She groaned against his mouth and then put a hand on his chest to stop him. He pulled back to look at her.

'Thor, wait, we need to talk,' she said breathlessly.

'We will. I promise,' Thor said, a desperate need for her erupting through him. He kissed her again. 'After,' he mumbled against her lips.

There were no more sounds of protest from her – instead she kissed him back.

He had never wanted anyone as much as he wanted her right then. He leaned over to grab his jeans from the chair next to the bed and wrestled a condom from his pocket. He kissed her again and then ripped the condom open and slid it on. He settled himself between her thighs and she wrapped her legs around him as he moved inside her.

'Oh god Eva.' Thor kissed her hard and then gathered her close, holding her tight against him. 'I can't believe you're here. You came all this way for me?'

He felt her wonderful warm body moving in sync with his, this was everything he needed right then.

'I came for Henry,' she teased.

He smiled against her lips as he kissed her again. 'I'll take that.'

He kissed her neck and felt her pulse racing against his lips as she ran her fingers through his hair.

He lifted her off the bed slightly and she arched back as he moved his mouth to her breast. She let out a gasp as he took her nipple into his mouth.

'Thor!' Eva moaned and he moved to kiss her again.

He felt her breath hitch, felt the change in her body at the same time he felt the change in his.

'Eva, I love you, I love you so much,' Thor said.

He kissed her hard as she clung to him, capturing the moans of her release on his lips as he fell over the edge, and fell impossibly even more in love with her too.

He collapsed on top of her, trying to catch his breath as he pressed his mouth to her throat, just below her ear.

And because he wanted there to be no doubt, he whispered in her ear, 'I really bloody love you Eva Blue.

Eva watched Thor move around the kitchen making breakfast for them. They hadn't really spoken, other than about Henry and what she wanted in her omelette, but there was an ease between them.

He loved her and, though they did need to talk, that was all that mattered right then.

He passed her a mug of tea and a plate with a delicious-looking omelette on it before sitting down opposite her with his own plate. She took a big bite; she'd not had anything decent to eat since their last meal in Stewart Island.

He took a sip of his tea, not taking his eyes off her.

'I still can't believe you're here, after the way I treated you.

I don't deserve it.'

Eva reached across the table to take his hand. 'You were scared and worried about your dad, I don't blame you at all—'

'But the things I said, I want to explain,' Thor said. 'It wasn't that I didn't want you here, I didn't want you to miss the rest of your holiday for me.'

'But I love you, you will always come first. You need to learn to let me in. We're not two separate entities any more, we're a team now, we stand together.' It felt weird finally talking about their future as if it now was a certainty but she also knew in her heart that this was how it was going to be. They belonged together.

He let out a heavy breath and brought her hand to his mouth, kissing across her knuckles.

'I'm sorry I never told you how I felt. I kept trying to push you away. I was so scared of falling in love again but I was already in love with you and denying it didn't change that.'

'It's OK, I shouldn't have pushed you when you weren't ready,' Eva said.

'Yes you should have. We both needed to be pushed out of our comfort zone on this trip and I think we needed the other person to do it. I watched you every day being brave and bold and it made me want to be brave too. You made me want to love again, you made me want a future. You knocked those walls down and made me stronger. You really are the most incredible woman I've ever met.'

'You changed my life too. You showed me the world, showed me how amazing it is and how much more exciting life is when you have adventure in it.'

'You found your own adventures Eva, and you would have

done all those things without me being there.'

'But it's much more enjoyable when you have someone to navigate the twists and turns with. I cannot imagine seeing the world without you by my side,' Eva said.

Thor sighed. 'I think that was partly what was worrying me when I lost my job. I could see you coming alive on this trip, how much you loved travelling and discovering new places, and I thought, without a job, how could we have that?'

'But that's silly. We can't spend our whole lives on holiday and, anyway, our trips don't have to be extravagant. We can buy a little camper van and travel around the UK. I've never been to Ireland, I've only been to South Wales and there are loads of parts of Scotland and England I've never been to either. And you promised me a camping holiday and I'm looking forward to it.'

Thor grinned. 'My tent doesn't have a chandelier.'

'I think I'll cope.'

He smiled as he took a bite of his omelette and Eva did the same.

'Tell me about the job here in Denmark?' Eva asked.

'Well, I wanted to find out a bit more about it first, mostly if I could work remotely and do the job from London.'

'And if you can't?'

Thor shrugged. 'Then I'd turn it down.'

'Why?'

'Because I'm not leaving you.'

Her heart soared at that comment but then she frowned. 'Is this a job you really want?'

'Yes, it's something I know I'd enjoy but my relationship with you is more important.'

Eva took another bite of her omelette. 'It seems you haven't considered something fairly obvious.'

'What's that?' Thor cut off another slice of omelette.

'We could live here together.'

He stared at her, his fork frozen halfway to his mouth.

'You'd really move here? You'd go through all that upheaval for me?'

'I know it seems sudden, but we've got on pretty damned well being together for twenty-four hours a day over the last few weeks. Maybe this has just been a wonderful holiday romance and it will all fizzle out in a few months but if it does I can move back to London. I can do my job anywhere in the world as long as I have my laptop and Wi-Fi. I sit in my house all day in my pyjamas, I can just as easily do that here. I don't see it as a big upheaval at all, I see it as a new adventure; living in a different country, learning a new language, living with the man I love. I think we owe it to ourselves to give this relationship its best shot and if you have an offer for a job you'll love then why would I not move here so you can take it?'

He stared at her in awe. 'Did I mention that I love you, Eva Blue?'

'It might have come up a few times,' Eva smiled.

'There'd be a lot to sort out,' Thor said.

'And we'll do it together.'

Thor smiled and then raised his mug to chink against hers. 'Well Eva Blue, here's to our next big, beautiful adventure.'

Epilogue

Eva stared up at the sky as she lay on her back on the banks of the Nakameguro canal. The sun was setting, leaving clouds of plum and tangerine across the sky. It looked very dramatic framed behind the delicate blooms of cherry blossom that danced on the branches above her.

It had been a year since she had found her mum's dreams in a box in the loft and when she had initially started researching how and where she could achieve those dreams, the one that had appealed to her the most had been seeing the beauty of the cherry blossoms in Japan, but the big holiday had started too late in the year to see them. But now they were here and she had never seen anything like it.

There were so many different shades of pink, from the palest almost white pink to the deepest flamingo pink. Cherry blossom trees were everywhere, in clusters, in rows, in every park, lining streets and rivers. The canal they were resting by had them all along the banks, their great heavy boughs almost touching the water. The surface of the water was a gorgeous pink, reflecting the majesty of the canopy above them beautifully.

To the Japanese, the cherry blossom was a symbol of how fragile and beautiful life was. The fleetingness of the blossom season was a reminder of how short life was. Eva loved reading that in her guide book. Life was precious and for some it was tragically cut short. It was important to Eva to make the most of the life she had, grab every opportunity that came her way.

After Henry had come out of hospital with strict instructions to diet, lose weight and exercise more, Thor and Eva had decided to carry on with their holiday. Although they had missed out on swimming with dolphins in Hawaii and going to Disneyland in California, they simply added those onto the trip at the end. They had managed to catch up with their itinerary in San Francisco, in time to ride a horse over the Golden Gate Bridge. They had spent the next two weeks ticking off all the American and Canadian dreams, including singing on stage on Broadway, even if it had been to an empty theatre, and singing in front of the Queen at Madame Tussauds in New York before returning to England.

They had even arrived back in the UK in time to meet up with her dad for dinner before he flew back home to LA. She liked Thomas and although most of their conversations were over text, he was definitely making an effort. They'd made plans for them to visit him in America later on in the year, where she was going to meet her half-sisters for the first time too.

Once they arrived back in England they had to pack up their lives and start their next adventure in Denmark. It had been fun living in a new country and the Danish people were so friendly. She had worked hard to learn their language but every time she tried to speak to any of the locals in Danish they would automatically reply to her in English. But Sofie, Henry and Thor had helped by talking to her in Danish. She certainly wasn't fluent, but she could hold a half-decent conversation now.

She watched the gentle breeze flutter the flowers above her, scattering them with confetti. A petal landed in Thor's hair as he lay with his head on her belly. She ran her fingers through his hair, removing the petal. She watched him smile, a look of complete contentment on his face.

She had wondered whether moving in with him so soon in their relationship would be a challenge, but it really wasn't. They had been together twenty-four hours a day while they had travelled the world, where they'd had all the stresses and exhaustion of travelling from one place to the next, and their relationship had survived. It seemed like the natural progression to then move in together. And it worked, they just... clicked. Of course they had little fights occasionally but they were always over before they had even started. And make-up sex was always fun. They had rented a small place in Skagen at first in a 'just in case this doesn't work out' kind of way, but it was quite obvious to both of them that this thing between them was going to last forever so she had sold her flat in London and together they had bought a bigger house just down the road from his parents.

Shortly after that, she had sold her mum's house too and bought a very small boat called *Juliette*. It had a bedroom, a tiny bathroom and a small kitchen–lounge area and that was it. But every time she looked at *Juliette* it made her smile. It was safe to say her mum would have definitely approved. They had spent many a weekend exploring the islands of

Denmark and Norway and, in some small way, it was like her mum was with them.

The hardest part of moving to a different country was leaving Laurel behind. While Eva spoke to her every few days, it wasn't quite the same as seeing her on a regular basis. Although Laurel and James had recently been talking about retiring to Skagen, something which Eva was a big fan of. She'd been sending Laurel links for houses for sale for the last few weeks and her aunt was clearly swayed. It wouldn't take a lot for her to be persuaded. James made her ridiculously happy and since their wedding a few months before they had been like teenagers in love. He would do anything for her, including relocate to another country.

Eva's friends had been delighted for her and they still kept in regular contact through WhatsApp. At their monthly meet-ups she was Skyped in just like Leila, so it didn't feel that different.

Thor sat up and looked at her. 'Shall we go for a walk?'

Eva nodded and he helped her to her feet. Still holding hands, they walked along the banks of the canal. Lanterns had started to come on, sending puddles of gold over the water, making the cherry blossoms glow in the dusky air. It looked magical.

More confetti petals rained down on them like gentle flakes of snow and Thor caught one in his other hand. 'How about Blossom?'

Eva smiled. Since they had discovered the wonderful news that she was pregnant the day before, Thor had been throwing out names randomly throughout the day, many of which were Norse gods, although she quite liked the idea of

THE SUMMER OF CHASING DREAMS

calling her daughter Freya. It was so endearing to see how
excited Thor was. She couldn't wait to meet their child. It
was the strangest feeling to be completely in love with their
baby already.

'Blossom would be lovely for a girl,' Eva teased. 'I'm not
sure it would suit our son.'

'No, probably not.'

They walked on in silence for a while, admiring the
lanterns amongst the pink trees.

'So, this is the last dream on your mum's list,' Thor said,
pulling her to a stop and taking her hands.

She smiled at that because they had finally ticked off all
the things on her mum's list. They had flown over to Svalbard
towards the end of the summer the year before to see the polar
bears and spent a week in Sweden at the beginning of
December to tick off all those winter activities her mum
wanted to do. It had been an incredible year, full of adventure
and surprises, although the biggest surprise she had never
expected was falling in love with such a wonderful man.

'Yeah, we finally did it,' Eva said, feeling a little bittersweet
about completing this mission. If her mum had been with
her, watching over her as she ticked off all her dreams, did
that now mean she would move on, and she would no longer
be there?

'I wanted to do something to mark the occasion,' Thor
went on. 'The last year, going on this adventure with you, has
been the best year of my life. I love you, Eva Blue, and I think
we should come up with a new list of dreams, new sights and
experiences we can do together. Life is an adventure and I can
think of no one I'd rather have by my side as we travel

through it.' He dropped to one knee and held a box up to her. 'Eva Blue, will you do me the honour of becoming my wife?'

Eva gasped as she stared at the ring, a sphere of blue and green turquoise swirls that looked like a tiny version of the world, surrounded by little diamonds. It was stunning.

'Of course I will,' she said, tears falling down her cheeks. 'The day you walked into the airport instead of Rebecca, you changed my world and I cannot imagine a life without you in it. I love you so much.'

He grinned and slid the ring onto her finger and then stood up and kissed her, resting a hand on their baby. As parents and husband and wife they were going to face the biggest adventure life could throw at them and she couldn't wait to take that next step with him. She wrapped her arms around him, knowing all of her dreams had come true.

The End

If you enjoyed *The Summer of Chasing Dreams*, you'll love Holly Martin's next gorgeously romantic story, *The Little Village of Happiness*, out in June.

To keep up to date with the latest news on my releases, just visit the link below to sign up for a newsletter. You'll also get two FREE short stories, sneak peeks, booky news and be able to take part in exclusive giveaways. Your email will never be shared with anyone else and you can unsubscribe at any time https://www.subscribepage.com/hollymartinsignup

Website:
hollymartin-author.com/

Twitter:
@HollyMAuthor

Email:
holly@hollymartin-author.com

Facebook author page:
www.facebook.com/hollymartinauthor/

Sunshine, Seaside and Sparkles –
The Holly Martin Reader Group:
www.facebook.com/groups/483957115452985/

Also by Holly Martin

Sandcastle Bay Series
The Holiday Cottage by the Sea
The Cottage on Sunshine Beach
Coming Home to Maple Cottage

Hope Island Series
Spring at Blueberry Bay
Summer at Buttercup Beach
Christmas at Mistletoe Cove

Juniper Island Series
Christmas Under a Cranberry Sky
A Town Called Christmas

White Cliff Bay Series
Christmas at Lilac Cottage
Snowflakes on Silver Cove
Summer at Rose Island

Standalone Stories
Fairytale Beginnings
Tied Up With Love
A Home on Bramble Hill
One Hundred Christmas Proposals
One Hundred Proposals
The Guestbook at Willow Cottage

For Young Adults
The Sentinel Series
The Sentinel (Book 1 of the Sentinel Series)
The Prophecies (Book 2 of the Sentinel Series)
The Revenge (Book 3 of the Sentinel Series)
The Reckoning (Book 4 of the Sentinel Series)

A letter from Holly

Thank you so much for reading *The Summer of Chasing Dreams*, I had so much fun creating this story and researching the wonderful locations. I hope you enjoyed reading it as much as I enjoyed writing it. If you did enjoy it, and want to keep up-to-date with all my latest releases, just sign up here. Your email will never be shared and you can unsubscribe at any time.

One of the best parts of writing comes from seeing the reaction from readers. Did it make you smile or laugh, did it make you cry, hopefully happy tears? Did you fall in love with Eva and Thor as much as I did? Did you like the beautiful locations? If you enjoyed the story, I would absolutely love it if you could leave a short review. Getting feedback from readers is amazing and it also helps to persuade other readers to pick up one of my books for the first time.

My next book, out in June is called *The Little Village of Happiness* and is set in a tiny Cornish village in the grounds of a castle.

Thank you for reading.

Love Holly x

Acknowledgements

To my family, my mom, my biggest fan, who reads every word I've written a hundred times over and loves it every single time, my dad, my brother Lee and my sister-in-law Julie, for your support, love, encouragement and endless excitement for my stories.

For my twinnie, the gorgeous Aven Ellis for just being my wonderful friend, for your endless support, for cheering me on, for reading my stories and telling me what works and what doesn't and for keeping me entertained with wonderful stories. I love you dearly.

To my lovely friends Julie, Natalie, Jac, Verity, Jodie, Gareth and Mandie, thanks for all the support.

To the Devon contingent, Paw and Order, Belinda, Lisa, Phil, Bodie, Kodi and Skipper. Thanks for keeping me entertained and always being there.

For Sharon Sant for just being there always and your wonderful friendship.

To everyone at Bookcamp, you gorgeous, fabulous bunch, thank you for your wonderful support on this venture.

To Kirsty Greenwood, thanks for answering all my questions with unending patience.

To Pernille Hughes, thank you so much for the help with the Danish questions and translations.

To the SPF community, you guys rock.

Thanks to the brilliant Emma Rogers for the gorgeous cover design.

Thanks to my fabulous editors, Celine Kelly, Kerry Barrett and Rhian McKay.

Thanks to Jason for help with formatting.

To all the wonderful bloggers for your tweets, retweets, facebook posts, tireless promotions, support, encouragement and endless enthusiasm. You guys are amazing and I couldn't do this journey without you.

To anyone who has read my book and taken the time to tell me you've enjoyed it or wrote a review, thank you so much.

Thank you, I love you all.